ONE LESS SNAKE

A DCI EVAN WARLOW NOVEL

DCI EVAN WARLOW CRIME THRILLER # 16

RHYS DYLAN

WYRMWOOD
BOOKS

COPYRIGHT

Print ISBN 978-1-915185-43-3
eBook ISBN 978-1-915185-42-6

Published by Wyrmwood Books.
An imprint of Wyrmwood Media.

CHAPTER ONE

THE FINAL THIRTY seconds of Matt Gittings's life not so much flashed before his eyes as rolled through the darkness all around him.

He screamed, but, through the gag, no one heard him.

He wrenched his hands in an attempt to free them from the zip ties gluing them to the car's steering wheel.

Blood flowed, but his hands stayed bound.

Through his bleary eyes, he could see lights bobbing on the horizon. Houses and farms whose occupants lay safe in bed, ignorant of him and the dark Merc jolting and bumping across the field. Across terrain not built for, nor even expecting to accommodate, a vehicle.

If he had regrets, they were lost in the bladder-voiding panic of realisation. And his brain, though fogged with booze and pills, understood that these were his last seconds of existence.

Gittings screamed through the gag and thrust with his right foot towards the brake, succeeding only in hitting the accelerator because his foot was locked onto it. He lunged against his seatbelt, the pungent smell of petrol filling his nostrils.

Fifteen seconds of the thirty had gone since consciousness dragged him back from the abyss. From when the jolting movement stirred him awake, assaulting his senses with confused panic and terror. Heat clawed at his skin as he became aware of the flames hungrily devouring the inside of the car. The acrid, pungent stench of petrol filled his nostrils, making each breath a burning struggle. His heart pounded in his chest, syncing with the guttural roar of the fire and the sharp, piercing scream that cut through the chaos—a sound raw with panic and terror, echoing his spiralling fear. Horror dawned when he realised he was in his own vehicle, locked and loaded and trundling forward and on the downward slope.

He tried the brake again to no avail. As before, his thrusts succeeded only in jolting the car forwards at increased velocity.

Seventeen seconds.

A flurry of bigger bumps and the world beyond the windshield tilted as stomach-churning weightlessness took hold and the vehicle became airborne, falling bonnet first through space. Through the silent nothingness – a nothingness broken only by the frantic pounding of his heart and his own choked gasps.

One hundred and fifty feet below, unforgiving ground waited.

Impact.

Metal screamed as it crumpled. Glass shattered into a glittering cloud. And in that same instant, the petrol tank exploded.

The interior of the car, Gittings's tomb, transformed into an inferno. In a blinding flash, the fireball consumed everything – metal, flesh, and the last fleeting moments of Gittings's existence.

In one second, both femurs were pushed backwards through their sockets. Five ribs cracked under the deceleration force as well. But neither of these killed the man.

The lethal blow came as the inferno erupted in the car.

He had time to bellow once as the flames burned through his gag and allowed him at last to open his mouth. But it was just the one noise he made before he inhaled. After that. He made no sound at all.

In the annals of tragic deaths, self-immolation stood apart – a desperate last act favoured by protesting monks or the deeply disturbed.

In such cases, bystanders often rushed to help, and sometimes the victim survived, albeit with horrific, life-altering injuries. Death, when it came, could be slow and agonising, stretching out over interminable hours or days.

But for Matt Gittings, trapped in his Mercedes-turned-fireball, there were no rescue attempts, no lingering suffering.

The conflagration surrounding him devoured the available oxygen in an instant, creating a lethal vacuum.

As he gasped, super-heated gases seared his airways. His trachea spasmed in a futile attempt to protect his lungs. But it was too late.

The intense heat ravaged Gittings's respiratory system, causing catastrophic damage. The flames consumed the surrounding oxygen triggered a desperate asphyxiation reflex. Making him suck in more poisonous, super hot air.

In a cruel irony, the conflagration raged outside just as Gittings's internal systems were failing rapidly. The very mechanisms meant to sustain life were shutting down under the extreme conditions.

If there might be one shred of consolation in such a gruesome end, it was that Gittings's death came swiftly. The human body, resilient in so many ways, succumbed quickly to such extreme trauma. Consciousness fled, the pain mercifully brief before oblivion claimed him.

Yet, whispers in dark corners suggested that even this rapid demise was too kind a fate for a man like Matt Gittings. There were those who, knowing the full extent of his sins, would have prescribed a far more protracted end – one that matched the suffering he had inflicted on others throughout his life.

The fire consumed all it could reach, reducing flesh to ash and bone to scorched calcium. Some might say it was the end of a dark chapter in which the man deserved no pity. But, in the smouldering aftermath, new questions arose.

Matt Gittings died not knowing who had orchestrated this elaborate execution.

Not knowing who he had wronged enough to trigger this act of horrifying vengeance.

That there were many people on this list was a telling epitaph.

EXCLUSIVE OFFER

Please look out for the link near the end of the book for your chance to sign up to the no-spam guaranteed VIP Reader's Club and receive a FREE DCI Warlow novella as well as news of upcoming releases.

Or you can go direct to my website: https://rhysdylan.com and sign up now.
Remember, you can unsubscribe at any time and I promise I won't send you any spam. Ever.

OTHER DCI WARLOW NOVELS

THE ENGINE HOUSE
CAUTION DEATH AT WORK
ICE COLD MALICE
SUFFER THE DEAD
GRAVELY CONCERNED
A MARK OF IMPERFECTION
BURNT ECHO
A BODY OF WATER
LINES OF INQUIRY
NO ONE NEAR

THE LIGHT REMAINS
A MATTER OF EVIDENCE
THE LAST THROW
DRAGON'S BREATH
THE BOWMAN

CHAPTER TWO

Piers Barber parked his Lexus and got out, stiffly.

This early, the air retained a coolness that suggested summer had yet to truly wake up, though June was threatening to make an appearance in just a few days' time. But all he did was zip up his tracksuit top and fiddle with the podcast app on his phone so that his lonely journey might be eased by some overly cheerful guru spouting the latest advice on wellness. What not to eat, watch, read, or think so that you could live forever. Or gibberish to that effect.

Jenny, his partner, had an addiction for them. He'd probably find something a little lighter after ten minutes, but he always liked to begin with the best intentions. So far, this holiday, he was sticking to the plan. Admittedly, not with a huge amount of enthusiasm, but sticking, nonetheless.

The kids and Jenny were due down from London in a couple of days, but he'd come down late Friday because Archie's sleepover at Rio's 10th birthday party in Notting Hill didn't need the two of them there. Besides, their youngest, Paloma, had a thing about trains at the moment.

Jenny, Archie, and Paloma would catch the Paddington to Haverfordwest train first thing on Sunday morning. That gave Piers a day to get the cottage shipshape in preparation for their first trip west. They'd return in late July and probably again in October for the school holidays. And autumn at Cludfan could sometimes be brilliant. His father never allowed him nor his sister to adulterate the name even though their Englishness tilted the pronunciation towards mud for Clud instead of the correct "Cleed".

The house, *Cludfan*, translated into cosy place or home. His father had loved the old place, though both Piers and Hatty Barber had secretly hated their Christmases in the dreary grey gloom of the Welsh winter when all their friends were jetting off to Dubai for blazing hot Yuletide festivities in the noughties.

As every British person knew, or rather decided to ignore as an inconvenient truth thanks to the Victorians, snowy Christmases were an affectation. Dubai and its brother Gulf states' sunshine had more in common with the Palestine of two thousand years ago than cold Britain. If anyone bothered to step away from the commercial nonsense and consider for one moment the events for which December 25th was celebrated, that is.

Of course, all that had long since gone by the by for more or less the whole population of an increasingly secular Britain, apart from the odd stalwart who pitched up to church at midnight on the 24th, driven by a sense of nostalgia rather than any true faith.

No, a proper Western Christmas called for dark days and nights, even snow, though that remained an unlikely prospect in Pembrokeshire's maritime climate.

Piers, however, found himself yearning for the cosy tradition he once despised. His pre-children Christmases in London with Jenny had been filled with expensive frivolity. Now, burdened with a well-paid but stressful job and an Everest of a mortgage, Piers appreciated the inherited cottage and its calmer atmosphere.

It was a blessing, and something of a shrine to his parents who had succumbed to gin and tobacco within months of each other only a couple of years ago. As for his sister, Hatty, she'd married a New York banker and had washed her hands of the place.

Local governments had attempted to make second-home ownership punitive, yet Piers had managed to satisfy the 182-day occupancy requirement per rental period, allowing him to run the property as a business. He achieved this despite reserving the lucrative weeks of Christmas, Whitsun, and August for family time.

This late May, coming down early had an added layer of necessity attached to it. As someone once famously wrote: one needed the odd secret hour or minute. And this time, it had grown into secret days, all thanks to the need for planning. A real and sustainable fitness plan.

Yet, even thinking about those words made him grimace.

'Piers, it's very simple,' his GP had said when he delivered the results of Piers' blood sugar level, leaving the patient shell-shocked. 'Lose weight, and it all goes away. Carry on as you are and, in a year or two, you will be a fully-fledged type two diabetic with all the delights that comes with it. Want me to list them?'

He'd said no. He'd said he'd do something about it. Honestly, he would. And had left the practice like a schoolboy on a last warning from the headteacher.

Of course, secretly, Piers wanted clarification and got all of that from Dr Go-ogle, much to his horror, and wondered immediately about a second opinion. But then he looked in the mirror, and the second opinion stared back at him with flabby confirmation.

Always slightly podgy, he was now carrying an extra two stone. He'd been heading that way since the job in London had layered on the late nights that always seemed to end up in a takeaway. And once married, his work had increased with little or no time to do anything but get up, go to work, come home, and find comfort in big meals out.

And then the kids came along, and the gym membership seemed an unnecessary, and wholly unused, expense. Finishing the food the kids left over became a guilty habit that he justified by his oft-repeated aphorism, "waste not want not". Unfortunately for Piers, that ended up being waste not, waist exponentially enlarging.

Therefore, drastic measures were called for. So here he was, at 6:30am on the last weekend of May, setting off for a three-kilometre walk around Craig Caled quarry near Middleton Mill in Pembrokeshire.

Not that Piers avoided walking in London. That was an inevitability. Even getting from a tube station or a bus stop to your final destination meant treading pavements.

But this kind of walking, up and down the sides of hillocks gouged out of the landscape by machines and men, angling ever upwards for the first kilometre and a half, you never found in London.

After five minutes, sweat soaked already, he consoled himself with knowing he was doing himself some good. He held on to that thought for the second half of kilometre one, realising it was poor recompense for the fry-up he really wanted until he reached the crest of the pathway and the roads previously used by vehicles. At least used when the quarry functioned to take away the hard blue stone hammered out of the earth here.

Piers paused frequently to catch his breath.

These very bluestones, he recalled, had been hauled over one-hundred and forty miles to Stonehenge nearly five thousand years ago. The feat remained an archaeological mystery, a testament to Neolithic ingenuity. He felt a sudden awe at the ancient history beneath his feet.

Puffing and straining, Piers reached the summit. Between laboured breaths, he huffed out the mantra that had become his lifeline through this ordeal: "Pain is temporary, achievement lasts." The words felt hollow, but he clung to them desperately as he pushed onward.

The path circled away from the edge of the quarry top. But today, since he'd only stopped twice on the ascent, the unfit Piers felt in need of a breather and the distraction of a view to allow all the lactic acid in his legs to leach away. Which would, given their chunky size, take some time.

From the top, you could either look out towards the Preselis, or down into the water pooled at the quarry bottom a hundred and fifty feet below.

He'd stood there before, of course. In days gone by when he was fitter and the kids were younger. When he ventured up here to give Jenny a break, or at least some time to get the dinner on and some food going. He knew what to expect.

Except today, his expectations, though not exactly exceeded, were certainly jarred. When he'd recovered enough to reassure himself that he wouldn't pass out, he noticed the smell. Petrol mingled with, what was that? A kind of greasy barbecue aroma?

Had someone been down there cooking?

That was a weird thought because he'd noticed no access to the bottom. But, curiosity piqued, Piers walked as near to the edge as he dared and looked down. Looked and saw both the source of the aroma, and horrifyingly, a suggestion with it, of what might be the originator of that cooked meat smell.

There, on the rocky boulders at the edge of the deep water, sat the battered and crumpled remains of a car. Its boot faced upwards; one rear door bent back, showing the colour to be dark silver, whereas the rest of the car had been blackened by the conflagration that had engulfed it. All in all, it was a black hulk.

He could see no evidence of a driver or passenger, but he didn't really need to. The smell and his imagination did the rest.

Piers, gasping for air from the exertion of his walk and fighting back the urge to vomit at what he was witnessing, found little comfort in knowing his trek was over.

With trembling hands, he pulled out his phone, stopped the podcast he'd been listening to, and dialled 999.

CHAPTER THREE

DCI Evan Warlow called his black lab, Cadi, back to him as a tractor trundled along the lane. Man and dog hopped up a bank and waited for the vehicle to pass, receiving a smile of thanks from the driver. Behind Warlow, the third member of the walking party also waited, having used a stick to help himself up the bank.

Detective Sergeant Gil Jones was still on sick leave, but about to go back to what the powers-that-be called light duties.

Both men knew that no such thing existed in reality. So far as either of them was concerned, violent criminals ignored memos telling them to take it easy because a member of the rapid response team had been shot in the line of duty.

Gil had wanted to return to work within a week or two of the surgery he underwent to remove a crossbow bolt stuck in his shoulder. A projectile that fragmented his scapula, aimed and released by a deranged serial killer. A man motivated by a twisted desire to experience killing someone with that specific weapon. And, as motives went, it ranked high in the sadistic charts.

The attacker, Hugo Milton, sat on remand in prison awaiting trial. Gil was making a good recovery but not yet deemed fit for full functionality by the occupational health gatekeepers. But he refused to sit at home and mope.

'Anwen said she'd understand if I wanted to give up,' he'd told Warlow more than once. A prelude, usually, to an accompanying qualifying remark that inevitably came loaded with sarcasm. '"Good one, Anwen," I said. "And if I do, who is going to pay for the caviar and champagne?" That usually stems the tide.'

'I bet,' Warlow replied, a willing participant in the routine.

'Guess what she said?'

Warlow stayed silent.

'"A rissole and a Tizer hardly qualify as sturgeon roe and Veuve Clicquot." *Mynuffernu*. That cut to the bone. Some people are just never satisfied, are they?'

Though likely fictitious, the purported conversation between Mrs Jones and her detective sergeant husband rang true enough. It signalled to Warlow that Gil, despite his shattered shoulder blade, wasn't ready to turn in his badge just yet. Comminuted fracture be damned.

This Saturday morning, Warlow's dog walk with Cadi took a roundabout route. He first stopped at Dyfed Powys' Carmarthen HQ to handle a sensitive matter face-to-face with senior officers from an ancillary investigation.

Meanwhile, Jess Allanby – his partner professionally, emotionally, and to his constant surprise, in a variety of other pleasurable ways – had taken her daughter Molly shopping in Cardiff. Warlow, baffled and drained by such outings, opted instead to drive fourteen miles east with the dog to a country park near Gil's home town of Llandeilo.

As they passed a barn housing the estate's photogenic white cattle, Gil casually asked, 'How's everything your end?'

The vague question left Warlow room to share as much or as little as he wanted, preserving their usual arm's-length approach to personal matters.

'You mean between Jess and me?'

Gil chose not to respond in any way, preferring to allow

Warlow leeway. The Y chromosome had a lot to answer for in terms of stoicism.

'We're good,' Warlow answered, surprising himself when his tongue took over unbidden. 'She's good. I mean, for me. Never thought I'd say that because I didn't think it would happen again. Once bitten and all that.'

'Run for the hills,' Gil said.

'Weird to think that if that landslide on the coastal path hadn't revealed Ken and Marjorie Pickering's corpses, we'd never have met.' Warlow didn't need to explain more as Gil was well aware of how that case had brought him back into the fold from an abortive early retirement.

'Straight out of the Stephen King book of romance, that one.'

'You know what I mean.'

'I do. But I take a more poetic view. Or at least a more fatalistic view. You've never stopped to consider what plan the gods have for you, Evan?'

'Gods? Never had the time or the inclination. And if they have a plan, they must have cooked it up after a night on the White Lightning and a spliff.'

Cadi, a few feet ahead on an extended lead, slowed to an attentive stop as a curly Labradoodle rounded a bend seventy yards away. The dog was off lead and came bounding forwards, ignoring the calls of its owner with Fentonesque abandon.

'Max!'

Warlow's rule in such situations was to let Cadi off, too. Let the dogs have a meeting, sort it out for themselves. After all, they were of the same breed and temperament. Different story if it was a sheepdog or a terrier whose general demeanour tended to be a little more protective or reactive and could often nip even the friendliest of passing dogs.

The dogs met, tails wagging, and soon got down to nose-to-tail canine protocol. Once the appropriate not-niceties were over, they decided to play zoomy tag for thirty hectic seconds.

'Well,' Gil said, ignoring the dogs, clearly not wanting to

let his philosophical moment pass. 'Perhaps not questioning it is the best answer after all when stars align.'

'Christ on a bike. Mills and Boone still looking to sign you, are they, Gil?'

'You may well mock.'

'Thanks for the invitation,' Warlow muttered, but instantly realised churlishness, though a useful shield against anything remotely maudlin, and one he not infrequently polished, had no place here. He suspected his private life might have been a topic of conversation around the Jones's dinner table. But that was no reason for peevishness.

'Gods and stars are well above my pay grade,' he said as a muted apology.

'Mine too. But if either tips their hat in your direction, my advice is to take the gift as offered and never dare glance into the equine bouche. Especially when you've also won over a teenage daughter into the bargain. They can be a tougher audience than a wet night at the Glasgow Empire.'

Gil would know, being the father of two girls. And there was that, Warlow conceded.

He and Molly Allanby were firm friends. A friendship whose complex machinery was kept well-oiled by the black dog currently chasing a brown Labradoodle called Max.

'She okay? Molly?' Gil's enquiry emerged not out of automatic politeness, which might have rendered it nothing more than a conversation filler, but a more genuine inquisitiveness borne out of an enforced absence from the team caused by his sick leave.

'Funny you should ask that. She and Jess are retail therapy-ing the hell out of Cardiff's shops. All part of Jess's need for them to spend some quality time together. Molly has suddenly announced that a cousin of hers had reached out via social media from Italy.'

'Is that a problem?' Gil watched as Cadi and Max sprinted past.

'It is if you've not spoken to that branch of your immediate family for forty-odd years.'

Gil and Warlow reached Max's owners, who seemed nice

enough, and apologetic about the behaviour of their dog, an apology that Warlow brushed off.

Pleasantries were exchanged, the dogs moved on. Warlow geared up to explain unfinished Jess and Molly business.

But that opportunity never arose. Instead, Warlow's phone buzzed a message from Superintendent Drinkwater, no less.

> Evan. Body found in burnt-out car near Solva

He showed the message to Gil.

'As party invitations go, that one could use a little work. At least it's near home.'

And it was. A harbour village on the south side of the St David's peninsula in Pembrokeshire, Solva was twenty-five miles from Nevern, where Warlow had his own refurbished cottage.

'But you'll be thin on the ground with Catrin still off,' Gil added.

Warlow grimaced inwardly but didn't let it show. Gil's reference to DS Catrin Richards and her fifth month of maternity leave came as a sharp reminder.

'I'll come back,' Gil said suddenly.

Warlow tilted his head in and smiled. 'They won't let you. We both know that. Christ, you can barely lift a bloody pint of beer.'

'*Esgusodwch fi?*' Gil used the Welsh term for 'excuse me', exaggerated to express his umbrage. 'Last time I looked, I had two arms.' He waved his undamaged left arm about.

'Well observed, but Anwen would kill me,' Warlow observed.

Gil made noise like a small donkey braying. 'She'd buy you a bloody ice cream for letting me do it. She says I'm cluttering up the place.'

'No,' Warlow said.

But Gil, like a persistent estate agent desperate to offload a bargain property, continued with the hard sell. 'Office only. Strictly no field visits. Mine would be a supervisory role. I'll man the phones, run the boards.'

'You're only just out of a sling, man.'

'The important bit of that sentence is "out".'

Warlow shook his head. But even as he did, the thought of having Gil back, if indeed the body in the car turned out to be an unlawful death, burrowed into his consciousness like the promise of a cold lager after a trek across the Sahara.

'I was going to come in on Monday, anyway. The nice people at Financial Crimes have finally got more of the files from Napier's stalling legal team, and I was going to cast an eye.'

Warlow nodded.

The reference to a recent case where solicitor John Napier ended up the victim of a vengeful killer called Roger Hunt seemed doomed to haunt the both of them. The repercussions of Hunt's targeting of Napier and two other men extended into cybercrime and coercion. Additionally, a messy dispute had developed involving the Napier estate, which was determined to sue the police for negligence after Hunt managed to get close enough to detonate the lethal pipe-bomb that killed Napier.

But allegations of fraud and larceny as a solicitor had emerged. And as a consequence, Napier's firm was now under investigation for a different reason.

This allowed Gil, called upon by the powers-that-be to look into the illegal recording and posting of images online that had led Hunt to target Napier and others in the first place, into accessing records. Records that he wanted to pore over in case there were any breadcrumbs that had anything to do with a missing child named Freddie Sillitoe.

Just how that most tenuous of links might bear fruit neither man knew.

But it was a pot that needed stirring. And who better to stir it than DS Gil Jones, a man who had years of experience working on Operation Alice prior to joining Warlow's team?

Gil was well used to following the white rabbit down dark holes. And his wish to use his time now that Financial Crimes had thrown a spanner into the Napier estate's delaying strategies was commendable.

Warlow sighed. 'Let me see if the case is for us first.'

He called Cadi to him, and both men turned back to retrace their steps, this time with purpose, rather than leisure, in their strides.

CHAPTER FOUR

IT WAS bright enough at 7.30 am that Saturday for Rhys Harries to wonder if he and the person he shared a house with on Tabernacle Terrace in Carmarthen should take a little trip.

Through the window, the dull sky of a barely noticeable spring looked to have disappeared, banishing, at last, the rain and the clouds that came with it.

He reached around and snuggled into a spooning hug with Gina Mellings, his partner. 'How about we shoot off for the day? It's going to be a warm one. I thought maybe a pub lunch in Pendine, and if it stays warm, even go for a dip. They're talking 25° today on my phone.'

'Sounds great,' Gina murmured in a morning croak.

But Rhys picked up on the slight hesitation.

'Don't fancy it?' he whispered from behind her on the pillow.

She did not turn around to face him when she answered, 'Promised Dan I'd take him to Swansea this morning.'

'Oh, right … there is a train.' Rhys's response carried a hint of exasperation he immediately regretted.

Gina still had not turned around. 'I know. But it isn't cheap. Besides, he said there's a chap who might offer him some work. I said I'd run him there and back.'

'Okay. What time?'

'He didn't specify.'

No, Rhys thought. He didn't specify. Specifics, just like cleaning up after himself, offering to replace milk from the fridge, along with bread, butter, cheese, and anything else he could lay hands on were not amongst Daniel Mellings' strengths. But Dan was Gina's big brother and … there was not much more to be said about it. Certainly not when it came to a termination date on his encampment in the spare room.

'Thing is, Rhys, he's got nowhere else to go,' Gina had replied when he brought up the subject.

Her eyes held a mix of pleading and desperation, seeking both understanding and the blind loyalty that bound families together. It was a look he now recognised as one that could twist its way into awkward situations.

And, as situations went, this was becoming more awkward by the day.

Rhys quickly realised that Dan was less a bad penny and more a tainted thruppenny bit, appearing uninvited and oblivious to his lack of welcome. He traded solely on the fragile currency of sibling tolerance – not quite love, but at least a lack of outright scorn from Gina. This was fortunate, as Dan's standing with other family members was poor at best, with no love lost between him and their parents.

A situation Rhys remained woolly about, thanks to a reticence on Gina's part to discuss the details. He found such familial animosity difficult to comprehend. His own family would do anything for him and the diaspora that were his aunts, uncles, and cousins. But as far as the Mellings were concerned, there were certain wounds that had never scabbed over. Not enough for David and Moira Mellings to offer their son Daniel shelter during this unannounced visit.

Consequently, Dan played the "just for a few days until I can sort myself out" card with Gina and came up trumps.

Rhys did not consider himself an expert in human nature, though, as a police officer, he was on a steep learning curve, but he knew a thick-skinned narcissist when he saw one.

Dan moved into the spare room in Rhys and Gina's tiny maisonette flat, took over control of the TV remote, and sprawled over a chair in one corner like a shaggy throw in dire need of a visit to the launderette. When Rhys and Gina were not present, he suspected Dan opened a window and smoked, not truly understanding the principle of airflow and that a breeze never emanated from inside a building, leaving the stale, blown in aftermath in pockets of air in the room. Stubs, like the spent jackets of ammunition, littered the path under the bedroom window.

It said a lot about Dan that tossing away a fag end so that it was no longer in sight had been, and still was, his idea of recycling. He drank Rhys's beer and ate their food. If indeed he was truly attempting to get himself sorted out, it was at pace matching a tardy stalagmite's growth.

"Give him a bit of space, Rhys," became Gina's stock answer on seeing Rhys's expression of exasperation every time he opened the fridge and found it empty again.

And so, Rhys did as requested.

Even on this sunny Saturday morning when the suggestion of a spring day with Gina laughing at his jokes and sharing their plans, ranking well above raindrops on roses or even bright woollen mittens as two of his favourite things, got shot down in flames.

Instead, Rhys got up and went for a run, alone. Then he took a shopping list to Aldi and stocked up on essentials and came back to find Gina, car keys in hand, waiting to take Dan to Swansea. Her brother, clearly only recently up from his bed, judging from the way his hair had shifted sideways, uncombed, on his head, grinned at Rhys and took the laden bags with a cheery, 'Alright, Greasy?'

Surprised by Dan's unexpected helpfulness, Rhys responded warmly. For once, he wasn't even bothered by Dan's snarky derogatory nickname and briefly wondered if Gina had followed through on her promise to talk to Dan about his behaviour.

'Hi, Dan. Good sleep?'

He threw Gina a glance and got a smile and an indulgent elevation of both eyebrows in return.

It took only a moment for the world to realign on its axis and for Dan to return to form. He reached into the bag and, after a significant rummage, took out a yoghurt and a banana, helped himself to a spoon from the drawer, grinned at Gina and said, 'Picnic on the go. Let's do it.'

He walked out.

Gina, a couple of unnamed emotions fighting for dominance in her expression, started to say something, pursed her lips instead, and pausing only to give Rhys a quick peck on the cheek, followed her brother out.

They were not back by lunchtime.

They were not back by 2pm

Warlow's call came a little after that.

Rhys, who'd eaten his lunch alone and put on some washing – mainly Dan's – tidied up the flat and ironed his own work shirts, and some of Gina's for the week to come, listened to Warlow outline the findings and immediately texted Gina.

> Called in. Something nasty in Solva.

She texted back.

> We'll do Pendine another time. Won't be long. Takeaway tonight?

> Great. I'll keep you in the loop.

She sent him a heart emoji.

And so, just after 2.30 pm, Detective Constable Rhys Harries got into his car and headed west. This wasn't exactly the afternoon he had planned. Not by a long chalk. But he consoled himself with the playlist that he and Gina had come up with and kept adding to. Rita Ora, Beyoncé, Taylor Swift, and Ed Sheeran from Gina. Rhys had some Foo Fighters on there, some Arctic Monkeys, the Killers, Sunami, Night Flight, and one or two more mellow, seventies tracks picked up from being in the car on long journeys with Gil and Warlow. As he hit the A40, one of Warlow's oldies kicked in with masterful irony.

Just the Two of Us. Grover Washington Junior and Bill Withers's smooth R&B jazz offering, emphasising the ebb and flow of a relationship.

Rhys felt a rueful smile shape his lips, and shook his head. Fate could be a smart-arse. But it tugged at him, and he wondered if he and Gina would ever be *Just The Two of Us* ever again.

'For God's sake,' he chided himself. He was being pathetic.

Dan would not be there forever. His plan, delivered as a mission statement with enthusiastic optimism, was to get some work, earn enough to get him through the summer and then go back to the Far East, where he worked in a bar that had been recently damaged by floodwaters.

'No point being there while it's refurbished, eh, Greasy?' Besides, he'd wanted to come back to see the "fam". A laudable sentiment not shared by anyone other than Gina and, in part, by her older sister who lived in Bridgend, but who had no room at the Inn for their itinerant sibling since the arrival of her third child.

No, Dan the cuckoo was his and Gina's problem. For now.

Rhys was negotiating the St Clears roundabout, exiting for all points west when his phone buzzed again and a quizzical grin cracked his features on reading the caller's name appearing on the dash display.

'Gil, how are you?'

'Never mind me, how is the A40 on this spring afternoon?'

'How do you know I'm on the A40?'

'Come on, don't you read the memos? All serving officers now have their phones tracked centrally. I've hacked into their system. My laptop screen here at Chez Jones looks like a cross between Air Traffic Control and the Marauder's Map.'

'No one told me.' Rhys sounded both confused and a little offended.

'No? As I say, read the memos instead of folding them up into paper planes with lovey-dovey messages for PC Mellings.'

'I don't send Gina notes at work, Gil ... sarge.'

Rhys, even after several months, still stumbled over calling his fellow sergeant by his first name. He'd acted up as a sergeant and that had meant first name status with Gil during that period. But not now. Rhys remained a detective constable, albeit one a few steps up along the ladder of promotion, if passing written exams counted.

'Really?' Gil countered. 'What about that one I found with an aubergine drawn on the side of it? At least I think it was an aubergine. *Mochyndra.*'

Rhys grinned. *Mochyndra* meant filth, as if any of it needed clarification. 'You haven't answered my question about how you know I'm on the A40?'

'Marauder's Map not hacking it, then?'

'No.'

'Well, it could be something to do with me being near DCI Warlow when he took the shout about something unpleasant in Solva. He immediately called his best people.'

'That explains it. And thanks for that.' Rhys grinned, still insecure enough to accept compliments – but this was Gil Jones he was talking to.

'Yes. Unfortunately, both Catrin and I are incapacitated, so then he called you.'

'Hilarious. I see that your injury hasn't improved the quality of your bants.'

'I'm an M&S cotton briefs man through and through. You?'

'I said bants as in banter, not pants as in—'

Gil finished his sentence for him. 'The word you are looking for is underwear. I see you as a microskin trunk man. Anti-chafing, obviously. And you'd need the extra material for holding said aubergine in place if that drawing holds any vestige of truth to it.'

Despite himself, Rhys gave in to a thin guffaw. 'Why are we talking about underwear?'

'No idea. You brought it up. But I am the bearer of good news. I will be returning to the fold to help man the office – or "person" the office to avoid melting any snowflakes in the vicinity. If this shout turns out to be … Gil used the Welsh word for unpleasant, '*Amhleserus*, that is.'

Does that mean you're fit and well?'

'Well enough to man a whiteboard marker. You and Gina okay?'

'Good, yeah.' Rhys's response sounded sufficiently hollow in his own ears to merit some explanation. 'Her brother is staying with us at the moment.'

'Ah. Relatives. Nice for him, I'm sure, but probably cramping your style in that little place of yours.'

Once again, Rhys was impressed by the senior sergeant's perspicacity. A trait honed by years of listening to people lie.

Gil put a cherry on his insight with one last phrase. 'I heard someone once say that their family was like a squirrel turd. Best avoided and full of nuts.'

This time, Rhys let out a full-throated laugh and immediately locked the phrase away for future use. 'I'm looking forward to seeing you in the Incident Room again, Gil. I've missed the insults.'

'I bet you say that to all the officers shot in the back with a crossbow bolt.'

CHAPTER FIVE

WARLOW KNEW SOLVA. There were many picturesque spots dotted along the coastal path, but this fairytale harbour village had stunned artists, authors, and poets for generations. The path itself ran right into the harbour car park and back out again. If you walked it, not calling in to the Inn for a drink was almost impossible, since when you crossed the bridge over the River Solva heading west, you were within spitting distance of the pub's back door.

Warlow and Cadi had sat at the picnic benches in the garden more than once. Gwadn Beach, an adjacent cove a quick ten-minute walk away, was one of Cadi's favourites. Easy access to the shallow sea and a river to wash off in.

Warlow's knowledge of the area was first hand. But that did not stretch to the river valley behind, which was where he'd been directed.

The A487 from Newgate to Solva had been slowly improved over the years to accommodate the influx of ever-optimistic tourists who preferred not to go abroad, hoping instead that the weather would be kind to them. But Warlow's destination took him on a poorly signposted right turn out of the village, along hedgerow-flanked roads, still quiet this time of year.

Once the schools broke up, this journey would be a very

different animal. A slow and gnarly animal, most likely. Felin Ganol, or Middle Mill, was the nearest habitation to where he needed to be. Luckily, a response vehicle had positioned itself in a rough delivery bay at the entrance to the Woollen Mill for which this little hamlet was known.

Warlow stopped the Jeep and got out to be met by a uniformed officer he had not come across before. She, however, knew who he was.

'Nice day for it, sir,' she said by way of greeting.

And it was. A proper, late spring's day at last. He'd met little or no traffic once leaving the main route west. But a Saturday in late May meant weekend revellers would be heading their way by the end of the day.

'Indeed,' Warlow replied. 'Where's the party?'

'That's why they've left me here, sir. I'm the signpost. Up the hill on the Fishguard Road, until you see a turning on the left after a hundred yards or so. That's the old quarry. Someone up there will direct you.'

Warlow thanked her and got back into the Jeep and followed her instructions. The turning, initially on a sealed roadway, gave way to potholes and gravel pretty quickly as it curved upwards.

Where the village had been Saturday-afternoon quiet, the quarry buzzed with activity. Scene of crime vans, more response vehicles, a rusting container that must have once been a quarry office, and dominating the horizon, but invisible from the roadway, stood a huge orange crane with its boom extending out at right angles.

Quickly, he checked in with the Crime Scene Manager and looked around.

Notable for their absence were the CSI Tyvek tents he was so used to seeing. The Uniform pointed up to the horizon. 'All up there, sir. Back to the road and another two hundred yards to a lane and into the field.'

'Walkable?'

'Yes, sir.'

Warlow retraced his steps, left his car and walked up the steep hill along the road to the rough track that climbed to a field. On the far side, the crane, a fire engine, and a line of observers stood under the boom, staring at a point he could not see.

A familiar voice called to him from the little group of onlookers.

Alison Povey waved and stepped across the field to meet him. For once, the senior CSI was not dressed in her snowsuit. Given that the temperature had reached mid-twenties, that, no doubt, came as a blessing to her.

She held out her hand. Warlow shook.

'Nice day for it,' Povey said.

'Second time someone has said that. You in cahoots with the Uniform down in the village?'

'The pretty one?'

'For God's sake, woman, you're old enough to be her—'

'Much more experienced guide in the ways of the world?' Povey grinned, and Warlow wondered, not for the first time, if he'd slipped through a crack into an alternate universe. One where it was okay for a woman to make quips about another female, albeit complimentary, when he would never dare for fear of being labelled a "sexist old git" of some stripe. Still a bit rich coming from Povey, who had a wife and a child of her own. That somehow made it even more galling.

Okay, not galling, more … befuddling. And Povey, judging from her ear-to-ear grin, knew full well that it was.

'Whatevs.' Warlow resorted to nonsense as the best way to climb out of the snake pit. 'Give me the pitch.'

'Early morning walker smelt burning and looked over the edge, expecting to find some campers only to see a burnt-out silver Mercedes. We've confirmed that there is a body inside. The walker is at an address in Solva if you want to see him.'

'Okay. And all this?' Warlow pointed to the crane.

Povey began retracing her steps upward to the higher ground. When they reached a point from where they could look down, she stopped. Below them, the car sat as Piers Barber had seen it, but now some firefighters in protective clothing were busily attaching straps to the vehicle.

'Too dangerous to go down. We've decided on a lift. We'll do the prelim up here. I'll go down to the crash site later.'

Warlow stared at the wreckage. The vehicle lay at an angle with the front end caved in and a portion of the driver's side submerged in a couple of feet of water. The rest sat perched on the rocks.

'What does the Fire Investigator say?'

'He's been down. Suspects the fuel tank burst on impact. Only thing that would explain it catching fire.'

'Registration?'

Povey sent him a side-eyed glance.

'Oh, God, don't tell me it's some eighteen-year-olds on a joyride.'

'No. The car belongs to a Mr M Gittings.'

'Do we know—'

'A.k.a, the ex-Right Honourable Matt Gittings. The disgraced MP.'

'He's the one who got caught drunk driving and almost killed someone, right?'

'Last year. One indiscretion too many. Even for him. The by-election was a fiasco, too, if you remember.'

Warlow didn't. Not that he was completely apolitical. But, like everyone else in the country, or at least a big majority, he yearned for someone to come up with some new ideas that stood for common sense, the value of meritocracy, science, and more money for the police. Especially Chief Inspectors. He'd vote for that.

'Right,' was the answer he came up with. 'And we have no idea if it's him in the vehicle?'

'Not yet. Not even sure if it's male or female. From the snaps the firefighters sent up, we can just about tell that there's only one body in there.'

'So, it'll be a while before we can tell if this is self-inflicted or not?'

Povey nodded briefly. 'The good news is that Tiernon is on holiday and Sengupta is still on maternity leave. So, it's Bryers again.'

'Hmm,' Warlow remarked. Which was tantamount to approval.

Bryers had been their HOP for the last case, deputising for Sengupta. He was a pathologist who played some half-decent music in the morgue when he sliced and diced. That, if nothing else, had won Warlow over.

'Said I'd text him as soon as the vehicle is recovered.'

'Any idea when that will be?'

'It's classed as a complex lift,' Povey said. 'Or so that man running the operation says. Lots of checks and balances before they dare start pulling it out.'

Warlow glanced across at the huge crane with its integral lifting gear and the words DAVIES emblazoned along the boom and everywhere else it could be stencilled against an orange background. They were a local firm, and their vehicles were a common site along the M4 corridor.

'It's been dry, so we can't tell how the Merc got up here. Tyre tracks non-existent against this hard-packed earth. Plus, we've had to compromise this access to get the vehicles in.'

'Okay. No point in me hanging around here until it's pulled out. First things first. We'll see if we can contact Gittings. That's one way of checking if it is or isn't him. Rhys is on his way down, so I'll get Gil to do the donkey work on that.'

'Gil? He back at work?'

'He's volunteering his services.'

Povey turned down the angles of her mouth. 'Some people would have taken as much compensation as they could after being used as crossbow target practice and headed straight for the allotment.'

'Gil … has some unfinished business in the job.'

'Does he now.'

Warlow turned away. 'Keep me informed. I'd like to be here for the unveiling with Bryers. And text me the witness's address, please.'

He walked back down to his car and spoke again to the Crime Scene Manager before stopping at the Woollen Mill and chatting to the officer on point duty.

Her name was Paula Kendrick, and her partner, PC Landor, had stayed up at the quarry. She was indeed an attractive girl with hair in plaits as she stood against her car.

'Landor's on his way down,' Warlow said. 'Familiar with this corner of heaven, Paula?'

'I'm Haverfordwest based, sir. But there's not much call to come out this way, usually.'

'No. Definition of sleepy village, I'd say.' He looked around. 'My map says there are only nine or ten properties in Middle Hill. It would be very helpful to me if you'd knock on some doors and ask if anyone heard or saw anything odd in the last couple of days or nights. PC Landor can sit in the car for a bit if you fancy the fresh air. I've sorted it with the CSM.'

She blinked and smiled, and Warlow suspected she was glad of having something to do. Something active. He gave her his card. 'Find anything, positive or negative, call me.'

Back in the Jeep, he retrieved Barber's address from Povey and rang Rhys. 'Waiting on the Tonka toys to lift out the vehicle. Nothing to do there. We'll chat to the witness. I'll send you the address.'

'Is there anyone in the car, sir?'

'Yes. No ID. There is the faintest whiff of fish about, but I am not counting my tadpoles just yet.'

Several seconds passed before Rhys replied. 'Tadpoles don't turn into fish, sir.'

'Excuse me for rushing a metaphor.'

'Sorry, sir.'

'Forgiven. You never know, the witness might have a kettle.'

Then he rang Gil.

'Matt Gittings, well, well.' Gil's response was as expected. 'Alright. I'll see what I can find out. I am on the way in having had the blessing of the Lady Anwen. Or rather, a sandwich bag full of her best salmon and cucumber on rye bread.'

'Good. We don't want you wasting away in front of our eyes in the Incident Room then. Have you spoken with Rhys today?'

'Yes. He knows I'm in.'

'Did he strike you as tetchy?'

'As in the fly?'

'As in being more pedantic than usual when it comes to amphibians and fish.'

'No, but he admitted that Gina's brother was staying with them in the flat. I got the impression his presence is being felt.'

'Might explain it. I'll find out soon enough.'

'And, as for the car, there is a corpse, I take it?'

'There is. I'd be delighted if you found out Mr Gittings is sitting in a pub somewhere, swilling tepid lager and enjoying the sun.'

'But your gut is telling you otherwise?'

'It is indeed.'

After a long pause, Gil said, 'Can I tell you what my gut is telling me?'

'Only if it doesn't involve any sound effects.'

Gil ignored him. 'It's telling me that if it is Gittings, we can kiss goodbye to keeping this from the press. He's someone they loved to hate.'

'Along with a good chunk of the population if I remember rightly. Meanwhile, I am meeting Rhys in the pub in Solva.'

'Police work is such drudgery, don't you think?'

'You take your pleasures where you can find them, sergeant.'

CHAPTER SIX

WARLOW WAITED in the harbour car park for Rhys. By now, it had become a warm afternoon. T-shirts were off, jean shorts on. Much pale flesh was on show and the majority, in his opinion, probably should not have been. What people did with their bodies was entirely up to them. But he didn't feel he needed to see the results.

Jess would probably tell him not to be so "bloody prissy". But if you bared your torso to the world, people looked. In his head, he could hear Molly's voice.

'What are you like, Evan?'

He had his answer ready. *Someone who didn't want to have to stare at a beached whale while sipping his spritzer.*

He smiled at that. Of course, he liked to think he was like everyone else, with a streak of common sense and humility. But then he was not in his early twenties, with a gym physique. Unfortunately, neither were the extroverts a few pints in multitasking by attempting to boost their Vitamin D levels and likely to end up with second-degree burns, judging from the erythematous forms on display. Still, no harm done, other than an increased risk of melanoma down the line.

One or two small groups of revellers made more noise than necessary, but on the whole, they weren't bothering the families with children, and letting off steam wasn't against the law. Meanwhile, the fish-and-chip shop was doing a roaring trade, and red-faced walkers descending from the coastal path crossed the bridge and, more often than not, paused to gaze thirstily at the pub's open door.

A true cornucopia of sights.

Rhys arrived in his own car, found a space, and got out to join Warlow in the Jeep.

'Pub's busy, sir.'

'Well spotted, Rhys.'

'Must be that big yellow ball in the sky.'

'Definitely has something to do with it. Thanks for coming down. I've ok'd it with Superintendent Buchannan for you to revert to acting sergeant for this again. With Catrin still off and Gil not fully fit …'

'Thank you, sir.'

Though Warlow had not expected a jig to be danced, Rhys's muted response to the temporary promotion took him a little by surprise.

'Sorry to have disrupted your Saturday.'

'I wasn't doing much, sir.' Rhys tried and failed to hide the bitterness in that sentence.

Warlow frowned. 'Why not? Big yellow ball and all.'

'Gina's brother, Dan, is staying with us. He's dragged his sister off today, so I've been at a loose end.'

Warlow could have unpacked that information there and then but decided to stick to the plan for now. 'Right, let's make ourselves useful, then. We'll leave your car here, and I'll fill you in while we find Mr Barber.'

'Who?'

'The witness. Here's the address. Go-ogle it for me, would you?'

'I can do better than that, sir. My dad's grandparents were from Solva. I have an uncle here. He'd know.'

Warlow nodded. 'Local knowledge? Always the best kind. But before we tell the world via your relatives, best to keep things under wraps for now.'

'Why's that, sir?'

Warlow explained about the car and who owned it.

Rhys responded as expected. 'The sleaze bloke?'

'Him.'

'I remember reading he had a place down here somewhere.'

Warlow drove out slowly, avoiding the milling tourists. The car park had a one-way system, and driving out took him to the far end of the loop, where car park became a path again.

On his left, some paddle boarders set off into the estuary from a slipway. Beyond, the steep-sided hills looked verdant from the spring rains and in the harbour itself, the naked masts of sailboats anchored in the sheltered waters swayed lazily. No super yachts here. You could moor in the centre of the harbour for a tenner. These were small boats, by and large owned by locals.

'A hideaway,' Warlow muttered.

'Not a cheap hideaway either, sir. You'd be lucky to get anything under £400k in the village.'

'Oof. Your uncle in the know, then, is he?'

'Well, yeah. Parish councillor and all that. I mean, they've been hard on second homeowners here for a while. But they've been smart about it. Using the hike on council tax to build affordable housing, because the houses that are for sale are way beyond first-time buyers.'

'What's a first-time buyer expecting to pay these days?' Warlow stopped to let a family of four cross the road. He kept the question general. This remained a touchy subject for Rhys and Gina.

'Now, around £200k. So, that's at least a £20k deposit. That's the ridiculous thing about all this second-home malarkey. They're hiking up the council tax to 150% and that will make some people sell. But they'll only sell to other second-home buyers who can afford them.' Rhys sighed, and the follow-up sentence held a twinge of frustration. 'Not that we're looking to buy here, sir, but sometimes me and Gina, we think we're almost there with a deposit, and then something happens to my car or Gina's or there's a bill to pay, or inflation puts the prices up another 2%. We could definitely do with a bigger place at the moment.'

Warlow, despite having more than half an inkling of the cause of his angst, said nothing and let Rhys speak.

'We only have the two bedrooms. Okay, Dan is nowhere near as big as me, but somehow he kind of fills the place.'

'Not a respecter of individual space, is he?'

'Not much.'

'How long is he staying for?'

Rhys's taut expression oozed frustration. 'It's been over two weeks already. It was meant to be for a couple of days. He's looking for work before he goes back to Thailand or Laos or somewhere. He's a bit vague about the details.'

'What does he do out there?'

'Works in a bar.'

'Owner?'

'I doubt it. I have asked, and he says he shares the profits.'

Warlow let his eyebrows ride up a millimetre or two. To his credit, Rhys spoke as he searched his phone for the address in Warlow's text. 'Head up Main Street and take a sharp left to stay on it heading west.'

Main Street, a quiet stretch of road, rose out of the harbour and climbed until houses with views appeared on the left. It formed part of the A487 trunk road, merging seamlessly into the High Street along a stone-walled section.

'I bet the people who built these cottages never thought they'd be going to £400k.' Rhys looked around, a glint of envy in his eye. 'I mean, there's the usual Iron Age stuff in the hills, but they mined silver here, too. And coal in St Bride's Bay. But it's lime that made Solva into a port two hundred years ago. My uncle said you could buy a ticket to New York on the ships.'

As they climbed, the houses became larger. A few terraced, mostly detached, rendered in earth colours, the odd stone cottage or bungalow, too.

Warlow took a left turn next to a well-tended park and then another left towards Fort Road and a jumble of houses.

'So, what would they have been quarrying out at Middle Hill?' Warlow asked.

'Igneous rock, sir. Solva's out on a volcanic peninsula. Road stone, that sort of stuff.'

Turret Cottage sat tucked away with two other houses, a hand-painted sign showing its location with a pointing finger towards a little cul-de-sac. Warlow parked up and walked past an assortment of kids' fishing nets, the odd wetsuit, small and large, and an inflatable paddle board stacked against the passage wall.

Barber answered the door after one knock. Rhys made the introductions.

'They said you might call,' Barber replied.

He led them through to a slate-floored living room with whitewashed walls and exposed wood over the log burner in the fireplace. The window lintels were old wood, too, with no attempt at making the plastering on the walls even. Nicely done to lend the place an authentic brushstroke. An exposed stone archway where there must once have been a door opened into a kitchen area where Warlow glimpsed some modern appliances next to a Belfast sink.

'Nice place,' Rhys said, his eyes lighting up.

'It was my parents'. We used to come down here as kids. The aim is to end up here one day.'

'You don't live here permanently, then, Mr Barber?' Warlow asked.

Barber shook his head. 'This is my haven. My family are joining me tomorrow. It's an in-service day for the kids' school on Monday. We'll drive back to London on Monday afternoon. We have the place on with Hideaway Cottages and rent it out most of the year.'

'Not exactly around the corner from London, is it?' Rhys said, clamping his mouth shut after the words.

'No. But worth it. Tea, gentlemen?'

Both officers accepted and waited while Barber did the necessary. Neither man minded. The cottage was cool after the heat of the car. Tea made, they sat around a gateleg table Barber pulled out next to the narrow stair leading up.

'We appreciate that you've given a statement, Mr Barber, but if you wouldn't mind going over it again for us,' Rhys said.

'Was there someone in that car?' Barber tried to swallow some saliva, but it seemed to stick in his throat.

'There was,' Warlow said.

'Oh, Christ.' Barber's mug clattered down onto the table-top, and he suddenly turned grey.

He was a big man. Not as tall as Rhys, but probably the same weight, if not heavier. A big lump to lift up off the floor.

Rhys got up quickly. 'You need to put your head down. Low down, between your legs. It'll help.'

Barber did as suggested. 'I think I might be sick.'

Warlow went into the kitchen, had time to think how tidy it was before grabbing a saucepan and returning to Barber and placing it beneath him on the floor.

'Deep breaths, sir,' Rhys said.

Warlow waited. He'd seen enough vasovagals in his time to know this would pass quickly.

When Barber eventually raised his head, the colour was back in his jowly cheeks.

'In your own time, Mr Barber. Why exactly were you at Middle Hill?'

As explanations went, it seemed as genuine as ever these things were. Barber wanted to kick off a fitness regimen. One look at him told Warlow that was believable. He'd chosen Middle Hill because he didn't want his neighbours, especially the ones from two doors down, also Londoners, seeing him. When he was a kid, he'd gone with his dad to hike the quarry. There were sometimes adders there and the odd flycatcher and redstart. He knew it was a good up and down pull.

They let Barber recount what had happened while Rhys made notes, underlining flycatchers and redstarts. Warlow simply listened. When Barber had finished, The DCI made a judgement call and decided to throw it out there, but to keep it light for now.

'Have you ever come across Matt Gittings in your time here, Mr Barber?'

'The ex-MP? Once or twice. He liked a pint. I'd heard rumours he'd moved here, but I've never seen him on the street, the sleaze ball.' Barber's reaction to the name was as expected.

Warlow had already noted a copy of *The Guardian* folded on the settee.

'Lucky for him because my wife thinks he's the spawn of the devil—' He frowned. 'Why are you asking?'

Warlow didn't answer directly. 'You say your wife and children are on their way?'

'They are. I'm picking them up from Haverfordwest tomorrow. They'll have been on the train for hours.'

'Good. Best not to be alone after a shock like this. Sergeant Harries will give you our contact details. We'll likely need to contact you again once we have more information ourselves. The vehicle has not been recovered yet.'

Barber swallowed. He still didn't look back to normal. 'What a way to do it, though.'

'It?' Warlow asked.

'Commit suicide. I mean, driving off a quarry cliff? Surely there are better ways.'

'Different ways, yes. Better, that's not for us to say, is it?'

'No.' Barber nodded. 'You're probably right.'

Rhys's phone buzzed. He read the message. 'Povey, sir.'

'Right, Mr Barber, take care. We'll be in touch.'

'You'll tell me who it was, won't you? None of my business, really, but I'd like to know.'

'As I say …' Warlow got up. 'We'll be in touch.'

CHAPTER SEVEN

POVEY'S TEAM had placed giant sheets of tarpaulin on the ground, on which the retrieved Mercedes sat, still attached to the boom of the crane by straps leading up to a steel rope. Warlow and Rhys watched the water leaching away from the front of the car, pooling on the impervious barrier beneath.

Bryers, the HOP, was dressed, as were Povey and her team, in a Tyvek snowsuit, overshoes and mask. He walked around the vehicle, pointing, photographing, and making notes. He seemed especially interested in the driver-side rear door where the paintwork kept its dark-silver colour despite structural damage from contact with the quarry's igneous rock.

From what Warlow could see, the corpse, still seated on the driver's position, had been completely incinerated. It did not look real – more like something from a post-apocalyptic film. And there were enough of those about.

The HOP crouched low, peering at the wreckage. Eventually, he got up, peeled off the hood of the suit and joined the detectives.

'Don't fancy melting in one of these, then, Mr Warlow?' Bryers unzipped his suit.

'No, I'll let you and the CSI kids have all the fun there.'

The doctor, his brow sweat-beaded, grinned. Warlow reciprocated, knowing that Tiernon, by this stage, would've been not so much spitting feathers as projectile vomiting them.

'The body is, as you can clearly see, a charred skeleton,' Bryers said. 'Just about enough teeth left for dental records from my cursory exam. They'd normally be my identification weapon of choice. But we struck lucky at the front end of the car.'

He scrolled through the photos on his phone until he found the one he wanted. Proximity to the vehicle had given the pathologist's suit, and very probably, his hair and skin, a charred flesh and petrol aroma, worse now that Bryers was close.

A murky image on the phone got clearer as it was enlarged. 'Difficult to make out but most of the right foot and half of the left one are intact. There's about four inches of skin above the ankle on the right side in a flare-shaped strip extending a third of the way around the leg where the water line was.'

Bryers used his fingers to enlarge the image further and from the mangled collage of metal and plastic, some stained pale flesh appeared.

'The water acted as a fire retardant where the car was immersed. This is what I wanted you to see.' He pointed to a uniform ribbon of black around the outer part of the surviving flesh just above the ankle. 'The feet were naked. My guess is this band marked the flesh as the heat increased and then the car might have settled into the water, dousing flame and preserving the flesh as one.'

'What is it?' Rhys peered at the image.

'Difficult to say. Might have been a burn where the skin rested against some heated metal.'

'You'll also get DNA from the foot, obviously,' Rhys said.

'We will. But that might take a few days. Dental records first. We'll wrap the head before extracting the body and use an acrylic spray for stabilisation too.'

'Will the teeth have survived?' Warlow looked over to the blackened remnants of head visible just feet away from where they stood.

'As I said, they are the most indestructible parts,' Bryers replied.

'Will your lot contact the dentist?' Rhys asked.

'If you give me the details of who you suspect it is. But we need to get the body out first. I'll do the postmortem as soon as possible, but probably not until Monday.'

'Fine. Sooner the better, but it will give us time to set something up and get the team together.'

'Today, sir?' Rhys asked.

Warlow glanced at his watch. Six p.m. had come and gone. 'No. We'll get cracking tomorrow. But since we're here, we need Gittings's address in Solva. It's his car. We'll assume it's him until proven otherwise. There may be someone there waiting for the poor bugger to arrive home.'

———

IT WAS APPROACHING 8pm when Warlow and Rhys finally got to Gittings's place. Eventually, Warlow reverted to Rhys's local knowledge and a quick phone call to his uncle, who, of course, knew where Gittings lived. More than once, when the ex-MP's grandiose antics had caught the media's attention, journalists had tracked him down to the village, made their own enquiries, and parked where they should not have. Such things always came to the notice of parish councillors.

The house sat next to Mynydd Seion Chapel as the land climbed on the northern edge of the village proper. A white-washed property, possibly an old farmhouse, sat on the road-side. A narrow lane to the side led to a nice stone barn conversion behind the farmhouse and accessed only via that lane. A name on the gatepost read: St Fagos

Warlow parked on the road outside, and they walked along the lane to a courtyard and an open carport with fire-wood stacked at the rear. From the tiny garden in front, there were views of the sea. A path to the right led through a hedge towards the bigger house next door.

'Not a saint I've come across before, sir, St Fagos. Definitely not one of the Welsh saints,' Rhys said as they walked towards the door.

'That's because it's not anyone's saint. It's made up. An acronym. Sod That For A Game Of Soldiers. Ever heard that?'

'My dad says it sometimes. When there's something he doesn't want to do.'

'Gittings's idea of a joke, I expect.'

Rhys made a face.

'There is no accounting for taste, Rhys.'

The barn had been converted and had access on one side through French windows and on the first floor via some stone steps guarded by metal rails. The evening was full of light, but no sign of occupation met them as Rhys climbed the stairs and knocked on a solid door.

Warlow walked to the side and tried the door of the French window. Through the glass, he saw a larger living space with seating and a table beyond a small vestibule that contained coats and shoes.

No one answered when he knocked. Rhys got the same response.

'No one home, sir?' Rhys called.

'Difficult to say. One thing's for sure, we have no grounds for entry. Not yet. For all we know, Gittings's car might have been left here and stolen. It could be the thief in the car.'

Rhys joined Warlow at the French doors. 'You don't sound convinced, sir.'

'Don't I? I'm not. But we play by the rules for now.' Warlow glanced at the gap in the hedge. 'Let's knock on the neighbour's door.'

Next door had a solid, long-house design, slate roof and a lean-to extension on the side. When Warlow knocked on the red front door, no one answered. He made a note of the address. This time, a Welsh name. *Am-Nawr*.

The interpretation was For Now. Or perhaps this will do for now. An interesting choice, but none of the sardonic slant St Fagos had. However, it must have held meaning for someone.

Once again, after several knocks, Warlow concluded there was no one home.

'Right. Well, we're getting nowhere fast here. I vote we let Povey do her thing and I'll ring Buchannan and get some bodies in the Incident Room tomorrow. Top of the list is finding Gittings so we can eliminate him.'

'I don't know much about him, sir. Except that he was thrown out of Parliament and came back here to reinvent himself in local politics.'

'That says it all, don't you think? I mean, these days, you have to do something pretty bad to get chucked out of Westminster. Ethical misdemeanours don't count anymore. But I've got Gil on that. He'll fill us in tomorrow. Now we'll call it a day. What are you doing for supper?'

'Gina's organised a takeaway. She'll keep some warm. That is if Dan hasn't snaffled the lot.'

Warlow smiled. 'Ah, well, maybe Dan will cook you all a nice meal tomorrow night for when you get off work.'

Rhys said nothing. He didn't need to. The eye roll he gave Warlow said it all.

———

WHEN HE ARRIVED home just after 9pm, he saw Jess's Golf parked on the gravel driveway outside their shared cottage, *Ffau'r Blaidd*, in Nevern. Darkness was still an hour away but the day had cooled and the sun was just above the horizon in the west. He liked the day's bookends, especially in summer. Often he'd be up early with Cadi, on the lanes as the sun came up, relishing the quiet and the promise the day held.

But tonight, there was catching up to be done.

Jess, too, had brought home a dine-in-for-two from M&S. Something they could enjoy alongside a glass of red.

She was in the kitchen in jeans and T-shirt, putting plates on the table when he opened the door.

'Sorry I'm late.'

She smiled. They both appreciated the fact that apologies

were unnecessary. She, like Warlow, was in the job as a Detective Inspector and knew the score.

He walked in, dumped his bag, and Cadi, who'd been with him most of the day, ran excitedly to Jess, as if she'd been away for six months. She reciprocated, kneeling to let the dog get as much contact as possible, while trying to avoid too many licks in the throat and face. A manoeuvre doomed to failure.

'Molly not here?'

'She's gone back to Swansea. It's the last weekend of Uni. Two of her housemates have stayed over, so they're making the most of it.'

'How is she?'

'No, you first.' Jess walked across and kissed Warlow on the cheek but wrinkled her nose as his aroma met her. 'Have you been to a barbecue?'

'Don't. You might regret that question in a minute. Let me shower and change because I can smell it, too.'

Ten minutes later, Warlow sat at the table with a glass of Nebbiolo already poured, telling Jess about the quarry and Matt Gittings's car.

'We'll start small,' Warlow said. 'If it turns out to be him, things will scale up quickly.'

'Press?'

Warlow shook his head, a mix of resignation and dark humour in his reply. 'I can hear the hyenas laughing already. But that's for tomorrow. Tell me about Molly and the Italians.'

Warlow tried to keep it light, but his hoped-for response – perhaps a ciao, or even a rueful smile – never materialised. Instead, Jess said, 'Molly's determined to follow it up.'

'By it, what do you mean?'

'You really want more Allanby dirty washing before supper?' Jess lifted one eyebrow.

'It's in the oven, right?'

'Another ten minutes.'

'The clock is ticking, then.'

Jess smiled, making the corner of her mouth dimple – a look Warlow found spectacularly attractive.

She paused thoughtfully, gaze fixed on her wineglass stem, before meeting Warlow's eyes again.

'Did I tell you I'm from Manchester?'

'You did. Born and bred.'

'Have you wondered why Molly never talks about her grandparents?'

'She does mention Granny WTF.'

'Granny Wart Face, yes – Ricky's mother.' Jess's voice carried bitterness.

Warlow narrowed his eyes and asked, gently, 'I know your mum and dad passed, so …'

His words faded out. Jess had never spoken about her parents, other than to tell him they had both died when Molly was very young. He'd given her space, but she'd never occupied it.

'Ricky's dad got lung cancer and died at sixty. His mother took her new freedom, and the insurance money, and moved to Spain. She never had much to do with me or Mol. Having had four kids of her own, in a way, I don't blame her. But she could have made an effort for Mol.'

'She's still there? In Spain?'

'Sends Molly a birthday card with ten Euros in it every year, so I assume so. It's always a week after her birthday. And then only after Rick has reminded her.'

'It's such a shame she missed out on your parents, though. That would have been the Italian connection?'

'My mother came over one summer with some mates,' Jess explained, her voice now a blend of nostalgia and a little pain. 'She met my dad in Manchester at an Elvis Costello gig in seventy-eight. She never looked at anyone else, or back. That's the bit that caused all the trouble. My dad's family were from Liverpool originally. Immigrant dockworkers and there's likely a bit of Irish in there somewhere. When the shipyards started to decline, my grandfather relocated to Manchester to work in construction. My dad came along with no siblings. My mother, born in Milan, had three.'

'So, Mol …'

'Never knew my mother and father. The only grandparent she had any contact with is WTF, and she is useless. '

'But—'

Though Jess's next words were spoken quietly, something about her expression stilled Warlow. 'My parents were in Thailand for Christmas in 2004. I'd just started as a PC and couldn't get time off.'

Warlow stayed silent as something cold rolled over inside him.

'They were in Khao Lak when the tsunami hit. Their resort had chalets built around a lagoon. They had no chance. My mum was found the next day. My dad was found four days later, half a mile away.'

'Oh, God, Jess.' Warlow reached out and took her trembling hand.

'I was twenty-five—same age as Gina is now.'

'I had no idea.'

'Why should you? I still don't talk about it much. Pathetic, but that's how I dealt with it. Still deal with it. What is there to say? But the worst thing of all, the thing I remember, is that at the service we had for them, only one of my mother's sisters turned up from Italy.'

'Why?'

Jess let out a thin snort. 'Let's eat first. I might need more wine, too, if I am going to drag that rattling skeleton out from its cupboard.'

CHAPTER EIGHT

THEY ATE, and Warlow put the dirty dishes in the washer.

Jess, who kept her promises, waited for him to sit before she began.

'I'm not religious, as you well know. That's no accident. My mum was Catholic. Lapsed. My dad was C of E at Easter and Christmas. I got christened to placate my dad's mother.'

Warlow, full of M&S Moussaka and on his second, this time smaller, glass of Nebbiolo, should've been tired after the sort of day he'd had. Instead, he listened with rapt attention to what Jess was telling him.

Cadi, intuiting a change in the normal atmosphere of lightness and joviality that Warlow strove for at home with Jess, sat next to the DCI. As he stroked the dog's fur, he realised she was offering comfort. She had already spent ten minutes doing the same for Jess. He was always amazed by the dog's perceptiveness; a canine's emotional intelligence should not be underestimated.

'It won't surprise you to learn that my Italian grandfather was Catholic. Staunchly so.' She tutted at her own words. 'That's putting it mildly. They had a name, but I can't remember it. But it was a kind of Opus Dei on speed. Santino Cardinale was my grandfather's name, which you couldn't make up if you tried because it means what it sounds like. He was wedded to the faith. Like nuns are supposed to be wedded to Jesus. I learned all of this from my mother who, born into the middle of a pack of five, felt strangled by it all. The reason she took off for the UK that summer was to get away from being smothered by the mixture of ultra strict tradition and superstition. No dancing, no TV, even music was considered a distraction from religious life. Hard for us to imagine, I know. And I know loads of Catholics and they aren't at all like that. But my mother committed the ultimate sin. She met a non-Catholic and fell for him. And someone less Catholic than Benny Furlong was difficult to find.'

'You were Jess Furlong?'

'Yep. In school, they called me Not.'

'Not Furlong.' Warlow chuckled.

'Until I got to thirteen, and then the boys stopped calling me that.'

'I wonder why?'

Jess gave him a perfunctory grin. 'As I say, my mother had a rebellious nature. After she met my dad, she went back to Italy briefly, but the relationship survived the distance. My grandfather was not happy. When an engagement was announced, he refused to acknowledge it unless Benny converted. Of course, he refused. In reality, my mother refused for him. They eloped to Manchester. Not quite Gretna Green, but it had the same effect. She was twenty-one by then. They had a registry office wedding with a couple of Benny's mates and someone from the registry office as witnesses. That triggered a seismic shift that caused mountains to tremble in Milan. Her father disowned her and banned all her siblings from contacting her.'

'Bloody hell. Who came to the funeral, then?'

'That's another story. I got a card from my grandfather. He wrote two words in it. *Deus volt*.'

Warlow gave a little shake of his head.

'God wills it. I read it as him suggesting it was divine retribution.'

'Jesus,' Warlow whispered.

'But my mother's younger sister, Vita, came. It's all a bit of a blur. I was in shock. She was lovely, really upset. But she didn't stay in touch afterwards. Santino, at ninety-seven, passed two months ago. I did not go to the funeral.'

'You think that's why someone is reaching out to Molly?'

Jess nodded. 'The Godfather is no longer sitting on his throne. No longer able to rule the roost.'

'How does Molly feel about that?'

'Molly knows the story. But she's nothing if not adventurous. And curious. You know her.'

Warlow watched Jess's expression remain stony. Attractively stony, but still stony. 'And you're not happy about it.'

'They made my mother very unhappy. Do I blame them for not upsetting the patriarchal apple cart? Lara, that was my mum's name, desperately wanted to share her triumphs with her mother and siblings. Me, especially. But her father stopped all that. He used religion like a whip.' Jess swallowed an inch of wine. 'It's hard to accept from here, but the faith can sink its talons in deep. You only have to read about the Magdalene laundries in Ireland that lasted until 1996. Some people believe religion has all the answers. I prefer to believe it has a lot to answer for.'

Warlow decided not to argue the toss. Instead, he let her talk about her mother and her regrets. Eventually, the confessional well ran dry. Jess looked at the bottle of wine but showed admirable restraint, got up, ran cold water, and drank a wine glass full before turning back to the table.

'So, Evan. Glad you asked? That's my stinky, dirty laundry laid out for all to see. Now, I'm going to put the cork in this bottle of wine and go to bed. Tomorrow, I'll have my game face on and we can head to HQ together.'

'Nothing like a burnt-out car and an incinerated corpse to get your mind off … things.'

'My take exactly,' Jess said.

———

Rhys found Gina alone in their flat when he got back.

'I saved you some curry,' she said. 'You must be starving.'

'I am a bit peckish. I won't lie.'

'Only half a naan left. Dan wolfed the rest before I could stop him. He'd already eaten his. I didn't open your curry. It's still in its tray along with a spare rice.'

'Hiding food now, are we?'

Gina looked very unhappy.

'How did it go in Swansea?'

'It didn't,' Gina said. 'The promised work won't be for a month. And the meeting took place in a pub.'

'Is that where he is now?'

'In town, yes. He has a key. I've told him to be quiet when he comes back.' She emptied a silver tray of Jalfrezi into a bowl and fired up the microwave. 'How was it with you?'

Rhys gave her the breakdown.

'We're expected in tomorrow?'

'Yes.'

Gina nodded. 'Dan will have to fend for himself, then.'

'He will. We'll be heading back down west. I spoke to my uncle on the way back in the car. I have the name of the guy who lives next door to Gittings now, too.' Rhys went to the sink to wash his hands. 'How come Dan's gone to the pub? I thought he was skint.'

'He is.' Gina had her back to Rhys. 'I bunged him fifteen quid.'

Rhys turned from the sink, genuine anguished exasperation distorting his features.

'Yeah.' Defeat softened Gina's reply. 'But I didn't want him here when you came back.'

Rhys nodded. 'It's weird, isn't it? After it being just us for so long.'

'I told him he'd have to sort out somewhere else to stay. I said it wasn't fair to you.'

'Me?' Rhys sounded surprised. 'What about you? He doesn't lift a finger here.'

'I've given him a week. I said that if this turned out to be a case, I'd be busy. We'd be busy. No time to—'

'Be his skivvy?' Rhys finished the sentence for her.

Gina's eyes were enormous when she spoke next. 'I'll make it up to you.'

'Nothing can make up for me only having half a naan.'

That made her smile. 'It's an awful thing to say, but I'm looking forward to getting stuck in if this turns out to be a genuine inquiry.'

'The Wolf thinks it will be.'

'Ah, well, if he thinks it's fishy ...'

'Exactly.'

Gina crossed the room and slid her arms around Rhys. 'I will make it up to you. I promise.'

'Can we eat first?' He meant it as a joke. Her reply took him a bit by surprise.

'You'll be full of curry in twenty minutes and half asleep.'

Rhys pulled her arms away and walked to the microwave. He pressed some buttons, and the machine stopped.

'Another half hour won't do me any harm,' he said.

'Half an hour? That'll be a first.'

'Oy,' Rhys said.

But Gina had already left the room, calling over her shoulder. 'You'd better shower first. You smell like a bad day at a hot dog stand.'

———

GIL, too, got home late. It turned out that, no matter how much or what you did to disgrace yourself, having been a member of Parliament offered protection when it came to someone tracking you down. Even the police.

Gittings had separated from his wife and family after shenanigans with a member of his Westminster team came to light. Younger, female, and, some argued, vulnerable. Revealed via security footage as nothing more lascivious than a snog worthy of every fourteen-year-old, it nevertheless exposed him as an unfaithful chancer.

The woman, not that young, never protested the advances that Gittings must have made publicly. And rumour had it, the relationship persisted. But that footage, along with spats with other junior party members, his vocal stance on a variety of topics, and his uncanny ability to make himself look like an idiot on TV, had made him a controversial figure and led to his demise.

Gittings's political career read like a snakes and ladder advert designed by a chameleon. Initially a Labour MP, he'd been removed from the party over harassment claims and remained as an Independent. He did not contest the seat at the next election. Instead, he dug up some tenuous Welsh roots and stood as an Independent for the Senedd, somehow bamboozling a rural population with his populist brand, drumming up money from supporters who liked his dubious style, promising to champion farmers and fight against the war on tourism, labelling housing policies and second-home council tax hikes as "racist".

Once in his seat in the Senedd in Cardiff, he made a nuisance of himself by rubbing almost everyone up the wrong way. Three months ago, for the second time in his political career, he'd been famously suspended as an MS for inappropriate behaviour and a variety of other "unspecified complaints". He'd vowed to return once his name was cleared.

Power, it seemed, was an addiction difficult to give up.

Gil, fed and watered by Anwen, sat in front of the TV, wondering, in a Warlow echo, why on earth he still paid a licence fee. Still, at least there was sport. His arm was back in the sling. It had ached earlier that evening, and as his physiotherapist had annoyingly predicted, the sling provided pain relief. It worked. As did the two paracetamol he'd taken with a fresh Anwen brew.

Feeling a little more comfortable, Gil turned off the TV and moved to the room he liked to call his study but which he now referred to as a maternity cave because of all the cots, buggies, and other childcare paraphernalia Anwen insisted on hanging, leaning, and stuffing into every corner, under the desk, and on the shelves of the room.

'You never know, another one might come along,' was her enigmatic argument.

Since both his sons-in-law had been snipped, all he could do was shrug and reply with, 'If one does, it'll be in December and carried on a donkey.'

That had earned him one of Anwen's looks.

He finally tracked down the ex-Mrs Gittings after leaving several messages with her. He'd found her contact details via West Mids police and, ironically, from one of the officers involved in reviewing the Bowman case the first time around, many years before. The same case that had resurfaced and resulted in Gil being used as target practice by the killer, Milton's, crossbow bolt.

When Gil explained who he was, the dynamics of the call changed dramatically. Slightly bored tolerance became enthusiastic support in a flash. Shattered scapulae, it seemed, could be useful after all.

But the call with Gittings's ex had not been helpful.

No, she had no idea where he was.

'When was the last time you spoke?'

'Last weekend. He still sees the kids.'

'And this weekend?'

'He is not around.'

Yes, she knew about the cottage in Wales. They'd had it for almost nine years, and it had been a welcome escape when things got too … irritating in London. She'd been there many times. Now she wanted nothing to do with him or it. And no, she did not think there was a new girlfriend, but she'd heard the old one had flown the nest.

The phone number she gave Gil rang but remained unanswered with each attempt. All of this had taken several exhausting hours, and Gil was now tired.

He scribbled a note to self for what he needed to do tomorrow. The beginning of what would no doubt end up a thick file.

But he would do no more tonight. Right now he needed to nurse his arm and find a position comfortable enough to sleep. A task that had been a real challenge over the last months. Initially, he'd slept half upright in a chair. At least he was able to lie in bed now.

But underneath all of that was a note of satisfaction. He'd take the tiredness and his aching arm if it meant he could get back in the hunt.

CHAPTER NINE

SUNDAY BECAME A WORKING DAY, and Cadi was a willing drop-off with the Dawes, her sitters.

09.00: a quiet Incident Room, fresh tea on the go with a chance for a catch up. And, of course, Gil was the source of everyone's interest. The first time he'd been back at work since the day he'd been shot by Milton at the killer's home near Myddfai on the edge of the Bannau Brycheiniog National Park. Or, as one of Gil's granddaughters called it, the Banana Brycheiniog. A slip of the tongue which had become Gil's choice of address whenever he had a chance. Like now.

They were all pleased to see him, sling free for now, back at work.

'What's the most difficult thing about only being able to use one arm, Gil?' Rhys asked.

Gil thought for a moment. 'Number one was not being able to have my hair in a ponytail.'

Gina grinned.

'Shoelaces,' Gil said after a little thought. 'But I quite enjoyed having Anwen genuflect twice a day.'

'I'd have thought you'd be on the Velcro trainers by now,' Rhys said.

'Nah,' Gil replied. 'They're a rip off.'

Jess groaned.

Gil held up both hands. 'Can I point out that it was not me who opened the Velcro joke box. Besides, we shouldn't make fun of Velcro as it is the anniversary of the inventor's death.' After a very short pause, he added, 'RIP.'

'Please, God.' Warlow groaned.

'I suggested some Velcro trainers for the grandkids, but Anwen said no. She worried it would make them too clingy.'

'Oh, my God.' Jess sent Rhys a glare. 'You started this.'

'Right.' Warlow stood up. 'I'm sure I speak for all when I say how much we've missed that level of stunning repartee. And I second DI Allanby's chastisement of Rhys for mentioning Velcro.'

Gil leaned into his junior colleague. 'Don't you worry, Rhys. Ignore them. You stick to your guns.'

Shaking his head, Warlow walked to the whiteboard where Gil had simply written up: Quarry Death.

'Okay. What we know so far. A walker who uses an abandoned quarry as his work-out finds a burnt-out car and calls it in.' Warlow wrote Piers Barber's name up on the board before turning back to the team. 'Rhys and I spoke to Barber yesterday. His statement rings true. He's overweight. Uses the quarry because it's out of the way and no one will see him exercise.'

'Why doesn't he want to be seen, sir?' Gina asked.

'Because he's embarrassed by how he'd look,' Warlow said. Though Barber hadn't said this, both he and Rhys had agreed that the sight of an overweight puffing Barber struggling up the streets of Solva would have been a talking point.

'Is the quarry accessible?' Jess asked.

'It is. An abandoned quarry in the middle of a rural area near a functioning Woollen Mill that is a bit of a tourist attraction,' Rhys explained. 'But unless you knew it was there, you'd never find it.'

'You could visit the mill a hundred times and not know about the quarry,' Warlow added. 'And before you ask, Barber goes there because in days past, his father used to take him and his sister to search for snakes and birds.'

'As you do,' Gil said.

'Rhys?' Warlow nodded to the acting sergeant who stood up, consulting with his notes.

'The car is registered to Matthew Gittings, the politician.'

'Ex-politician,' Gil added.

Warlow continued, 'Gittings has a property in Solva. We could not contact him yesterday when we called. Rhys has posted images of the car both as seen at the bottom of the quarry and on recovery after the crane lifted it out. Those are on the local database. We'll get one of the less gut-churning ones up here, too. Looks like it was driven over the quarry wall, fell about a hundred and fifty feet, and caught fire. The sole occupant was incinerated except for some flesh around the feet.' He outlined Bryer's finding.

'How do you see this?' Jess asked.

'Depends on which angle you examine,' Warlow replied.

They'd already discussed this the previous evening, but it would do no harm to let the others in on their thinking.

'Possibilities. Rhys, if you will?'

'It's Gittings's car, we know that. But Gittings could be somewhere else. Maybe his car was stolen and somehow, the joyrider drove over the quarry wall.'

'Is that likely?' Gina sounded dubious.

'Unlikely, but we can't rule it out. Until we locate Gittings or confirm it was him in the car, we need to keep this possibility in mind.'

'What if it is Gittings in the car?' Gina persisted.

'Then we have a further two possibilities. From the local geography, there's no way you could accidentally drive over the quarry wall. Access is through a locked gate and across a field to a fenced hedge. The fence was down. The gate chain cut. Therefore, Gittings either drove to the quarry himself and made a choice to take the plunge, or the car was driven by someone else.'

'But the body is in the driving seat?' Gina required clarification.

'Exactly.' Warlow turned to Gil. 'Where are we with tracing him?'

'No phone response. That's my first job today, chasing up his mobile provider. But, of course, if it is him and the phone was in the car ...'

Warlow nodded. A phone would not have survived the fire.

'His ex has not spoken to him for a week,' Gil went on. 'They did speak last week. He has kids. Both early teens. But since his eviction from the Senedd, he's lived down here.'

'The Senedd, that's the Welsh Parliament, right?' Jess asked.

Being from Manchester, Jess still sometimes struggled with the intermingling Welsh and English words, and the insistence that some Welsh words only were used. Banana Brycheiniog being a prime example after decades of the Brecon Beacons.

'Correct. It's a druid's get together in that petrol station above the west terrace in Cardiff,' Gil replied with a grin and a little sardonic nod to the aesthetics of the parliamentary building.

Warlow stifled a smile as Gil responded more fully to Jess's question.

'Scotland just has the Scottish Parliament, and Northern Ireland has its Assembly. Wales gave it a Welsh name. Was it five years ago that they passed legislation to turn the National Assembly for Wales into the Senedd?'

'Might as well give us the background on Gittings now, Gil, since you're in full flow,' Warlow suggested.

'Right. Are we all sitting comfortably?' Gil looked out at the expectant faces, a slightly manic smile on his face. 'I promise I'll stick to the quick version. Matthew Gittings, maverick politician. Started in the Midlands as a Labour MP. Big on levelling up. Somehow grabbed the immigrant vote. This was before Gaza. Unfortunately, he was even bigger on sleaze. There were rumours of him partnering with investigative journalists to catch out opposition MPs in a scam. That backfired. Then there was the snog-gate affair where, as a junior minister, he got caught via a security camera fondling an aide – a willing partner, it transpired – who turned out to be his then girlfriend. He left his wife in the fallout and sometime later, the girlfriend left him. He got over that but lost the Labour Whip over accusations of bullying. That was upheld and so continued to sit as an Independent, but wisely did not stand at the following election. Instead, he moved to Wales to avoid the limelight. But then had the bright idea of standing as an Independent MS or Member of the Senedd, and had enough popular support after suggesting farmers should get recompensed for rewilding and the plummeting price of lamb. If you remember, he called the New Zealand lamb industry Kiwi Cutthroats. That went well down-under. Added an extra tongue poke to their Haka.'

'What is it with politicians?' Gina said. 'It's as if they want people to hate them.'

'Not all of them are narcissistic power-mad twits,' Gil said. 'But it helps to be one, so it appears. Anyway, he lasted in the Senedd for three years before that all blew up in his face when someone accused him of pestering a young researcher by text. He or she has not been named. No dick pics, but almost as good as.'

Jess was shaking her head. 'He sounds a real charmer.'

'Not the worst of them, but in contention, I'd say,' Gil replied. 'Anyway, he was banned after a unanimous vote by other MSs. Who knows if he'll stand again? But he attends local council meetings and makes a nuisance of himself. He is particularly animated when it comes to council policy on second homes. Since he still lists his primary residence as the house he used to share with his wife and children in Warwickshire, he is subject to the 150% extra council tax for the house in Solva.'

Warlow walked to the board again. 'Povey now has the car, and the body has been extracted. Bryers said he'd do the postmortem tomorrow. He's on the case with dental records. I got some Uniforms to do house to house in Middle Mill. No one heard or saw anything, which, given the noise that car would have made and the conflagration that followed, is surprising.'

'But you said the quarry was abandoned and not visible from the road.' Jess made a good point.

'True. Priority one is finding out if it is Gittings in that car. Until then, it's all an assumption on our part. While we wait for Bryers and Povey, I think we have enough concern over Gittings's whereabouts to keep it top of the list. Let's at least find out where his phone was last pinged.'

'What about the car. Any ANPR?' Gina asked.

'That's your job today.' Warlow looked at his watch. 9.30am He needed to ring Povey. 'And let's chase up any missing persons' reports from the last couple of days. In case whoever is in that car is not Gittings. Oh, and I've spoken to Buchannan. For the duration of the case, Rhys, you're it again.'

'It?' Gina asked.

'Acting sergeant. That okay with you?'

Despite a valiant attempt, Rhys failed to hide his grin of delight.

―――――

THE CALL that shunted the investigation forward came at 10.25. Warlow took it in the SIO room.

'Dr Bryers. I thought you said the postmortem would not be until tomorrow?'

'It won't be. But my forensic odontology colleagues like to have first dibs. And since we had a name in the frame, I got that ball rolling last night. The ante-mortem dental records of Matthew Gittings match those of the corpse.'

A tiny, careful bit of Warlow wanted to ask if Bryers was sure. But of course, he was sure. Otherwise, he would not have rung.

'I'll be doing a thorough analysis tomorrow to see what I can find, but I would suggest none of you or the team attend. It's more painstaking than usual, and if the body is severely charred, sometimes establishing whether death occurred beforehand may not be possible.'

'Do I take that as a warning?'

'It's a matter of fact. But there is one more thing. I also

had a quick look at the feet. You remember the area of darkening that looked like a band?'

'You thought that the foot might have been resting on something metallic that scorched the flesh?'

'I've changed my mind. I'm sending you through some images. Bottom line, it is a burn, but there is extraneous material.'

'How do you mean?' Warlow felt a prickle on his neck.

'The band ends where the preserved flesh ends and it is burned away. But on the skin, it looks like a piece of plastic has melted, melded with the flesh and stayed there when the water cooled it down.'

'That's important?'

'It is if the diameter of the material is exactly the same as that of a zip tie.'

Warlow stayed quiet.

'You still there?'

'I am. And you're sure?'

'I'll be surer when I get full access. But I'm willing to hazard a guess.'

'That—'

'Changes everything. I know. I'll try to confirm tomorrow. But I would assume the worst if I were you.'

'That should be our team motto,' Warlow muttered.

'I'll be in touch.'

Once the call had ended, Warlow walked into the Incident Room. All eyes swivelled his way.

'That was Bryers. The deceased has been confirmed as Gittings through dental records. He also noted that there are marks on the skin of the victim's foot which appear consistent with a zip tie.'

'*Diawl*,' Gil muttered.

'What does that all mean?' Gina asked.

'It means,' Warlow said, 'we need to get back down to Solva.'

CHAPTER TEN

THIS TIME, Jess travelled down with Rhys in the job Audi. Warlow used the Jeep with Gina as passenger. Another spring day.

A week ago, it had been a bank holiday weekend and travelling down to Pembrokeshire on a bright day like this would have been a very different proposition. As it was, the unending road improvements between Whitland and Haverfordwest added another fifteen minutes to the journey.

'Makes you wish flying cars were a reality,' Warlow muttered as traffic slowed to a crawl again.

In truth, he didn't mind because he had some delightful company. And much quieter company, if the mastication decibel level was considered. If there was one caveat, it came as Gina's normal buoyant outlook wallowed in the doldrums.

'I hear your brother has dropped in with you and Rhys for a few days.' Warlow took the male bovine by the horns.

'Yeah.' It emerged as a half sigh. 'Rhys told you, I suppose.'

'He did. Over from Thailand, is it?'

'Thereabouts. You know that part of the world, sir?'

'No. Never been. It's on my list.'

'Mine, too. Dan has been there yonks. He's seven years older than me.'

'Works out there?'

'He's supposed to have shares in a bar.' She made eyes at Warlow. 'His place is on the Thai-Cambodia border. It looks lush out there. But they had some floods, and the place was damaged. I mean, it's right on the beach and low-lying. They're prone to that sort of thing, aren't they?'

The word tsunami stepped out of the shadows of Warlow's mind, but he had the sense to not say it. Not after what Jess had told him.

'How long is he staying for?'

'Good question. He's not the easiest of people to pin down.' She kept it light, but the little undercurrent of desperation fluttered like a trapped bird under her words. 'He says he's going to find some work and then go back, but things move slowly over there. No telling when the bar will be up and running. At least that's what he tells me.'

'I'd like to go,' Warlow admitted. 'I keep telling myself that one day I'll go out there. Far East, I mean, for a couple of months. Visit my son and grandchildren and perhaps make a trip to Vietnam, Cambodia, and Thailand.'

'You and DI Allanby?'

He thought about telling her that perhaps Jess had no desire to go anywhere near the place, given what had happened, but again gave a non-committal answer. 'You never know.'

'Dan has never actually invited me or anyone else from the family. I think his accommodation out there is … basic. But he seems to love it.'

'Does he have commitments? A family?'

Gina smiled. 'He's not "ready" for commitment. Not according to him. I wish he'd hurry up, though. A beach wedding could be fun.'

She added the beach wedding idea as an afterthought to what sounded like a heartfelt wish that he'd commit sooner.

'Anyway, I'm hoping that he'll sort himself out. The flat isn't made for three people.'

'No, I'm sure it isn't. Especially when one of them is the size of Rhys.'

Gina switched gears. 'Sir, this Gittings doesn't sound like a very nice bloke.'

'Controversial is the term I think you're looking for, Gina.'

'I suppose. I've been looking him up. It's the sheer volume of his … controversies that get me.'

She wasn't wrong there. He'd discussed this with the person he debated these things the most with, Molly. Her degree in psychology and criminology prompted the odd dinner-table chat. Her take on mindsets provided excellent discussion material. He remembered what she had to say about politicians and offered it up to Gina now. 'I have it on good authority that politicians craft their responses in order to appease an audience.'

'Lie, you mean?'

'Possibly. But it's more to do with maintaining popularity and approval because they want to stay in power. That may be why they sometimes come across as not authentic. They may tow a party line and be terrified of saying something the press would hang around their necks. But ensuring popularity sometimes conflicts with truth. Then again, if we take Gittings, he pokes around until he finds a seam of popularity gold, then mines it for all its worth and sod the consequences.'

Gina shivered. 'Who on earth would want to do that job?'

'Someone has to. And it is wrong to tar everyone with the same brush. Look at the guy who helped the sub-postmasters and fought with them. And a Tory to boot. Lots of teeth were gnashed when he turned out to be a good'un.'

'I suppose,' Gina said.

They arrived at St Fagos before the others, got out, and stretched their legs.

'Are we going to break in, sir?' Gina asked.

'Not if I can help it.'

Rhys and Jess pulled in, and Warlow waved to them. 'I'm going to try the neighbour again. You hang on here.'

Warlow left the three of them in the garden and headed for the hedge and the path to *Am-Nawr*. This time, his knock got a response. A slow and shuffling one that ended with the door opening a crack to reveal an emaciated man in his seventies with thinning hair and a grey, close-cropped beard, one hand on the door, the other leaning on a walking stick.

'Hello, sorry to disturb you.' Warlow held up his warrant card. 'I'm Detective Chief Inspector Evan Warlow. We're here trying to find Matthew Gittings.'

'Isn't he at home?'

'No. His car isn't there.'

'Then he'll be off somewhere, no doubt.'

'Look, Mr ... uh.'

'Talbot. Barry Talbot.' The man shifted his grip, moving the walking stick to his left hand and holding it and the door frame as one before extending a hand towards Warlow. Two spots of colour high on his cheeks seemed unnaturally flushed and threaded with veins.

Warlow shook. 'I won't keep you, Mr Talbot, though I may come back, or send someone over to have a conversation later if you'll be in.'

'I will be. What's this about?'

'I can't tell you why at this moment, but I can tell you we need to get into Mr Gittings's property as a matter of urgency. You don't have a key, do you?'

Talbot peered over Warlow's shoulder. 'Are you alone?'

'No, there are another three officers waiting for me to return from my fishing expedition. We really do not want to have to break in.'

'Break in? That sounds serious.'

'It is.'

Talbot hesitated, but then said, 'I have a key. For when Matt isn't here. I let the cleaners in. But I'm not sure about letting you into his house. I mean—'

Warlow showed him his warrant card. 'I should have shown you this earlier. We will get in, key or no. But this is a very serious matter. We don't want to cause damage. If you do have a key, I'd be grateful to borrow it.'

'Can I see that warrant card again?'

Warlow gave it back to Talbot, who adjusted his glasses on his nose. 'I've seen your photo on TV and on my computer. That's how I read the news. You caught that crossbow bloke.'

'I was part of the team, yes.'

'Wait here.' Talbot turned away.

Warlow stood on the threshold, the door open a foot. He couldn't make much out inside the dark interior, but what he could see looked clean and tidy.

Talbot walked with a stiff gait, his polo shirt and jeans hanging off his wiry frame. There was no car in the drive, but under a car port sat a blue enclosed cabin scooter that had not been there the previous evening next to an eBike.

Talbot came back with a key on a plastic fob. 'It's the Yale lock for the front door. The other is for the back.'

'Thank you. Can I ask when you last saw Mr Gittings?'

'Friday night. In the pub. I left before he did. Haven't seen him since.'

'Which pub?'

'The Anchor. It's where I generally end up.'

'Okay. Someone will be back shortly for a chat, Mr Talbot, but I appreciate this.'

'I'll be here,' Talbot said and turned to go back inside.

Warlow dangled the key as he approached the others along the path and through the gap in the hedge. 'Let's hope there isn't an alarm.'

There wasn't.

Inside were three bedrooms, two bathrooms, one ensuite upstairs. Downstairs, a kitchen, nook, living room, and sunroom. Definitely not only a cottage. This had been a second home before circumstances made Gittings turn it into his primary residence.

Jess and Rhys took the downstairs, while Warlow and Gina took the upper floor.

Only one bedroom appeared occupied judging by the ruffled and hastily made bed, with southwest views over the town and sea – views that added significant value to the place, no doubt. The bed was made, but haphazardly. Gittings's approach to clothes storage was chaotic, with chairs, radiators, and an ottoman used as surfaces to drape things over. The small stand-alone wardrobe contained jackets and suits, but shirts were conspicuously absent. The ensuite was tidy enough, though the soap-stained shower door hinted at a disregard for housework.

None of this mattered. The bathroom cabinet contained nothing unusual or concerning – just shaving gear and some empty bottles of expensive aftershave. Crucially, no prescription drugs. Later, when they gathered in the kitchen for a briefing, Warlow emphasised this point. 'Nothing pharmaceutical of note.'

'I found some statins, Ramipril, and aspirin in the kitchen drawer,' Jess said.

Warlow felt obliged to comment, 'Tom says every man over a certain age should be on those.'

'A certain age?' Rhys asked, smirking.

'Something you haven't reached yet,' Warlow retorted. 'Since you are barely out of nappies. However, they are not the drugs of choice for suicide victims.'

Gina looked surprised. 'Is that what we're investigating here, sir?'

'We're looking for any evidence – violence, suicide, anything,' Warlow replied.

'We've found nothing like that,' Jess said. 'But there was something interesting on the living room table.'

The downstairs area had dividing walls to maximise space, but few doors. Rhys led them to the kitchen table, which sat behind one of these low walls. He opened a black, plastic, album-style folder with a nitrile-gloved hand. Inside were newspaper clippings, all featuring Gittings. Some were neatly cut, others folded or torn.

'Has he kept a scrapbook of himself?' Gina asked, her tone more disdainful than incredulous.

'Looks like it,' Rhys replied, flipping through the pages.

'A bit outdated, isn't it?' Gina remarked.

'He probably had someone do it for him,' Warlow said, examining a few cuttings. 'These go back to his Westminster days.'

'Why not just have a file on his laptop?' Rhys suggested.

'Giant ego?' Gina chipped in.

'Ease of access?' Jess suggested.

'Probably both. I spy a laptop on the table.' Warlow nodded in its direction. 'We'll get someone to look at that. But first, I want to know what happened Friday night. His neighbour says he saw him at the pub. It's after midday, so the pubs will be open. Let's split up. Gina and I will talk to the neighbour. Jess, you and Rhys take the pub.'

Rhys grinned, but Warlow nipped it in the bud.

'And no food until we join you.'

'Pub lunch?' Rhys went into bouncy puppy mode.

'We'll meet at 1:30 at the Anchor,' Jess said and walked out with Rhys in tow.

Gina hung back with the DCI.

'What was that tune Rhys was humming?' she asked.

'I believe it was, "Oh, we do like to be beside the seaside".'

'I've never heard him sing that before.'

'Must be all the time spent with Sergeant Jones,' Warlow observed. 'And the promise of food at the end of the rainbow.'

Gina smiled. 'That would cheer him up.'

'Right, let's you and I chat with Mr Talbot.'

CHAPTER ELEVEN

THE PUB SAT on Main Street, leading up from the harbour car park, just off the busy road and narrow pavement. As Jess and Rhys entered, they noticed all the doors and windows were open. Wooden tables with padded chairs and benches, filled the space. Many tables were set up for food, and the place was busy. The riverside garden at the rear was the busiest, with kids running around and waitstaff hurrying to and from the kitchen. The main bar led into a second room with an enormous fireplace, not needed this time of year, but Jess thought it would add a nice touch come winter.

The place was bustling with a queue at the bar.

Rhys made a quick recce and spotted a recently vacated table under the dartboard in the second room.

'Let's nab it. If there are bookings, someone will tell us,' Jess suggested.

It didn't take long for an apologetic young woman in an Anchor Inn T-shirt to tell them exactly that.

'We're not here to eat,' Jess explained.

A panicked Rhys added, 'Not yet, anyway.'

'Can you find the manager for us, please?' Jess held out her warrant card.

The waitress took fright and hurried away.

'Ever been here?' Jess asked Rhys.

'Once or twice. I have relatives in Solva, ma'am. I may have mentioned that.'

'You did.'

'They do a roaring trade in the summer. All the pubs do.'

Jess took in the roughly rendered walls and the boating motif. Paintings by local artists, with prices attached, hung on the walls. Polished floorboards underfoot, string lights on the beams. The background music sounded like an oldies compilation playlist. Warlow would like it here.

A man appeared at their table. Early forties, barber-trimmed stubble, white shirt and jeans and a tea towel draped over his shoulder. He peered down at the officers with a slightly harried expression.

'Janine here tells me you're the police?'

'That's right,' Rhys explained. 'And you are?'

'Paul Atkins. My wife and I own the place. What's this about?'

'Were you here Friday night?'

'I was on bar duty until about eight. Then I was in the kitchen.' He looked from Rhys to Jess, waiting for more detail in an expectant tit-for-tat stance.

Jess obliged, 'We're making Enquiries about a Matt Gittings.'

Atkins's face softened with amusement. 'The Git? What's the bugger done now?'

'His neighbour tells us he saw Mr Gittings here on Friday evening.'

'You mean Barry?'

'A Mr Talbot,' Rhys clarified.

'That's him. Then yeah, I suppose he did. They're regulars. I definitely saw Barry because he always sits on a stool at the bar until he gets company and then moves to a table, poor chap.'

'Poor chap?'

'He's not well. Still rides a bike to the pub, though. He's started doing that again. Like I said, I disappeared at eight. But I can ask Luke. He manages the bar mostly. He's off until this evening, but I can text him.'

'If Luke could confirm an arrival and leaving time for Mr Gittings, we'd be grateful,' Jess said. 'And we might have some more questions for Luke, too.'

'Right.' Atkins saw someone signal from a table in the other room. He turned back to Jess with an apology. 'Look, give me half an hour, and I can come back to you. I'll text Luke.' He didn't move away before adding, 'We're going to need this table, too.'

Jess got up. 'Of course. Any chance of a spot of lunch at, say, 1.30?'

'There's a function room we can use. We're fully booked in the restaurant and bar, but no function today, so let's say 1:45?'

'Not too late for lunch, then?' Rhys blurted out the question.

'No. We serve until 2:30. But you'll have to excuse me now.'

When he'd gone, Jess made her way out of the pub. 'We have fifty minutes. How about a tour of the sights?'

'It'll be a quick tour, ma'am. Solva's a sleepy place.'

'Once news of Gittings gets out, it won't be.' Jess looked up and down the street. 'Let's make the most of it.'

———

'MY WIFE WAS WELSH,' Barry Talbot explained in response to Gina's question.

They were in a living room that looked as if it had been untouched for a decade. A relic of faded wallpaper and worn-out furniture, its musty scent mingling with the memories of a forgotten past.

Gina had asked if he'd always lived here. And his reply, though not complete, went some way to explain his presence. He wore a polo shirt and jeans that looked too big for his stick-thin legs.

'We used to come down here on holiday. She loved the place. We had no kids. I worked in logistics and we had a tiny house in Surbiton. I retired at sixty-three and we moved down here. My wife died five years later after a long illness. Lupus.' He paused at the word, lingering over it before going on. 'I've been here ever since.'

He waved a hand at them. He wore Crocs on his feet and above them, Warlow saw that his skin looked red from the sun, or something else. 'I haven't done much to the place since Marlene died.' He looked around at the room.

Warlow followed his gaze, and the furniture, though dated, looked solid, but the shelves were dusty, with a cobweb up in the ceiling's corner. He wondered how often Barry came into this room. He wondered if it held too many memories.

'Had to give up driving a year ago after a seizure.' Barry's resigned smile seemed to show too many teeth in his thin face. 'You're wondering about the bubble on wheels outside? I still use my bike to get into Solva. I can just about manage that for now, but only with a battery. Electric bikes are a godsend.' Another grin. His skin had a greasy sheen. 'I used to do two hundred miles a week on a bike. Me and Marlene … that had been the plan when we moved here. Not now,' he muttered.

There was no mistaking the wistfulness. 'I'm going to hold on to the bike for as long as I can. Even if it's only down to the village and back. I'm better in the afternoons, you know? But now I need the Mobility scooter for shopping. It gets me into St David's and back when I need to. I won't be entering this year's TT race, but it does the job. Tea?'

He put an arm on the armrest to lever himself up.

'Will you let me make it, Mr Talbot?' Gina offered.

A trained Family Liaison Officer, this kind of situation, albeit where the grief that still so obviously affected Barry Talbot was a great deal more raw, was one she found very familiar.

He looked up at her with tired eyes and shrugged. 'If you like. Kitchen is on the right. Excuse the mess. Tea bags in the caddy marked … tea bags.'

Gina got to it, and Warlow heard the rumble of a kettle within half a minute of her vacating her seat in the living room.

'How long have you known Matthew Gittings?'

Talbot shifted in his seat, trying to get comfortable. 'He bought the place eight years ago. Did it up. My wife had passed the year before and the barn Matt bought needed a lot of work. But he and his wife had kids, and they were great. He rented it out mostly and came down during holidays. The kids and his wife were always polite.'

'What about him?'

Talbot fidgeted in his chair again, his face creased with pain. 'I won't lie to you. Things were not great after he moved here permanently. Not to start with. Silly little things that seemed to annoy him no end.'

'Such as?'

'I had some security lights up and sometimes a fox would walk through and set them off. He claimed it woke him up. I apologised and took some of them down. Then there was the drive. I had a tree with some branches hanging over and he wanted those cut down. In fact, did it himself and did a lousy job of it. Very belligerent he was. This was when I first got ill. I didn't want a fuss. But he's calmed down a lot.'

'What's your relationship like now?'

'Much better.' Another shuffle, another wince of discomfort. 'Sometimes, he drives me back from the pub if the weather is foul. Chucks the bike in the boot and we share a can or two in his kitchen or here. I have a key, as you know. I monitor the place when he's gone, which is one or two nights a week. Longer when he was a Member of the Senedd.'

'Okay. And when he goes away, where does he go?'

'To see his kids, I think. Back to Warwickshire. He's sad about them. At least, I think he is. Hard to tell, sometimes.'

Warlow half smiled. 'In what way?'

'He's thick-skinned, I'd say. Argumentative when he's had a drink.'

'Does he work?'

'Not now. There's talk of him writing a book. An exposé of life in the commons and all that. The truth about those politicians.'

Warlow smiled. 'Not a thriller, then.'

Talbot made a noise in his throat that might have been derision. 'Someone will read it. Anything with a bit of sleaze.'

Gina came back in with the tea. She didn't need to ask how Warlow liked it and handed him a mug. She put hers down on the table. 'How do you take it, Mr Talbot?'

Talbot looked up. His neck appeared stiff. 'Just milk, please. And strong.'

Warlow waited until Gina found a seat before continuing. He glanced around the room. On top of a chest of drawers he caught sight of some framed photographs and an upright, wooden, shield-shaped military plaque. He was too far away to see the details.

'Barry here was telling me that Mr Gittings is writing a book,' he said as Gina settled herself.

'Well, there's a ghostwriter doing that,' Talbot explained. 'But Matt is giving her all the gossip.'

Warlow sipped his tea. Too hot for a day like this, but you never turned down a cuppa. 'Would you say he was depressed after his marriage broke up?'

'I wouldn't say depressed. More hacked off.'

'Is he better now?'

'Oh, yes. We mostly talked in the pub. He was one for putting the world to rights, you know.'

Talbot picked up his tea in two bruised and spotted hands. As he turned his face up, Warlow noticed that the whites of his eyes were yellow.

'And what about visitors? Have you seen anyone unusual about the place of late?'

'No. Hardly any visitors except this ghostwriter person. Matt was always on his computer in the garden or with the French doors open, writing letters to the council and such like.'

'Does he have any other friends in the town?' Gina asked.

Talbot made a 'tuh' sound. 'Hardly a town. Only about eight hundred people in winter. More in the summer, of course. It's still small. Still a village. That's what I like about it.'

'What about friends?' Gina persisted.

'Not that I know of. Except maybe me, I suppose.'

Warlow put his tea down. 'Mr Talbot, I think you ought to prepare yourself for a shock. We found Mr Gittings's car yesterday. Burnt out.'

'What?' Talbot's relative lack of mobility meant he did not jerk or move in response to this news. 'What about Matt?'

Gil had been on the phone to a colleague in Warwickshire. Matt Gittings's wife had now been informed that the body found in the car was very probably her ex-husband's. Gil had texted to confirm.

'Both the car and the corpse were badly burned. But we believe it is Mr Gittings.'

A loud exhalation from Talbot. And an exhalation of shock, though his features – again Warlow suspected because of whatever disease had hold of him – gave nothing much away. 'You're sure?'

'We are.'

'Oh, God. He never … I never thought … how?'

'The car was driven over the edge of a quarry cliff.'

Talbot leaned forward, both hands on his bony knees.

Gina got up and put her hand on his shoulder. 'It's a bit of a shock when you hear something like this, Mr Talbot. Take some deep breaths.'

Warlow waited. Gina knew what to do.

After a while, Talbot's head came up. 'Where did it happen?'

'Not far away. Near a Woollen Mill. I'd say about a mile away.'

'Middle Hill?'

'That's it. We've recovered both car and body. I trust you to be discreet, Mr Talbot. We're just beginning our inquiry. Obviously, we are treating this as suspicious.'

'Suspicious?' Talbot's lower lip had begun to tremble a little. Perhaps through grief, perhaps simply shock.

'For now,' Warlow said. 'We'll come back for a formal statement. But if there's anything at all you can remember that might shed some light on what's happened, contact us.'

Cards were left. And then the officers did.

'Poor chap,' Gina said. 'He was upset.'

'Can't be easy living alone out here.'

'Oh, I don't know, sir. At least there is a community. People rally around.'

'Yes, they do. But he does not look well.'

Gina nodded just as her phone chirped a message. 'Text from Rhys to say they've booked a table for 1.45.'

'Better get our skates on, then.'

'Are we driving?'

'No, thought we'd walk. Get a feel for the place. That alright with you?'

Gina smiled. 'Good idea, sir. I could do with stretching my legs, too.'

CHAPTER TWELVE

RHYS ATE A FULL SUNDAY LUNCH. Warlow decided against it. A meal that size would have him dozing in half an hour. He opted for the salt and pepper squid starter and shared some whitebait with Jess. Gina had hummus and toast. Alcohol was not consumed.

At twenty past two, desserts were turned down, much to Rhys's disappointment, and Paul Atkins joined them as promised.

Jess introduced Warlow and Gina.

'How was the food?'

'Very nice,' Warlow said.

'Top-notch beef, and the Yorkshires were amazing,' Rhys, animated as always after food, gushed.

'We have some leftovers if you want to take some away with you?' Atkins offered.

Rhys's eyes lit up. Gina said nothing but half rolled her eyes.

'Mr Atkins.' Warlow brought things back to business, 'DI Allanby has told you we're looking into Mr Gittings's movements on Friday evening.'

'Am I allowed to ask why?'

'You are. We're investigating a very serious incident. That's all I'm at liberty to say.'

That took Atkins completely by surprise. He blinked at Warlow and frowned. If he picked up on the fact that the DCI had said incident and not accident, he did not mention it. Instead, he shook his head and aimed for humour to dilute the tension. 'Has he put his big foot in it again?'

'I'd like to hear about that big foot, too. But first, can you confirm he was here on Friday evening?'

'I've spoken to Luke, who was managing the bar. Gittings came in at about nine and left at eleven.'

'And did he drive, do you know?'

Atkins shook his head. 'I don't know that. He'd have parked in the harbour car park if he drove. The Inn may have CCTV, but I don't think the council does.'

Warlow looked at Rhys, who nodded, notebook out.

'I asked Luke about Barry Talbot, too. He left a good hour before Gittings. But then he has to get back to Upper Solva on his bike, so I don't blame him. I mean, it's quiet then. Best to leave before last orders and the punters all go home.'

Warlow tried to imagine the journey home for the sick-looking Talbot after a night at the Anchor Inn. But he put that aside for now.

'Mr Gittings was a regular, I take it.'

The muscles under Atkins' eyes bunched slightly. He leaned forward, lowering his voice. 'He is. If you want to know the truth, it's the only place he's allowed in. He's been banned from all the other watering holes in Solva.'

'Why?' Jess asked.

Atkins sighed, running a hand through his thinning hair. 'Take your pick. Threatening other customers after losing an argument. Being inappropriate to the staff. The female staff especially. Swearing too much. Being an obnoxious … git.'

The last word didn't strike Warlow as the one Atkins would have chosen in different company.

'How come you let him in, then?' Jess asked.

'He was on three strikes and you're out and knew it. Having already received one strike for calling a local coun-cillor a shortsighted twat. This is a family pub. Most of our profit comes from the food. But in the middle of winter, it becomes more of a drinker's spot.' His expression softened slightly. 'And, so help me, Gits was a character. He had a few good stories about Westminster and the lunatics that run the asylum up there. When he was in good form, he could be entertaining.'

'Any altercations recently?' Rhys asked.

Atkins shook his head emphatically. 'Not in here. None that I can recall. Gits is … was a creature of habit. Didn't come in every night.'

'Barry Talbot told us he'd travel to the Midlands regularly,' Warlow interjected, watching Atkins closely.

'Yeah. Never saw him mid-week. Usually a Friday, and he'd come in full of it. He never seemed down.' He paused, lowering his voice once again. 'Or he'd been on the wacky baccy before coming in. But it wasn't every Friday. It's just that it was a Friday when I saw him.'

'Did he partake?' Gina asked, sharply.

Atkins dropped his chin. 'Definitely. I've smelled it on him more than once.'

'Does he have many friends in the pub?' Rhys asked.

Atkins pursed his lips this time. 'Not friends. Drinking opponents, yes. By that I mean on the politically. Barry Talbot was always happy to speak with him, though. Some of the other guys saw him as someone to poke a stick at and see him dance.'

'And his journey home? Which way would he go?' Jess asked.

'The only way. Out of the harbour car park, hang a sharp left up Main Street, through the High Street, and then a right at Whitchurch Avenue, turning towards the chapel. Half a mile, I'd say. Five minutes by car, no more. Probably fifteen for poor old Barry Talbot.'

Warlow nodded. He'd already made that journey.

'Gittings sounds argumentative,' Gina observed, her tone neutral.

Atkins barked out a laugh. 'Politician, right? Always

wanted to debate bloody everything. If you said white, he'd want you to tell him why not black. Could be exhausting.'

'Enemies?' Rhys asked.

'Oh, he'd fall out with people and then they would avoid him. But by enemies, you mean someone wanting to hurt him?'

'Yes.'

The landlord shook his head decisively. 'No. Not in this pub. You could ask in the others, but I can't give you any names. This is a small place. Gits held certain views that didn't sit right with other people. Not an easy man to warm to, but he wasn't like some of these namby-pamby buggers whose views changed depending on which way the wind blows so as not to upset their army of keyboard warriors. But it's a free country, thank God.' A wry smile tugged at his lips. 'And if you don't want your opinion aired, you can always hide behind your phone and annoy people on Twittex.'

Warlow noticed Rhys about to correct what he perceived as an error. But then, realising that Atkins's mispronunciation was deliberate, he closed it again.

Jess suddenly straightened. 'Do you have CCTV?'

'For the bar and the outside area, yes.' Atkins gestured towards the corners of the room.

'Someone will be in touch for a copy of Friday night's if that's okay.'

'No problem.'

Warlow cleared his throat, preparing to wrap up the interview. 'Thank you for your time, Mr Atkins. We'll be in touch if we need anything else.'

As they stood to leave, Atkins called after them, his voice tinged with a mix of curiosity and concern. 'Look, Gits may have been a pain in the arse but he wasn't a fighter or anything. What I'm saying is, there were never any fisticuffs. Just piss and vinegar.'

The detectives nodded solemnly before stepping out into the cool air of the harbour.

Outside, Warlow recommended a quick walk along the street

for doorbell CCTVs and then suggested revisiting the scene. He wanted the others to see it, and a walk after that lunch would be a good idea to shake off the post-prandial slump. Besides, Povey was still there and wanted to show him a couple of things.

After the CCTV doorbell recce – Rhys found three – they headed for their cars. By now it was mid-afternoon and a proper warm spring day. Bare-chested kids ran on the little beach in front of the pub, eating ice creams. Dogs chased sticks and splashed in the river, cavorting through the pebbles and sand and the seaweed-frosted rocks towards the ocean. The tide was out in the narrow harbour. The moored boats either sat on the harbour basin sturdy on bilge keels, or leaned drunkenly, waiting for the Atlantic to give them back their buoyant dignity.

Gina and Jess both stood at the edge of the car park, staring out with smiles on their faces.

'This is special, isn't it?' Jess said.

'No jet skis. No high-rise hotel,' Rhys added.

'Timeless, I think is the word,' Warlow agreed.

'My mother would say it's like the cover of a chocolate box.'

Warlow turned to Rhys. 'Right, but inside there is always one orange cream.'

'What's wrong with orange cream?' Rhys took offence.

'The least loved of all the gooey fillings.'

'I like them.'

'Why am I not surprised by that?'

'Oh, come on, sir.' Gina took Rhys's corner. 'This is an … what's the word I'm looking for?'

'Idyll?' Rhys suggested, pleased like someone who got the last crossword clue.

'I doubt it. Not big enough. The nearest one's in Haverfordwest. Though the shop in the Post Office isn't too bad.'

That confused Rhys no end. But not Jess.

'German supermarket puns?' She stared at Warlow openmouthed. 'He's only been back a few hours but you're channelling Gil already?'

Warlow kept his powder dry with an enigmatic smile.

'Why haven't we been down to visit your uncle more often, Rhys?' Gina asked with a mildly accusatory air.

'We have an open invitation. I think one of those boats is his. I suppose it's because it's an hour from us and a bit out of the way.'

'That might be the attraction,' Warlow muttered. 'Come on, let's get it done.'

He timed the journey two ways. First, he sent Jess and Gina back out on the A487 until it split on a street called Prendergast to follow the River Solva to the Woollen Mill. He and Rhys followed the route Barry Talbot would have taken up from the village to the chapel, but kept on towards the hamlet of Whitchurch, took a right, and met the others at the Woollen Mill. He parked there and walked up to the cordoned-off quarry entrance to show Jess and Gina where the car had ended up, pointing out the ridge it had fallen from. They trudged up the hill and the lane to the field where the crane had parked to recover the car and where Povey's team was still busy.

'Alison,' he called out to her. For once, she wasn't snow-suited. Instead, she wore trousers and T-shirt.

'Had an ice cream yet?' she asked.

'Not yet. Too much of a queue at the shop.'

She turned back to where the car had taken flight. 'Two points of interest. The fence barring the way to the hedge that marked the border of the quarry cliff has been cut cleanly with wire cutters.' She showed them the downed fencing and the place where the vehicle had flattened vegetation, clearer now that the area was not blocked by large machines.

'No other signs of vehicles?'

She shook her head. 'It's been dry.'

Jess and Gina looked down to where other members of the crime scene team were working. These were white-suited techs poring over the fire-blackened rocks.

An evidence tent had been erected nearby on the ridge.

Povey led the way to a table where she had some photographs to show the team.

'Usually, we come into the tent to get away from the wind or the rain. Today, it's the sun that's a pain.'

Warlow didn't object. He was sweating after the stroll uphill from the quarry.

'The gate into the field had a chain and a padlock. Someone used bolt cutters on the chain.' Povey pointed to the image of the cut metal.

'We're to assume that whoever did that to the gate – and we are not discounting it could have been Gittings himself for the moment, right?' Jess looked around at the gathered faces. 'Whoever did that to the gate had planned for it.'

'And if it was not Gittings?' Gina asked.

'Then we have local knowledge and premeditation,' Rhys said.

'Still not discounting Gittings, ma'am?' Gina probed.

'We need to be sure about the zip tie. That we won't know until tomorrow at the earliest.'

After a few more minutes of examining the site, Warlow suggested going back to the cars. He rang Gil as they walked down the hill.

'How are you getting on?' Warlow dispensed with niceties.

'I managed to get hold of this ghostwriter. Of course, she thinks that she's won the lottery now that Gittings is dead. People will want to know the truth about the man.'

'Is that what she's going to give them? I thought ghost-writers wrote on behalf of someone else. They surely can't put his name on the book?'

'It'll be posthumous now, obviously. But she's keen to cooperate. She sees a new chapter for the book, no doubt.'

'Okay. We're no further forward except for knowing how much of a … git Gittings was. It's almost four now. I vote we call it a day. Recommence battle in the a.m.'

'Agreed.' Gil rang off.

Warlow turned back towards three expectant people. 'Let's go home. DI Allanby and I will go in my car. Gina, you and Rhys take the Audi. And much as you'd like to take the thing on the autobahn to see how fast it can go, I suggest staying vigilant for now. There are lots of innocent tourists about.'

CHAPTER THIRTEEN

RHYS DID AS SUGGESTED and kept the Audi under the speed limit all the way home.

'At least we don't have to think about food tonight,' Gina said.

'Don't we?' Rhys asked, clearly discombobulated by the suggestion.

'I can warm up your Yorkshires if you like.'

'I love it when you talk … heating food.'

Gina thumped him gently. 'I'm having cheese and crackers.'

'What about Dan?'

'He's a big boy. He can sort himself out for once.'

'He certainly can,' Rhys agreed, reassured by Gina's stance.

He left the Audi at HQ and they travelled back into town in his car. They'd moved into a house on Tabernacle Terrace two months before Dan pitched up. Within walking distance of just about anywhere in Carmarthen. But not their forever place. Far from it.

They arrived outside the property and parked in a designated permit spot on the other side of the narrow street, only to be met by a glum-faced Hakeem, their Afghani neighbour.

'Where you been, Rhys? You went out and left the TV on loud. It's blaring, man. We're trying to get the baby to sleep.'

Rhys frowned. A cracked-open window let the noise out, muted audience laughter and someone asking questions. It was indeed loud. It would have been much louder at the rear where the TV was situated.

'What?' Gina looked perturbed.

Rhys was contrite. 'I'm so sorry, Hakeem. I don't remember leaving anything on.'

'We been knocking for hours. Is there someone else in there?'

Gina and Rhys exchanged the slightest of knowing glances.

'We'll sort it,' Rhys said and opened his door.

Gina, distraught, added more apologies, 'My brother … he's staying.'

'Yeah, I've seen him around.' Hakeem was already assimilating the West Wales accent.

'He's probably fallen asleep with earphones on or …'

Rhys had the door open. Gina followed him in with a final, 'Sorry again.'

Rhys walked through to the living room, Gina in pursuit. The flat they'd left this morning neat and tidy had been transformed into …

'It's a bloody pigsty in here,' Gina said, raging.

Magazines were strewn all over the floor. Empty pizza boxes open on the coffee table, congealing cheese on uneaten slices mingled with the smell of meat to give the place a stale odour. Empty bottles and beer cans cluttered the table and floor.

'Was this lunch or breakfast?' Rhys asked, not expecting an answer.

Dan lay sprawled on the settee, earphones on, and the TV at full volume.

Gina immediately switched off the set. Dan did not stir. And then Rhys's eyes caught on something at the top end of the sofa.

'Oh, no,' he muttered in a heartfelt moan.

There, on its side, half its contents spilled on the floor, was a bottle of whisky. He stepped across the flotsam and set it upright, staying on his knees to survey the damage.

'Tell me it isn't,' Gina said, looking like she might throw up.

'It is,' Rhys said. 'The bottle of Penderyn I was going to give my dad on Father's Day.'

'Dan!' she yelled, though it had no effect. 'You shit.'

But her brother did not move because the earphones he wore, which in fact were Rhys's expensive earphones, had excellent noise-cancelling properties.

Gina moved forward to put her hand on Dan.

'Don't,' Rhys said, his eyes still on the bottle.

Gina stopped. 'What do you mean, don't? He's going to clean up his mess, not me and you.'

'Don't wake him. I need to be not here while you wake him. I don't trust myself.'

'Rhys.' She spoke his name and injected it with apology and an appeal for forgiveness.

Rhys got up, walked into the kitchen and put the bottle on the drainer.

'I'll make him buy another bottle,' she said from behind him.

At the sink, Rhys nodded. 'I can buy another bottle. I'd rather he didn't use the money you lend him to buy another bottle for me. That's not the point. It had my dad's name on it. A label that said for Father's Day. Dan's taking the piss, Gina.' He spoke calmly enough, facing the window that looked out into the patch of garden. Only the slight tremble in his hand as he ran water to wash alcohol from his fingers signalling the anger consuming him.

'I know he is.' Gina put her hand on Rhys's arm, but he didn't respond.

'I can't do this. I can't trust myself. I'm going to go over and see my folks. Dad's had a cough for a few days, so I said I would, anyway. Just a cold, he thinks, but I ought to call.' He turned around and held her gaze.

'What time will you be back?' Gina's question held a note of alarm.

'I'll text you, okay?'

Gina nodded. She didn't object. 'Your mum will probably have leftovers for you, too.'

A standing joke. But Rhys barely smiled in response. 'Make sure he cleans this up and not you.'

He leant down, kissed her on the cheek, picked up his keys, and left.

———

WARLOW MADE use of his late evening walk with Cadi to mull over the day. Jess had wanted to catch up with Molly, and so man and dog had gone alone. Tonight, he'd chosen some recently cut hay fields to let Cadi run around in and fetch the ball he threw with the aid of a green chucker that provided extra leverage, and thereby distance, to the ballistics.

The sun wouldn't set until well after 9pm, darkness an hour later, and the heat of the day hung in the fields and on the lanes. The forecast was for temperature to build all over the country over the next few days. He thought about the boys, his sons.

Alun would laugh like a drain at the promised high 20s that constituted a scorcher in the UK. He lived in Perth, Western Australia, the sunniest city in Oz, and that was saying something. As for Tom, London always managed a few degrees more than what he and Cadi got in the wild West of Wales. But London's heat felt stifling; the street smells and all the people mingling with the traffic fumes trapped breathlessly between the buildings sometimes made it intolerable.

Warlow had the T-shirt. He'd walked enough of those streets in his time. And thoughts of London brought his mind back to an annoying conundrum.

Fern.

The enigmatic name Jeez Denise, his ex, had left him with and which his brain had come to associate with his time in the capital city. That association, though vague and unformed, was as far as solving the world's worst crossword clue as he'd got despite weeks of pondering who, or what, the hell Fern was.

He'd even discussed the name with Molly and some old Met colleagues, who listened, bewildered, to the story of how Denise had mentioned the name in a deathbed letter to Warlow. Adding how she'd been visited by some people who'd asked about his association with a Fern. Mostly, he parked the annoying puzzle at the back of his head. But sometimes, like now, he revisited it for no obvious reason. But then, that in itself threw up new and tantalising ideas.

Why was he thinking of it now? On a warm, fine evening. Was there a link? The time of year? A particular time of day? Or the heat?

Who knew?

Cadi trotted back for one last throw of the ball that she dropped at his feet. He used the thrower to retrieve it in all its slobbery glory, threw it, and she sprinted after it.

Okay, that would be enough. He didn't want her over-heating.

Back at *Ffau'r Blaidd*, he found Jess in the kitchen pensive over a glass of already poured red wine. They'd tacitly agreed to wine only on weekends. Maybe a G&T twice a week. A win in this heat for certain.

Still, only as required.

But today was Sunday. Still a red wine day.

'Molly okay?' he asked, washing Cadi's ball under the tap in the sink.

'Oh, yes. If announcing that her cousin from Milan is coming over next weekend to stay with her in Swansea quali-fies as okay.'

Eyebrows raised, Warlow turned slowly to look at her. 'Not okay, then?'

'Do I have any say in it?'

Aware that he was probing very close to an exposed nerve here, Warlow took baby steps. 'Knowing your daughter, as I do, no.'

The plan had been for Molly to stay in Swansea, at the

student flat she'd already paid twelve months rent for until July, and visit Pembrokeshire and her mother – and Warlow, but mainly Cadi – as and when. At least one of her flatmates had the same approach to getting value for money for the rental. The other two were well-off enough to visit occasionally, take the loss, and spend the summer with family in England.

Molly, having secured a job in a Mumbles ice cream parlour to help them accommodate the extra tourist demand, was being admirably self-sufficient and used visits home as sporadic Cadi and good food fixes.

A bit like Warlow and Jess's mid-week G&Ts. As and when required.

Warlow suspected, therefore, that angst would be at the heart of Jess's disquiet. He knew the history of Jess's relationship with the Italian side of her family now. He decided to test it out.

'You like Italy, though, right?'

'I have nothing against it. As a country.'

'You certainly like their wine.' Warlow nodded at her glass.

'Hilarious.'

He refilled Cadi's bowl with fresh water and, seeing her sitting patiently with eyes fixed on his every movement, gave her a post-walk reward in the form of a dried fish-skin stick that crunched magnificently in her jaws as it scraped plaque from her teeth. At least that was the claim on the packaging. The dog did not object.

Then he sat next to Jess and let her pour him a glass of the wine.

'The cousin is the granddaughter of the aunt that came to your parents' funeral?'

'She is. And her name is Nina. She's in a university in Milan and her grandmother, my aunt Vita, is the youngest of my mother's sisters.'

'Sounds—'

'Perfectly reasonable. I realise that. This is all my prejudice. I understand that too. Just as projecting my hang-ups onto Molly is nonsensical. I can hear her now.' She changed her voice into a Welsh lilt, half an octave above her own. Not that Molly had much of a Carmarthen accent, but it did the trick. 'We can't be held responsible for the sins of our fathers, Mum.'

Warlow dropped his chin and looked at Jess. 'She said that?'

'As good as.'

'Blimey, as Rhys would say. Or as Gil would say, according to his granddaughter, Ay Crumbaba. From what little I read online, on that bastion of well-reasoned and intelligent source material, the Internet, her generation generally says the exact opposite. I thought, and I speak as a boomer par excellence, that we, according to certain theories, critical or otherwise, are responsible for everything bad that has happened in the world since the year dot. We should all be wallowing in guilt for just being alive. Aren't we supposed to apologise first and apply logic later?'

'Molly doesn't run with the ideological herd on everything.'

'And I will certainly drink to that.'

Jess let out a heavy sigh. 'I'm not sure how I'll react if I meet Nina. Mol is going to want to bring her here, obviously.'

'You'll be fine. If needed, I'll be an intermediate. I can even act as an interpreter. You know I speak fluent Italian.' He made some vague hand gestures as per the Italian propensity to do likewise as he spoke. 'Chianti, Sangiovese, Primitivo, Amarone, Valpolicella, Barolo Nebbiolo.'

It elicited a grudging smile from Jess. Warlow felt content with that since it had been the object of the exercise. He saw her switch out of her negative self-obsession and return to the here and now.

'By the way,' she began, 'how come you've got out of the postmortem on Gittings?'

'Bryers is a sensible chap. He says there'd be little point. Having already looked at the corpse, I agree a hundred percent. He'll contact me if he finds anything relevant.'

'That's very nice of him.'

'Isn't it just?'

'Tiernon would've been his insufferable self, no doubt.' Jess put the glass down and then looked at Warlow with fresh eyes. 'Early thoughts on this one, then?'

Warlow sniffed deeply. 'I have a gut feeling that all the worms will leap out as one once we open the can.'

'Me too.'

'Better watch some telly, then.'

'Good idea.' Jess slid off the chair she'd been sitting on. 'Something light and frivolous by way of distraction.'

'Right. A party-political broadcast it is.' He ducked in time to avoid the lobbed cushion that sailed his way.

CHAPTER FOURTEEN

MONDAY MORNING in the Incident Room. The first day of June. Gil held court while they waited for Rhys to arrive.

'He stayed at his parents' last night,' Gina explained. 'The cough his dad had turns out to be Covid.'

'Oh, no,' Jess said. 'The sodding gift that keeps on giving. And this summer strain is a sod, I hear.'

'Rhys made him test last night. He's OK, but because of what happened …'

She did not need to elaborate. Rhys's father's heart attack had been a worrying time for their acting sergeant not so long ago.

'He's at home, though? Not hospitalised, I mean?' Warlow asked.

'At home, yes. But Rhys is coming from their place. He texted to say he's hit some traffic.'

That had not been the only text exchange between Gina and Rhys. And though their content had been frank and open, there remained some unresolved issues that needn't concern the team. She'd hoped to catch him before the briefing, but the traffic issue was genuine. She'd made Dan apologise, albeit by text. And he had bought a fresh bottle of whisky. But not the Penderyn Rhys had wanted.

'It's bloody whisky, isn't it?' Dan had argued.

But she hadn't backed down. Not this time. She'd sent him out this morning, with the receipt to replace like with like. His one job for today.

Gina wanted to tell Rhys directly, but fate had conspired against her. That tête-à-tête would need to wait for the right moment.

Meanwhile, Gil brought them all to order.

'Rhys knows all this, so we might as well start. Matthew Gittings. Aged fifty-one. Married, separated, two kids. Ex-member of Parliament, now a Member of the Senedd, in the Welsh Parliament – currently on gardening leave pending an inquiry. To summarise – a bit of a plonker.'

Warlow, for Gil's sake, filled him in on their findings at Solva the day before. For once, the timeline seemed indisputable.

Gil, unlike his erstwhile colleague Sergeant Catrin Richards, whose maternity leave Gina was deputising for, preferred the expanding sticky note technique. Catrin was a whiteboard marker person.

Now, Gil had three Post-it notes up for Gittings's movements after Warlow had given him the intelligence.

The first noted Gittings's arrival at the pub at around 9:00pm, the second his time of leaving the pub at 11:05pm, and the third the time Barber had dialled in on finding the car in the quarry the following morning.

'The bits in between will follow,' Gil said.

'Yes, we gathered that.' Warlow tapped a pen idly against his open palm. 'House to house at Middle Hill turned up nothing. Talbot, the neighbour, heard and saw nothing.'

'So, did he jump, or was he pushed?' Gina asked.

'Could not have put it better myself.' Gil began writing something on the board to that effect.

At that moment, the Incident Room door swung open and in walked Rhys, hands up in apology. 'Sorry all. Bloody broken-down lorry.'

'How is your dad?' Jess asked.

'Not too bad. Nasty sore throat, aches and pains, and a cough that won't stop.'

'It's still bloody horrible,' Warlow said, 'even if it is not as bad as the first-time round. Give him our regards.'

'I will, sir.' Rhys walked to his desk. Gina caught his eye, and he gave her a tepid smile.

'I forgot to bring you a fresh shirt,' she whispered.

'I had one still at Mam and Dad's. But it's way too small. I'll pop back lunchtime to fetch one. This thing is like a strait-jacket on me.'

Gina wanted to go to him then. Hold him and say she was sorry. It would have to wait.

'Since we are all here, I'll tell you about the brainwave I had last night.' Gil's voice drew their attention back.

'I can't wait,' Jess said, her eyes large, cynical ovals.

'No. This one was genuine. And not the kind I get from eating too much cheese at night.'

'What happens when you eat too much cheese, Sarge?' Gina asked.

A genuine question from the least experienced member of the team. And one which drew despairing glances from the other three.

'Funny you should ask, Detective Constable Mellings. It's known to make you dream. In fact, sweet dreams are made of cheese. And who am I to diss a brie, as Ms Lennox once famously sang.'

'Oh, God,' Warlow said. 'No cheese puns. Not yet.'

'Feta complis, I'm afraid. But no, this brainwave was genuine. So listen … Caerphilly.'

Gina grinned. Warlow simply shook his head very slowly. But, he let Gil continue.

'I think we already know Gittings's life was … compli-cated. After reading about him and his exploits for a couple of hours, I felt like I needed a pilot to guide me through the choppy waters.'

'And?' Warlow asked. 'And please don't let this drift into sea puns.'

'I could, but I will keep this on the straight and narrow even if it krills me.'

'Gil,' Warlow's use of the sergeant's name carried a warning in the tone.

'The ghostwriter,' Gil said. 'She who has been privy to all Gittings's history and foibles.'

'Poor sod,' Jess muttered.

'Indeed. But she is on the way to us as I speak. Dead keen, too. I thought a quick chat with her might help us sort the wheat from the chaff, etc.' He paused there, awaiting comment.

'Good idea,' Jess said. 'What's her name?'

'Lucy Sanders.'

'When is she due, Gil?' Rhys asked.

'Tennish.'

Warlow smirked. 'Don't mind if I do. I'll bring the nets, you bring the balls.'

'A Connery-Wimbledon double-header this early, Mr Warlow?' Gil said with a smile. 'Impressive.'

'Just keeping up with the Joneses.' Warlow returned the smile.

'Well, there is more news,' Gil continued. 'The mobile provider confirmed the last known location of Gittings's phone placed it near Solva at 1am. After that, nothing.'

'What time are they releasing details to the press?' Jess had her notebook out.

'Rumours are already spreading on social media,' Gil replied. 'I've spoken to Sion Buchannan, and it'll be this morning. Probably about the same time as our spectral scribbler arrives.'

'What do we know about her, sarge?' Gina asked.

'I've had a peek at her bio. Smart cookie. Writes fiction, too. But she's done a couple of biographies. One on an Olympic cyclist who got drug tested and lost his medals, and one on that actor who outed the toxic director bloke.'

Jess made her mouth into a shape that implied a wary respect. 'Not scared of a bit of controversy, then?'

'It doesn't sound like it.'

'Let's hope she isn't a female version of you know who,' Rhys muttered.

'Do not mention the Lane word,' Gina warned him.

'You just did,' Rhys pointed out.

'Lane's book isn't out yet, though, is it?' Jess asked.

'No. End of this year, maybe early next is my understanding,' Warlow said.

Geraint Lane, the journalist referred to, was not writing a biography. Though there would undoubtedly be biographical details in the book … about more than one person. It was mainly about Roger Hunt, infamous pipe bomber, murderer, and kidnapper, but also about members of Warlow's team, especially their absent colleague, Catrin Richards, who had been abducted by Hunt. No one was looking forward to the book.

As an example of a reputable journalist, Lane left a lot to be desired. As an odious serpent, he was top-notch. No one believed the book would be even-handed or neutral; it was a matter of just how much anti-establishment rhetoric he could squeeze into every paragraph.

'Let's give her a chance,' Gil said. 'Let's not judge Sanders by Lane's example.'

Warlow's phone broke up the discussion by pinging a notification. He glanced at it and excused himself.

'It's Bryers, the HOP. I'm going to take it in the SIO room. Jess, see if you can cadge a conference room for our chat with Sanders. I think we should all be in on it.'

'Cheeses of Nazareth,' Rhys blurted out the words.

'Pardon?' Jess looked genuinely baffled.

'Cheese puns. I was trying to remember the one I saw at Christmas online. I'm sure there was a shop by the same name, even.'

'That's why you were so quiet, trying to remember?' Jess asked.

'Yeah.' Rhys looked pleased with himself.

———

Bryers' voice over the phone came through over a background of prog rock.

'Are you in the morgue?' Warlow asked.

'How did you guess?'

'Because that's the Alan Parsons' Project in the background. So, where else?'

'I'm impressed yet again, Evan. Few people would have recognised the Parson. I have some information for you. First, bilateral acetabular fractures. The legs were driven backwards in a sitting position consistent with the car's engine block being forced back on impact.'

'Okay. No surprises there.'

'It would have been painful.'

'Not enough to kill him?'

'No. There is no neck fracture, so my guess is that the airbags deployed. No sign of them now, of course, after the conflagration. The Fire Investigator tells me a car fire can reach up to nine-hundred degrees centigrade. He's full of cheerful facts like that.' Warlow imagined Bryers wry grin. 'Almost cremation level heat. Lucky we had pooled water at the bottom or there would be nothing left to examine. But, and here is the better news for you, the band on the leg is definitely a zip tie. The actual locking mechanism had fused with the flesh on the burnt side of the leg above the ankle. It was not visible until I dug it out. There's no doubt in my mind.'

'I see. Nothing on the other leg?'

'No. The minimal amount of retained skin on that side is consistent with how the car lay in the water. Any tie would have burnt away. But I also have a preliminary toxicology report.'

'That was quick.'

'We took samples yesterday while the forensic dentist did his thing. Congealed blood in the foot went for analysis and the lab runs an automated immunoassay for a standard panel. We have positive results for alcohol.'

'Again, no surprises, he was in the pub Friday night.'

'Okay. But he was also positive for cannabis and Zolpinam.'

'Which is?'

'A central nervous system depressant which blocks GABA receptors.'

'You'll need to explain.'

'Gamma-aminobutyric acid receptors.'

'I'm still none the wiser.'

'It's a sleeping pill. And mixed with alcohol, not good. We'll have to wait for actual blood levels, but this guy was sailing.'

'That's useful to know.'

'The question is, what was he doing in the car with all that on board? Trying to forget something permanently?'

'Well, that might work. But the zip tie is a real fly in that particular ointment.'

Bryers made a noise in his throat that might have been some kind of condolence. 'I'll leave that side of it to you.'

Indeed, Warlow thought as Bryers rang off.

CHAPTER FIFTEEN

LUCY SANDERS GREETED everyone individually when she came into the conference room. Gina had met her in reception, brought her up, and offered her tea. She opted instead for instant coffee.

Warlow had long since stopped letting preconceptions rule. Still, the short-haired, nose-ring wearing person who breathed out a toothy 'Hi,' when he offered his hand, had not featured in his imaginings. In that scenario, he'd envisaged an Oxbridge accent and hair held back in a band.

Lucy Sanders had no need for a band. Her carpenter's jeans had rolled-up cuffs and on her feet were baseball boots. Thick glasses correcting her myopia made her eyes look smaller behind the lenses.

The team had already sorted out their own beverages; everyone else had gone for tea and the *Human Tissue For Transplant* box had been opened to display its wares. So as not to frighten their guest, biscuits had been decanted onto a plate.

'Thanks for coming,' Warlow said. 'Sergeant Jones says that you might help us.'

Sanders smiled. 'I'm still a little in the dark. As, it appears, are you. Your DS thought I could shed some light into the darker corners.'

'Interesting choice of words,' Warlow said and glanced at his watch.

The press announcement was imminent and ideally, he would have wanted to wait, but this woman deserved an explanation.

'You've come down from Bristol, I hear?' he asked.

'I left at seven on the dot. Google maps said two hours, so I stopped for a coffee on the way.'

'How far along with the book are you?'

'About three quarters. I have a few interviews left. In Cardiff, as a matter of fact. But I finished interviewing Matt a month ago.'

'Just as well,' Jess said, noting her use of the first name.

Lucy Sanders lowered one eyebrow, her suspicions raised. 'That's a bit cryptic.'

'It's not meant to be,' Jess explained. 'Matt Gittings was found dead two days ago. His car had been driven over the edge of a quarry a mile from where he lived in Solva.'

After swallowing dryly three times, Lucy Sanders took a sip of her coffee before whispering a question, 'He's dead?'

'I'm afraid so,' Gil said. 'When I contacted you, we were not one hundred percent certain for reasons that will become obvious. We knew then it was his car, but not who the driver was … I wasn't trying to mislead you in any way. And you will be amongst the first people to know officially, if that is any consolation. The press announcement is this morning.'

Sanders nodded, clearly shell-shocked.

'How well did you know him?' Warlow asked.

'I'm writing his biography.' The reply was sharp. Delivered with a nervous laugh that suggested she found the question ridiculous.

'Let me rephrase that. Was your relationship with him purely professional?'

'Totally,' Sanders said, her tone crisp. 'He was not my type. Not even in the same galaxy as my type.' She cast a fleeting glance at Gina and Jess, so quick it was almost imperceptible.

But Warlow caught it. That lightning-fast look told him everything he needed to know: Lucy Sanders and Gittings were about as likely to tango as oil was to mix with water.

She recovered quickly. 'Am I allowed to ask questions?'

Jess nodded.

'Was this suicide?'

'Did he strike you as suicidal?' Warlow threw a question back at her.

'No. Absolutely not. Never. He had too big an ego to contemplate suicide.'

Jess picked up on this. 'You seem very sure.'

'That's my opinion.'

'Sometimes, people are good at projecting. Hiding behind a mask,' Warlow said.

'I'm sure they are,' Sanders agreed. 'But not Matt Gittings. What you saw was what you got. He was an agent of chaos, yes. An argumentative twit, yes. But if you think there might be something deep or sensitive behind all of that bluster, you'd be wrong.'

'But his career—' Rhys began.

Sanders interrupted him. 'He was a biographer's dream. Contentious, pugnacious, some might say weak-willed, in many respects. But he was a survivor. In fact, I'm thinking of calling the book *Chameleon*.'

Warlow saw immediately that Sanders had analysed what they'd told her. Yes, it had shocked her, but she was already weighing up the opportunities it was all affording. Callous? Perhaps. After all, a man was dead. But death left only memories. And how people remembered Gittings might be up to this woman in front of him.

'So, suicide?' continued Sanders. 'And nothing else?'

'We are examining every angle,' Warlow answered.

'Oh, my, God. You are, too, aren't you? You think someone else might have done this?'

'As I explained, we're at the very beginning of our investigation,' Gil said carefully. 'That's why I contacted you to get a better handle on our man.'

Lucy smiled. 'Good luck with that. I'm still trying after twelve months.'

Warlow looked around at the team. The cat had very much got out of the bag and was now scratching at the door to be let out into the big, wide world.

'Okay. Cards on the table,' he said. 'Enemies. That's what we're interested in.'

Sanders had brought her laptop. 'Funnily enough, I have a file labelled exactly that. It's a large one, too. But I guess you're after only the big stuff. Political spats I think we can ignore. If you want them, we'll be here all day.'

Warlow exchanged a look with Jess.

Sanders typed in a password and then spent several minutes concentrating and opening files. 'Let me run through the list of names left smouldering in the wake of Matt Gittings's slash-and-burn approach to life. Shall we start with Westminster and the reason no party wanted to touch him with a bargepole?'

'Snog gate?' Rhys asked.

'Indeed.' Sanders's eyes never left the keyboard. 'Her name, in case you've forgotten or lived in a cave when it all blew up, is Marissa Wilson, and I'm pretty certain she'd be happy to drive a stake through Matt Gittings's black heart any time of the day or night.'

'That's—'

'Her words,' Sanders said. She paused, staring at Warlow. 'I am obviously more than happy to cooperate. But some of what I am going to tell you has been said to me in confidence.'

Warlow sat back. 'I understand. But this is an investiga-tion into what might be an unnatural death. That means we could get a warrant for that information.'

Sanders smiled. 'I could run for the journalistic high ground on that one. But, as I say, I am more than happy to cooperate.'

'But?' Warlow repeated the caveat.

'Where is the quid pro quo?'

'We can't involve you in the investigation.'

Sanders broke into a sly smile. 'You already have, though, haven't you?'

Warlow didn't engage.

The journalist pressed home her advantage. 'All I'm asking is that if you find someone, you let me in on the process and the evidence. If it goes to court.'

'The CPS would never agree to that,' Jess said.

'Alright. But then you let me interview one of you. When it's appropriate. Horse's mouth and all that. I mean, the book's on hold now, anyway.'

'We can do that,' Warlow said. In his peripheral vision, he saw glances thrown his way from more than one source. But they were fleeting. He'd do what needed to be done.

Sanders nodded and turned to her screen.

Around the table, people started taking notes.

————

THEY SPENT a good hour with the journalist. Gina saw her out after profuse thanks from Warlow and a promise that he would be in touch with more questions and … information when and if. By then the press announcement had been made, so Warlow insisted they have a briefing before lunch to analyse what Sanders had told them and put it all into context.

Back in the Incident Room, Gil wrote THREADS on the board and spent a good five minutes populating the white space. When he finished, Warlow stood, and his index finger worried at the tiny patch of stubble he always managed to miss while shaving.

'Let's go through them one at a time,' he said.

Turning to Rhys, Gil asked, 'You still have that laser pointer?'

'I do. Would you like to borrow it?' Rhys replied.

'No, I want you to be my audiovisual assistant. Something to keep your mind off lunch. If your stomach grumbles any more, we'll have to get some earplugs.'

'On it,' Rhys said, retrieving the gizmo. A red spot appeared on the board.

'Okay. First, the Westminster angle. Top of the list, Marissa Wilson, the woman in the snog scandal. We know it didn't last, and she has threatened to kiss and tell. According to Sanders, she's still bitter.'

'She's a definite, then. Need to check on her movements over the last weekend,' Jess said.

'I'll do that,' Gina volunteered.

Gil wrote "DCGM" next to Wilson in red and Rhys lit up the next item with his pointer.

'Next, it's the Smart Motorway controversy,' Gil said, and then caught himself. 'Is everyone familiar with this concept?'

Gina hesitated. 'Vaguely, but I could use a refresher.'

'I had to research it myself,' Gil admitted. 'Traditionally, motorways have a hard shoulder – a lane reserved for emergencies. Smart Motorways repurpose this lane for regular traffic. There are two main types.' Gil wrote on the board, speaking as he wrote. 'There are hard-shoulder running sections. This is where the emergency lane opens for traffic as needed. Overhead gantry signs show whether it's open with a speed limit, or closed with an "X". Second is the "all-lane running" type. Here the hard shoulder becomes a permanent traffic lane. In emergencies, drivers must use designated refuge areas spaced along the motorway.' He turned with a toothless grin. 'All clear on that?'

Everyone nodded.

'According to Sanders, Gittings faced public backlash after commenting on a tragic incident. A car broke down on a Smart Motorway and was hit by a lorry. Gittings suggested the driver shouldn't have stopped at all, effectively blaming the victim.'

'Did he say this publicly?' Jess asked.

Gil nodded. 'On television. The car had suffered a complete electrical failure. Gittings's insensitive remarks were made worse by his connections to pro-Smart Motorway lobbyists. It soon emerged that a hauliers' association, which had donated significantly to Gittings's campaign, supported these motorways. This led to online death threats against Gittings, including one from the father of the deceased driver.'

'Rhys,' Warlow turned to the acting sergeant. 'You know the drill.'

'Identify, investigate, eliminate, sir.'

'Yep. Establish the relevant parties' movements, but approach with sensitivity and firmness. This is probably still raw for the people involved.'

Gil wrote Rhys's initials next to "Smart Motorway" on the board. Below, he added another potential motive: Hate crime moratorium.

'Gittings made a speech promising to campaign against any Welsh government attempt to pass a hate crime bill similar to Scotland's. He got a real backlash.' Gil said. 'He claimed a law allowing feelings to determine what hateful meant made a mockery of the whole thing and was a gut punch to free speech. He said being offended was a part of being a grownup. He argued this was a recipe for disaster, saying many agreed with him but wouldn't speak up for fear of the shrill minority throwing their keyboards out of the pram.' Gil flipped a page of the printouts he was reading from. 'Someone even threw a milkshake at him during one of his surgeries.'

'Okay. We talk to the milkshake thrower, too,' Warlow said.

'The thing is, I have some sympathy with that. Life is about as fair as a rigged horse race and politicians are just the bookies taking your money and playing double or quits,' Gil muttered.

'That sounds about right,' Jess agreed.

'So, that leaves the inappropriate behaviour claim in the Senedd he's been suspended for,' Gil added.

'That's undergoing an internal investigation, isn't it?' Jess asked. 'Why don't I chat with one of the other MSs? Hopefully, they can fill us in and provide some insight into the milkshake thrower, too.'

Warlow turned from the boards. Now they were getting somewhere. 'Anything else?' He left the question open.

No one answered. This, they all knew, was more than enough to be getting on with.

'Then I'm heading down to Solva to talk to other pub landlords. See what else I can find out about our agent of chaos. As if we don't have enough already.'

CHAPTER SIXTEEN

IT TOOK Rhys eight minutes by car to get from Police HQ to Tabernacle Terrace. He planned to change his shirt and do a quick detour to Gregg's in the retail park at Pensarn on the way back. It could be worse.

But even as he slid the key into the door of the house he shared with Gina, and now Dan, Rhys sensed something different.

Music drifted down from the spare room, followed by a peal of laughter. Not Dan's voice. A woman's and another man's.

Rhys, one hand on the bannister of the stairs, shouted up. 'Dan, it's me, Rhys.'

The laughter stopped abruptly, followed by the sound of movement. The music died down, and Dan appeared on the landing.

'Hey, Rhys. You're back early.'

'I need to pick up a shirt. You have visitors?'

'Yeah. Couple of old mates. We're just catching up, but we're just about to go out to the pub for a sandwich and a pint. You up for that?'

'I'm at work, Dan.'

'Yeah? Pity.'

The mates appeared from behind Dan. Much younger

than him, in their twenties. The man in a tracksuit top and bottoms, the girl in a denim dress and trainers, thin and pale with hair bleached almost white.

'This is Jared and Lowri.'

'Aya,' the girl said.

'Alright.' Jared nodded.

'Can I smell smoke?' Rhys asked.

'Probably. These two are like troopers.' Dan laughed. 'But I made them go outside. I would not want to upset my sister, now, would I? Anyway, we're off, like I said.'

Lowri and Jared hurried down and stood in the narrow hallway. Dan ducked back into his room, before emerging with an overshirt that he eased into. When he closed the bedroom door, Rhys heard the Yale lock that had been on it from when the place had been a rooming house slide closed.

'Why are you locking the door, Dan?'

'Can't be too careful.'

'We've never locked that door.'

'Extra layer of security, right? I found the key in a drawer in my room.'

My room.

'That is smoke.'

'It's them two. In their clothes and stuff. It'll go. Right, I'm starving. See you later, Rhys.'

No "Greasy" this time. Dan was in a hurry.

The trio exited, the chatter and laughter starting up again as soon as they were through the door. If Rhys had been asked to describe its nature, relief at some kind of narrow escape would have come to mind.

He took the stairs and tried Dan's bedroom door. The lock held. Okay, the place was a mess, and he didn't want Rhys to see it. On the other hand, the place might be full of smoke, and he didn't want Rhys to smell it.

Rhys sniffed. There was smoke. Up here, it was much stronger. And he'd put money on it being marijuana.

'For God's sake, Dan,' Rhys muttered.

He stood outside the door, contemplating breaking it down. But how would that look? If Dan had any sense, he'd have opened the window and fresh air would have done the rest. In which case, it would be his word against Dan's by the time Gina got home.

Again.

Rhys fetched his shirt from the drawer in his and Gina's bedroom. In here, it smelled of lavender and fresh laundry. If Dan was smoking cannabis in their house … if someone caught sight of him … Dyfed Powys had a zero-tolerance policy on that kind of thing.

He'd need to talk to Gina. He took out his phone. She was still at HQ, but she needed to know. And in his mind's eye, he saw her face. The expression he recognised whenever they discussed Dan. Resignation, guilt, resentment, and loyalty. An expression he'd come to fear. An expression that told him she hated having to take sides.

But this wasn't sides. This was something else now.

He put the phone away, his mind as conflicted as that look on Gina's face, as he walked down the stairs. He had the front door handle in his hand when a thought occurred to him. Turning, he rushed through to the kitchen and exited into the small garden, mown with his dad's old, corded mower, and featuring a patio set his parents no longer wanted.

At the beginning of summer, Rhys had planted some shrub, the idea being that he and Gina could enjoy a coffee out there on the odd sunny morning.

But that was BD. Before Dan.

Rhys took a couple of steps towards the fence between him and Hakeem to a spot under Dan's bedroom window. There, on the floor, were some burnt ends. Rhys shook his head. How could anyone trying to pretend not to be smoking be so feckless? And thick. Tossing stubs out as if they would magically disappear instead of putting them in a bag and dispose … his thoughts screeched to a halt. A little further on, at the edge of the path where the lawn began, he found it. Fatter and tapered, the remains of a discarded roll-your-own. He slid on the gloves he always carried, picked it up, and sniffed.

Definitely cannabis. There was no doubt in his mind.

Rhys fell into a sweat, looking up at the window above and the fence, hoping that Hakeem was not seeing this. He had to do something. He had to follow Dan to the pub and have it out with him … didn't he? Gina would understand that this was way too much.

He's my brother, Rhys.

Shit.

The second idea he had, a much more complicated idea with several moving parts, flashed into his head. It would be asking a lot, but if someone asked it of him, he knew he'd say yes.

Quickly, Rhys bagged up the cigarette ends. A quick search found another discarded spliff, this one much longer. Had they panicked on hearing him on the stairs and tossed out the bigger one? He put them all in an evidence bag.

Then, acting Sergeant Rhys Harries left his house, got in his car and made a phone call.

'Gil, it's Rhys. I need a favour. Something's come up and I need an hour to sort it out. Okay if you start the ball rolling on that Smart Motorway enquiry?'

'No problem. Is your dad okay?'

'Yeah. It isn't Dad. But—'

'I don't need to know, Rhys.'

'Okay. Tell Gina I bumped into Craig and we went for a coffee.'

'How is Craig?'

'Tell you later.'

Only then did Rhys ring Craig Peters, fellow police officer and husband of DS Catrin Richards.

———

GIL RELAYED the message to Gina. She waved a vague acknowledgement as she chatted with someone on the phone.

He fished out the number of the officer from West Mids he'd contacted to get Mrs Gittings's address. This time, he asked for and got a number for the father of the man killed on an all-lane-running section of the M5.

Gil took a moment before dialling. Not an easy call to make, but it had to be done. He doodled on a scrap of paper, steeling himself for the conversation ahead. The number he rang answered on the fourth ring.

'Mr Austin,' Gil said, his voice formal, but tinged with apprehension.

'It is.'

'My name is Detective Sergeant Gil Jones. Apologies for the out of the blue call.'

The briefest of pauses signalled George Austin's wariness at talking to a police officer. 'What can I do for you?'

'I'm not sure if you've heard the news, Mr Austin, about Matthew Gittings.'

Another pause. 'What news? I'm in the park with my grandson.'

'Mr Gittings was found dead two days ago.'

A longer pause. The tense silence was broken only by the sounds of a child's laughter in the background. 'Why are you telling me this?'

'It's not my intention to upset you, Mr Austin, but your name has emerged during our investigation into Mr Gittings's death.'

'My name? How?'

'It's been flagged as part of our screening. Anyone who made threats against Mr Gittings—'

'Hang on. Did someone kill that snake?'

'We're not ruling out the possibility of foul play.' Gil chose his words with caution.

A noise that was half snort, half grunt escaped Austin. 'Well, it wasn't me. Though I'd happily buy the man or woman who did it a drink.'

'You threatened Mr Gittings in a series of tweets, I understand.'

'I did. After my son died and I saw that shit Gittings on TV saying that Smart Motorways were safe, and that if drivers were careful, there was no need for any change of policy. That the sodding increase in capacity and decrease in congestion was important for productivity and growth. More important than my son.'

A tremor had crept into George Austin's voice.

'I understand the government has shelved all plans for further smart sections—'

Austin's voice rose, raw emotion bleeding through the phone line. 'Imagine me sitting there,' Austin carried on, oblivious of Gil. 'In front of the TV, listening to … that! I was numb. I was in pain. We all were. I was expecting this, this turd, because he wasn't a man, not in my book, to take a stand. Imagine hearing all that shit when we'd just learned that our Lee's vehicle had been concertina'd into something three feet long by an articulated lorry. What he should have done was demand an immediate closure of all Smart Motorways. They're death traps. Insist on a return to hard shoulders as safe spaces for broken-down vehicles. But no. Instead, he said that drivers in trouble should always head for the emergency refuge and that some common sense needed to be applied. Lee's car had no power. What was he supposed to do, get out and bloody push? No one came to help. He was there for just four minutes with no barrier to jump over—'

Gil squeezed his eyes shut. 'I'm sorry you had to go through that.'

'So, why are you ringing me?'

'I have to ask you where you were on Friday night?'

'Where was I? You think I did this to him?'

Gil gritted his teeth. 'No. But you had threatened him, and I'm obliged to ask about your movements.'

'We had the grandchildren for the weekend. Their mother was having a break. She's a widow at thirty.'

'Were you at home?'

'No, we visited a place where there's a play area and had an ice cream. You want the sodding name and a photo?'

'It would help.'

Austin told him. Gil wrote it down. Then Gil apologised again and prepared to ring off, but Austin had one more question.

'How?'

'How what?'

'How did it happen?'

'He was in a car that drove into a quarry.'

'Did the car smash?'

'Caught fire.'

'Then I'll play that image in my head over the one I have of my son being crushed by that lorry.'

Gil pinched the bridge of his nose, trying to imagine what this man had been through. 'I'm sorry for your loss, Mr Austin.'

'I'm not sorry for yours, Sergeant. National Highways still think they're safe, did you know that? Controlled, dynamic, all-lane running. Just different fancy names for bloody death traps. At the last count, eighty people have died. And they can put up as many emergency bays and radar checks as they like. How many deaths is it going to take? They should be ashamed of themselves. Like that snake Gittings should have been.'

Gil let him have his say. He deserved it. But he ended the call with his stomach churning from a mixture of sympathy and unease. Then he rang the officer in West Mids and asked him to send a Uniform around to Westholm Farms Ice Creams with a photo of Austin so that they could eliminate him formally.

Because someone had to do it.

CHAPTER SEVENTEEN

THE FIRST THING Jess discovered in her attempt at getting hold of an MS (Member of the Senedd) was how complicated the devolved Welsh government is. Unlike Westminster, where every person in the United Kingdom had a single representative as an MP of a particular political party, in Wales, every individual had five. One constituency MS elected by first past the post, and four regional MSs selected via a party vote. Said party then might appoint a second or even a third representative according to some complex calculation.

'Ah, yes, the D'Hondt method, as in D'Hondt ask me to explain the damned thing because it makes my ears bleed,' Gil said when Jess made the mistake of asking him exactly that as she did her due diligence before contacting someone about Gittings.

'Sounds like something you do in artificial insemination, doesn't it? The D'Hondt method,' Gil added cheerfully. 'Come to think of it, you'd be better off asking Catrin and Craig, as they are our resident experts on that side of things.'

That earned him a single raised eyebrow from Jess, which Gil ignored.

'Come on, they've had the baby now, so it's fair game. I am well aware of D'Hondt because one of my sons-in-law works in local government, God help him. I've therefore had to listen to the explanation over several suppers. Even managed to stay awake for almost half of the whole thing once. Bottom line, it's a formula for proportional representation also known as Regional D'Hondt. Don't tell Rhys the truth, though. Someone told him Regional D'Hondt is a French international who plays on the wing for Chelsea.'

'Was that someone you, by any chance?'

'Moi? Haw-hee-haw.' Gil twirled an imaginary moustache.

Jess parked the information. Since Gittings had sat as an Independent regional member, she looked up who the other three regional members were and randomly chose a woman named Sali (spelt with an I) Tranter.

Jess rang the number, reached a screening service, explained who she was, and got through to a secretary. After further explanation and a significant amount of Muzak, a fresh voice came on the line.

'Detective Inspector Allanby, this is Sali Tranter. How can I help?' The politician's voice came over as crisp and pragmatic.

'Ms Tranter, I wasn't expecting—'

'I take it this is in relation to Matthew Gittings?'

'You've heard the news?'

'I had. An alert came out from the Senedd press office as soon as it was announced.' Tranter's reply was matter of fact, the rustle of papers audible in the background.

'Are you up there now? In Cardiff, I mean?'

'No, I'm at home, prepping for a debate on Welsh language education on Wednesday. We need to expand the language skill base, and that means legislation.'

'Any chance we could chat face-to-face?'

'Not about the Welsh language act, I take it.' Tranter's tone shifted, becoming more guarded.

'No.'

'I actually live in Narberth. Have you ever visited? From your accent, I can tell you aren't local.'

'I'm not. But I'm familiar with Narberth. I've visited the crematorium and the shops.'

'A sweet and sour day out if ever there was one. Two p.m. suit you?' The politician's voice softened, a touch of local pride evident.

When Jess agreed, Sali Tranter texted her an address.

———

THE MAN who'd thrown a milkshake at Matthew Gittings had an address in Powys. A long way away, but still on the Dyfed Powys patch. As a result, getting hold of the records took Gina seconds.

He'd been charged with common assault and criminal damage, found guilty, and ordered to pay costs; to pay Gittings £75 and to carry out one hundred and fifty hours of unpaid work, as well as an eighteen-month suspended sentence.

She found footage of the actual incident online. And, of course, it had gone viral, delighting a portion of the public who enjoyed that sort of thing, now that milkshakes had become, like eggs, a humiliation weapon of choice.

Some people, no doubt, considered milkshake throwing a fairly innocuous thing. Even amusing as an abstract form of protest. Designed to embarrass the target by besmirching clothes, or a face if the delivery was accurate enough. And that may well have been the point. Expose, capture it on video, and humiliate.

But, from a policing perspective, the milkshake could have been something else altogether. A knife, or a gun, or acid. And then no one would have been amused, except those few radicalised individuals who considered assault a valid form of communication with anyone they did not agree with.

Prosecution, therefore, was always carried through where possible. Throwing an eggy milkshake was no yoke, as Gil inevitably put it, no matter how much you wanted it dripping and congealing on the target's face.

A couple of phone calls to the probation service quickly

established what kind of community payback work Tyler Collins had been ordered to do. Luckily for Gina, he was, at that moment, repainting an old hall as part of its renovation in Newtown – ironically, where the attack on Gittings had taken place.

Five minutes later, Gina was in touch with the supervisor who promised to get hold of Tyler to chat to him after outlining why she was keen to talk to him.

'Hang on. Tyler!' The shouted name signalled a lull until a different voice appeared. Male, unwelcoming.

'Hello?' The voice was gruff and impatient.

Gina introduced herself and went straight into the reason for her call. 'Matthew Gittings. That's why I'm calling.'

'Huh. He's dead.' Tyler couldn't suppress the note of triumph.

'He is. You're right. I'm ringing to find out if you had any contact with Mr Gittings after your court case.'

'No.' Collins was twenty-nine, but the way he spoke was more in keeping with a thirteen-year-old. Truculent and defiant.

Gina took a deep breath.

'If I ask you to tell me where you were last Friday night, you'd be able to do that?'

'Yeah.' Another upturn at the end of the word. He might as well have added a "so what?".

'Let's try that, shall we? Where were you last Friday night?'

'I don't know, do I?'

Gina sighed. 'Do I need to remind you that you are under licence, Tyler?'

'Hang on, I just got to think … yeah, I was probably over my mate's house. We played some Apex Legends. Had a few beers.'

'Give your mate's name and number to the supervisor.'

'Okay.' A small silence followed, and Gina thought she could hear the gears grinding in Collins's head. 'How did he die, Gittings?'

'In his car.'

'What, like an accident?'

'We're still looking into it.'

'I hope the twat suffered.'

'What?' Gina asked, her grip tightening on the phone, her jaw clenching.

'Suffered, like I fucking suffered.'

'Why have you suffered?'

'What? Unpaid work. I lost my job because of him.'

Gina remembered reading that Collins had a good job working for an estate agent. And, of course, he'd convinced himself he was the victim in all of this. But the truth was very different. 'You lost your job because of what you did, Tyler. Your choice.'

'What? Chuck a milkshake at someone?'

'That's assault. And Matt Gittings had no idea it was a milkshake. It could have been anything.'

'Why did he have to take me to court, though? Why not forget it?'

'You did it in full view of the videoing public. The police had no choice.'

'It was a laugh, is all. I'm proper fucked, though.'

Gina was well aware of what he meant. He now had a criminal record, which would affect a whole slew of things he might want to do at twenty-nine years of age. It would have to be declared on job applications, any volunteering. Travel to certain countries would not now be possible.

'You made a choice, Tyler,' Gina said, her voice firm and brooking no argument.

'My mates were telling me to do it.'

With that one sentence, Gina sensed what sort of kid Collins would have been. The kind that would kick a bin off a wall or eat a worm if his "mates" challenged him to do it.

'Alright for them,' he muttered. 'They got nothing.'

'That's because you carried out the attack.'

'It wasn't an attack. Just a bloody milkshake.'

'As I said, you did it in front of dozens of cameras. What did you think might happen?'

'Not this.' Tyler's voice cracked slightly. A hint of regret finally showing.

Gina lost patience. 'Give that name to the supervisor. And it'll be one less thing to worry about.'

'He was such a Nazi bastard, though.'

Gina sighed. 'He was not a Nazi. And calling people you don't agree with Nazis doesn't get you anywhere. In fact, the exact opposite. I'd remember that if I were you.'

'Yeah, right.' He muttered out the words.

'That name.'

'Alright, alright. Jeez.'

'Hand the phone back to the supervisor, please.'

Gina explained to the team leader what would now need to happen in terms of checking, and made sure the supervisor had her number.

———

It took Rhys twenty minutes to get from HQ Carmarthen to Tumble, where Craig and Catrin lived. With family close by, and easy access to the A48, Rhys had always admired her practicality and organisation. Now tea had been made, and they sat in a bright, modern kitchen.

'Where is she, then? Queen Betsi?'

'On her second nap of the day,' Catrin explained. 'She's up at 6:30, sleeps again from 8.30 to 10.30, and then 1 to 3pm. Bath at five and back to sleep at seven. Exactly what the sleep trainer recommends.'

'Sleep trainer?'

Catrin nodded. With a smile. 'Worth their weight in solid gold. Of course, my mother thinks it's hysterical. But start as you mean to go on is my motto, and Craig's all for it.'

'You're looking good on it, anyway,' Rhys said, bouncing his bent leg on the floor using the ball of his foot.

Catrin tilted her head. 'Okay, I know I'm not back to my fighting weight yet, but there is no need to be sarky.'

'I wasn't,' Rhys protested, eyes wide.

Catrin grinned. 'I know you weren't. I'm teasing. Thank

you. I am better than I was a couple of months ago. Sleep is a very underrated commodity, IMHO.'

'I like sleeping too.'

'Yes, well. It becomes a bit of a preoccupation when you have a little one. I have no idea how people with twins manage. How is Gina?'

'Great.' Rhys delivered this with an over-eager grin that made Catrin narrow her eyes. 'But you know how she is. You speak now and again, don't you?'

'We do. But she's been quiet on Insta lately.'

Rhys let out a big sigh, shoulder slumping.

'Oh, dear,' Catrin said. 'Trouble at t'mill.'

'Sort of. That's why I came. I mean … it's partly why I came … obviously, I came to see you and Betsi.'

Catrin shifted her jaw to one side. 'Flannel alert. It's one o'clock on a Monday afternoon. No one comes to visit at one o'clock on a Monday afternoon unless you're a midwife. There must be a good reason.'

Rhys looked defeated. 'You ever think about being a detective?'

'Spill the beans, cowboy.'

'I know you're not working, but … I need to talk something through. Personal, I mean.'

'Do you want to lie down on the couch like they do in the films?'

'I don't need a psychiatrist. I need a good copper.'

'Just as well, then,' Catrin said. She picked up her tea in both hands, elbows on the table. 'Go on. I'm listening.'

Rhys dropped his eyes and then brought them back up to look at the woman opposite him. 'Did Gina tell you about her brother Dan?'

CHAPTER EIGHTEEN

On the long and winding road back to Solva, as he negotiated the roundabouts in Haverfordwest and headed out towards the cathedral town of St David's, Warlow took a call from Molly Allanby.

'Not working?' was his pithy opening remark with more than a hint of amusement in his voice. 'When does the café job start?'

'Wednesday,' Molly replied, following it up with what sounded like a yawn.

'Ah, so you're still on student time. Breakfast, is it?'

'I wish. I've been up for hours, thanks. Tilly is moving out, and her parents arrived bright and early to lug her stuff downstairs. So, no chance of a lie-in.'

'Just Tilly moving out, is it?'

'No, so is Rhian. She and Tilly were third years. So, yeah, they write off that extra month.'

'Can't you get a couple of surfers in to help with the rent?' He navigated a sharp bend in the road.

'I wish.'

He'd been to the Fringe in Edinburgh twice, where tenement student flats had ten-month rental contracts from September to June. Ostensibly so that the landlords could get the flats spruced up for the next lot. But in truth, it was so that they could charge an extortionate price for the month of August when the Fringe ran and punters, desperate for accommodation, would pay through the nose.

'All okay, Mol?'

'Yeah. Thought I'd give you a ring and see how you were since I haven't seen you for three weeks.'

'Me or Cadi.'

'It's her I'm asking about, really.'

Warlow laughed. 'I never had a moment's doubt. She's good.'

'Give her a hug from me,' Molly added, her voice soft with affection.

'Consider it done.'

A slight pause followed. Warlow surmised that the other reason for Molly's call was now being loaded into the barrel. He could almost hear her gathering courage on the other end of the line.

'Mum mention anything to you about the Italian problem?'

'That sounds like something a 20th-century newspaper might have had as a headline when Mussolini came to power.'

'Who?'

'Some bloke who thought that the Roman Empire needed resurrecting and decided the best way to do that was to throw in with the Fascists. I'm oversimplifying, of course. And it has nothing to do with your Italian problem.'

'So, you do know about it?'

'I know that you have someone coming to visit you shortly.'

'It's not just anyone – it's Nina, and she's great.'

'Met her, have you?'

'No, but we've been chatting. She's in Uni like me, but she's never been to the UK. Just like I've never been to Italy.'

'Right,' Warlow said because he could think of nothing else.

'No, it's not right. This stupid feud thing has been going on, and …' Molly sighed. 'What did Mum say?'

'She quoted you. We can't be held responsible for the sins of our fathers.'

'Oh.' Molly sounded genuinely surprised. 'Did she actually say that?'

Warlow picked up on the mix of hope and disbelief. 'She did.'

A long beat followed. 'After I said it, I thought maybe it sounded a bit … insensitive.'

'Your mother realises that you shouldn't be burdened with her prejudices. She really does. But she's anxious for you.'

'What do you think, Evan? I'm not doing this to upset Mum. It's not some rebellious solar flare.'

'No. I know that. And my take is that you should do what feels right. I'm only too well aware how rifts can occur in families. Before you know it, people go to their graves with things left unsaid that should have been said.'

'Are you talking about Denise?' Molly's voice dropped a notch or two lower.

He was indeed. Yet it still remained too painful to admit. 'Let's just say that I speak from experience.'

'Thing is, Nina's already said I have to go out there before the end of the summer. She says it'll cost me nothing, and she has a mate with a place on Lake Maggiore.'

'Well, that's a different discussion, but I don't think your mother is going to disown you for chatting with a cousin.'

'Are you sure, though?'

'On that point, a hundred percent.'

'I wish I was.'

Another silent beat.

'Oh, God, Evan. I bet you wish you'd never met the Allanbys with all their baggage.'

'I helped carry your trunk up those stairs to your room, so I agree with that.'

He got a chortle for that. 'You know what I mean.'

'I do. And I can honestly say that I have never regretted meeting either of you two from day one. Not once.'

Molly sniffed a couple of times, followed by a deeper inhalation as she composed herself.

'You okay?' he asked.

'Yes. I haven't done my makeup, so I'll let you off. Where are you, in the car?'

'On the way to Solva.'

'Ooh, nice.'

'Yes. You might think so. Only the reason for my visit isn't so nice.'

'Matt Gittings?'

'Yes. You still read the news, I see.'

'Sounds horrible. But then horrible is what you and Mum do, isn't it?'

'Someone has to.'

'Thanks, Evan. For the listen.'

'I'll expect an extra scoop of ice cream on my cone when we visit you in Mumbles.'

'Deal.'

———

SALI TRANTER'S house was in Templeton, a couple of miles from Narberth. A detached property in well-tended grounds. Plenty of warm brown exposed stone was on view as Jess pulled up and parked next to a large all-electric Nissan.

Box ticked there, then.

Tranter opened the door before Jess could ring the bell. 'You found us okay?'

'Good instructions, that's why,' Jess said.

Tranter wore her auburn hair shoulder-length, and a cashmere top over high-waisted baggy trousers.

'Tea is made. We'll take it in the study.'

Of course, she would have a study, Jess thought. The room looked out onto an enclosed garden, with lots of lawn and a stone patio adorned with shrubs and conifers. One wall of the room was filled with framed photos of Tranter shaking hands with dignitaries and other members of her party in the Senedd and Westminster.

'How many years an MS now?' Jess asked as Tranter

poured tea into matching cups. No mugs here, and the milk jug was in the shape of a Friesian.

'Fifteen.'

'Wow. Surely, there'll be honours somewhere soon?'

Tranter laughed. 'You never know. But let's just say I am not holding my breath.' She pursed her lips as she handed Jess a cup. 'No matter what anyone says, what's happened to Matt Gittings is horrible.'

Jess adjusted her position in the chair, feeling the tension in the air. 'Are you expecting things to be said?'

'Of course. Matt was a contentious figure. He liked to be that. I doubt there'll be a parade in his honour.'

Jess waited for more, watching Tranter closely.

'Surely, you have gathered that by now, Inspector?'

'It's Jess. And yes, I had gathered that. You wouldn't classify yourself as a friend, then?'

'Colleague, yes. Friend, no. Matt was not the friendly type. I'm sure he had people close to him, but not in politics.'

'Is that because of the complaints?' Jess's gaze didn't waver.

'Before and after the complaints.'

'I understand a vote was made to suspend him from the Senedd.'

'We, that is the Senedd, agreed on a ninety-day suspension beginning April of this year.'

Tranter's fingers swept an imaginary crumb off the table before she resumed speaking. 'Can you tell me what happened?'

'I'd like to, but as of yet, we don't know. I mean, we know he died in the car, probably because of it exploding on impact.' She paused, and then asked, 'I understand no charges have been brought against Gittings. My colleagues in South Wales Police have not been asked to investigate.'

'No. But we like to think that, as politicians, we should be held up for scrutiny. The Standards Committee and Commissioner's report upheld the complaint by the complainant.'

'Which was?'

'Matt Gittings went out with some co-workers. He is independent of any party but inevitably ends up in some working groups. This was one of those groups. They'd finished their work and wanted to let off steam. Anyway, he got drunk, made some lewd comments, and ended up grabbing hold of a younger female member of the group to dance with her. He pulled her a little too close in a "hug" and used offensive language in a suggestive way. Now, if you read the newspapers, every day those standards I mentioned get lower. But we are in Wales, and we decide what we consider appropriate behaviour from someone in public office.'

'How did he react to the ban?'

'Accepted nothing. Criticised the process for its lack of transparency.'

Jess noticed Tranter's grip on her teacup tightening. 'Won't there be a by-election?'

Tranter's smile was a brief and fleeting thing. 'In Wales, there is no such thing as a recall petition that might trigger a by-election. He can sit until his term ends.'

'But he wasn't sitting now?'

'He had a month to go on his ban.'

'The people involved in this episode, there was no suggestion of any overt sexual misconduct?'

'No. Though touching of any kind is now considered inappropriate.'

'I realise that. What I'm asking is—'

'No. There was no overt sexual element to this. Although the recipient might have felt differently about it all.'

'It's a grey area.'

'Indeed.'

Both women sipped their tea. 'What's your impression of Mr Gittings, may I ask?'

Tranter sat slightly more upright. 'He liked attention.'

As damning accusations went, that didn't seem particularly mortifying.

'I get that he was a bit full of himself. How did you find him?'

'Testing. That's the kindest way to put it. He'd be probing you all the time. As if he was working out if you were worthy of his time. If you were, he could be charming. If you weren't, he'd ignore you.'

'Which group did you fall into?'

'I like to give as good as I get, Inspector. We had several heated discussions across the Senedd floor.'

'And personally?'

Tranter gave nothing away. 'As I say, we were colleagues. He had been chosen by a democratic process and had every right to be there. However, though we represented the same region, we had very little in common politically.'

Jess leaned forward, her tone sharpening. 'Apparently, he received death threats for some of his more contentious views around stating blunt facts.'

She nodded. 'Trawl through any politician's social media and you will find extreme reactions from those who do not agree with one's views.'

'Enough to attempt murder?'

Tranter adopted a prim and very much closed-mouth response. Jess noted how her fingers tightened around the delicate handle of her teacup, a subtle sign of her discomfort.

'These ideas polarise people. And those who are offended can be … vociferous. Now, whether the clamour ever translates into violent action, I couldn't say. But Matt Gittings's social media would, I am certain, make for very interesting reading.'

Someone knocked, and a head appeared around the door. Female, mid-twenties, a fixed smile of apology in the look she gave Jess before addressing the Senedd Member. 'Sorry, Sali. You remember the Education Minister has a group call in five?'

'Thank you, Branwen.'

Tranter pushed her cup and saucer back on the tray with the teapot. 'My PA. Terrier doesn't even come close.'

Jess remained seated. 'What about his political opponents?'

'You mean the whole of the rest of the Senedd?'

Jess shrugged.

'There have been many occasions where more than one

member would happily have throttled Matt Gittings. But that would be in the heat of a debate. I know of no one who would do anything as … extreme as what you've described. Politicians can be many things, but on the whole, we don't kill our opposition colleagues.'

'Of course,' Jess said, though she was thinking, *but there is always a first time for everything.*

Tranter got up. 'You'll have to excuse me.' She waved vaguely in the direction of her PA. 'Duty calls. Sorry, I could not be of more help. I don't suppose you've learned anything much, have you?'

'More a confirmation of what we suspected. It looks like it's going to be more difficult to find Matt Gittings's friends than it is his enemies.'

CHAPTER NINETEEN

WARLOW EASILY FOUND a space in the harbour car park because there were nowhere near as many cars as the day before. Schools had not broken up yet, and you didn't need to be a DCI to twig that the post-weekend demographic had changed. On the rocky shore today were people of a certain age. Either fit retirees walking themselves or dogs, silver hair poking out from under hats and caps, or younger parents with babies and toddlers not yet of school age. No bare-chested drinkers shouted on the patio today. And the rowdy raised voices had been replaced with the odd toddler's tantrum. Just as strident but tinged with innocence.

The Inn was all wooden beams, with wood panelling on the walls, and a slate floor in the main bar. But this wasn't some designer's idea of a kitsch theme. This was the real deal. The specials in chalk on the wall listed leek and potato as the day's soup offering.

Warlow went to the bar, showed the staff his warrant card and got chatting with the owner. Donna Reeves explained her partner had gone to the cash and carry. She suggested they find a table in the restaurant as it had not yet filled up.

Donna, who'd clearly come out from the kitchen, waved away Warlow's apology.

'Like I said, we're not busy yet. You're fine.'

'Not like yesterday,' Warlow said.

She gave him a tired smile. 'Start of the season. And the weather was good. Lethal combination.'

'Matt Gittings.'

'Oh, God. I heard. And someone has been in touch for CCTV footage on Friday night. That's all in hand.'

'Good. That'll be useful. He didn't come in here, though, on Friday, right?'

Donna's mouth thinned into a line. 'No. We wouldn't serve him.'

'Can you tell me why? What did he do to deserve that?'

Donna had brought them both a glass of iced water. She'd already drunk half of hers. Being in the kitchen made for thirsty work.

'We get our share of rowdiness, especially in July and August, with all the tourists,' Donna said, setting the glass down and meeting Warlow's gaze. 'But Gittings was different. He had a mean streak. Enjoyed arguing, he did. Could be a bolshy drunk. Insulted the staff one too many times.'

Warlow nodded, noting the seriousness in her voice. 'Can I ask about the final straw?'

Donna sighed, placing both hands on the table. 'Last summer, he had one too many and started berating one of my bar staff. Called him all sorts of names – he was just a kid. I couldn't have that, so I barred him.'

'Any reason they'd fallen out?'

'Yes. Tim caught the idiot lighting up something, definitely not tobacco. He was outside, off the premises, but even so ...'

'Marijuana?'

'So Tim said.' Donna shrugged. 'It smelled like it. We can't have any of that nonsense. This is a kid-friendly pub.'

Warlow glanced around, watching a couple of patrons at the far end laughing over their drinks. 'Tourism must be a double-edged sword for you, then.'

'It is,' Donna agreed, following his gaze. 'Brings in the

money, but also brings in trouble. Some people forget their manners when they're on holiday.'

Warlow smiled slightly. 'I bet. And summer is your big season, right?'

'Lots of Airbnb visitors now, too. But summer is when we make our money. We try to give people value here, though everything's gone up. Beer prices, food, utilities. Hard to keep the place running, sometimes.'

Warlow leaned in closer. 'So, Gittings. Did he come back after the ban?'

'No,' Donna replied, sipping her water. 'He knew he wasn't welcome. It's only the Anchor he visits now. Word gets around.'

'Did he have any friends here? Anyone who might know more about his movements?'

Donna thought for a moment. 'Not really. Not the type to make friends easily. Tried to impress people with his political talk. One of our regulars, his neighbour, used to chat with him sometimes. Talk to him.'

'Thanks, Donna, I will,' Warlow said, standing up. 'You've been very helpful.'

'Anytime,' Donna replied with a nod. 'And if you need anything else, I'll most likely be here peeling spuds or washing lettuce.'

Warlow gave her a grateful smile before heading towards the door, his mind already piecing together the new information.

So, Gittings liked the Mary Jane …

Somehow, he wasn't as shocked by that as he ought to have been as he strolled back out into the car park and turned right up the hill. His next stop was The Cooper's Arms, right next door to the Anchor. Might even be a good place for a spot of late lunch.

The Coops had a more modern feel to it. More open and restaurant-like than the other two, with a bigger garden area. The menu said *Bwyd Cymraeg onest ar yr arfordir*. Honest Welsh fare on the coast.

Warlow opted for potted crab with a mixed leaf salad and crostini. Local crab, of course. The pub owner wasn't on site, but the manager, John, a mid-thirties metal-head judging by the tied-back hair and the Viking mythology tats on his arms, knew all about Matt Gittings. Who didn't in the town?

Warlow repeated his questions and much the same by way of answers. Gittings had been a loud and belligerent drinker – but not an alcoholic. That was the weird thing. He'd often come in only for a couple of hours but get drunk quickly on a few pints with the odd whisky chaser.

'Think he'd been drinking before he came in?'

'Yeah … or something else.'

Warlow, lunch now finished and nursing a cappuccino, listened without making notes. He sensed an emerging pattern.

'Why do you say that?'

'I don't want to speak ill of the dead and all.'

'John, we're not at all sure what happened to Mr Gittings. This kind of thing is important.'

John held Warlow's gaze and seemed to decide. 'Well, there's what I've just told you. Sometimes, you could tell he'd been smoking cannabis before coming in. It makes some people relaxed, but with Gittings, it made him mouthy.'

'What made the owners ban him from here?'

'He upset some customers in the garden who were eating and recognised him. They asked about removing the military from Castlemartin firing range. Not locals – looked a bit alternative. I saw their VW camper in the car park; it was impressive. Anyway, Gittings started arguing with them. He could really debate, you know? He had the experience to back it up, I suppose. It ended with the customers accidentally breaking some glasses. It looked worse than it was, but it did for him. He was no longer welcome.' John used an index finger to stroke some hair back over his ears.

'I see.' Warlow stirred his coffee. 'Anything else?'

John looked torn between shaking his head and speaking.

Warlow caught it. 'It doesn't matter how weird or harsh it sounds. You can't libel the dead.'

'I guess. It's just that some of my pals, we surf and that. Bike sometimes. One guy who goes up to the old airfield a lot said he's seen Gittings's car up there in the car park. Late evenings, like ten or eleven. Now that it's almost summer and light enough, he goes up there a lot, my mate. Twice that happened. Always on a Thursday. Gittings just sitting in his car up there. My Kate thought he'd been up there doing a bit of dogging. I said that was stupid, but after what's happened …' John shrugged.

Warlow thanked him, finished his coffee, and left the pub.

An airfield near Solva came as news to him. But perhaps now was the time to check it out. It took only five minutes to cover the two miles from the harbour to the airfield in the car.

The parking area, a lonely outpost along the quiet stretch of the A487, had space for only half a dozen cars. He googled the place and read for a few minutes before reaching back into the Jeep for his coat, shrugging it on as he stepped out. The spring sun was a weak rival against the chill of the sea mist rolling in from the north. Before him, the disused St David's airfield stretched out in a vast, empty expanse of cracked concrete and wild, unkempt grass. A weathered sign on the gatepost warned of snakes, making him glance down reflexively, half-expecting to see one slither across the path.

He knew about Brawdy, the much larger airfield nearby. But from his brief read while sitting in the car, St David's had its own storied past. Opened in late summer 1943 for RAF Coastal Command's use, it once buzzed with the activity of Meteorological Halifaxes, anti-submarine patrols, and training aircraft. Now it lay almost silent. The distant cry of a skylark and the soft whisper of the breeze ushering in the encroaching mist were the only sounds.

Warlow followed the concrete path, the hedge on his right a meagre barrier against the encroaching wilderness. Gaps in the hedge led to a vast open expanse that must have been a runway once. In the silence, he imagined the roar of engines, the shouts of airmen, the tense anticipation of wartime operations.

As he walked, he passed the remains of a stone circle, an

odd anachronism in this place of military history. Erected in 2002 for the National Eisteddfod of Wales, it stood as a symbol of peace and cultural celebration, a stark contrast to the airfield's martial past.

He kept to the path, angling right and following the perimeter, the hedge banks on both sides growing more imposing as the mist thickened. Visibility dropped, reducing his world to a few yards of grey. The path led him to a kissing gate by the road, where he paused, considering his options.

Choosing the loop along the raised path of compacted stone, Warlow turned left and continued. The mist now pressed in on all sides, creating an otherworldly atmosphere. Hard to believe that half an hour ago, he'd been sitting in the heat of a pub garden. The air was heavy and he breathed in the scent of damp earth and distant salt.

According to his research, St David's had shifted to non-operational duties after 1944. The Royal Navy took over in the 1950s, running a civilian-manned Fleet Requirements Unit with de Havilland Mosquitoes and Sea Hornets. But things wound down slowly until it ended up as a relief landing ground for advanced jet trainers until 1992.

Now, the snakes and skylarks were reclaiming the area, and the National Park Authority was busy restoring wildlife habitats. The heath and wetland areas had become a nationally important Site of Special Scientific Interest (SSSI).

Warlow's thoughts returned to the present as he approached the loop's end. Just as suddenly as it had arrived, the mist cleared for a moment.

He stepped through another gate, turning left to finish in the parking area. The fog had blurred the lines between past and present, history and memory. St David's airfield was a place of stories, both told and untold. Perhaps Gittings had been a student of that history.

Maybe not.

What struck Warlow was how utterly alone he was in this spot. Whatever Gittings had done here, he'd been sure of not being seen by locals or tourists. The mist would not be here every day, but without it, you could see people approach for miles around. See them and avoid them.

The visit hadn't been very fruitful, but it sharpened his resolve.

There was something out here, hidden in the quiet expanse. Something that had drawn Gittings to the place, and Warlow needed to uncover it.

CHAPTER TWENTY

WARLOW STOOD a few yards from the gate marking the footpath entrance, phone in hand. He'd opted for a video call so he could see Jess, and behind her, the boards of the Incident Room.

'How's it going your end?'

'Slow but steady,' Jess replied. 'I've had a useful chat with the regional Senedd Member.'

'That's what Gittings was, right? Before his suspension?'

'Indeed.'

'What did she have to say?'

'She had quite a lot to say. That he was a loose cannon and that in any other electoral system, he'd have been booted out for good. But we are in Wales.'

'Does that make a difference? Are we a more forgiving nation?'

'You're a complicated lot. Ever heard of Regional D'Hondt? And please do not say he plays on the wing for Chelsea.'

'Don't be daft. It's Fulham. But no, regional de-whatever means nothing to me.'

'Right. Then you'll have the pleasure of me being able to explain all that to you this evening.' Jess's eyes drifted up over Warlow's face to the moving landscape. 'Are you outside?'

'I am.' He strode back to the gate and showed her a large orange sign with a cartoon bug-eyed "friendly" snake centre stage and the words "Stay calm, no harm" #ThinkZigZag.

'What is that?' Jess asked.

'This place is adder heaven, apparently.'

'Ugh. I really dislike snakes. What are you doing there?'

'Not catching a business class flight to Oz, much as I would have liked to. It's an abandoned airfield. One of Gittings's haunts, according to some locals.'

Warlow panned the phone's camera around to show Jess the vast emptiness.

'What's there?'

'Nothing, except adders in season. That's the intriguing thing. It's an SSSI. But Gittings hasn't struck me so far as a nature lover.'

'So, what are your thoughts?'

'It's a meeting place. Away from prying eyes. And this meeting place is about as far away as it is possible to be.'

'You're not coming back here, are you?'

'I was going to, but Alison Povey just texted me. She's at Gittings's property, and it was a "you-need-to-see-this" kind of text.'

'Okay. Don't let me keep you. We'll catch up later. The plan is to stay till about six, and then I'll let the troops go home.'

'Sounds like a good plan.'

Warlow pocketed his phone and turned one last time to look at the expanse of the airfield runway. Across the valley, to the north, the mist was retreating. As if some cosmic prankster had sent it his way just to make his life difficult while he'd been walking the airfield, and now that he was leaving, had withdrawn it.

Fitting that this spot was a haven for snakes. Gittings was turning out to be quite the serpent himself, if the reports on his behaviour were anything to go by. A loose cannon in the Senedd, a man with too many secrets and not enough shame at home.

Warlow couldn't help but think that this choice of meeting place, or even solitude, said a lot about him.

A desolate spot, perfect for someone who thrived in secrets, wanting to avoid the light. Especially for a man who did not shy away from the light in his professional life. The irony wasn't lost on him, standing there in the lingering mist.

Snakes in the grass, indeed.

'Bring it on,' Warlow said, and headed for the Jeep.

———

SEVERAL VANS SAT PARKED outside St Fagos. One van had its door open to receive anything of interest, or which needed more analysis. The sun still sat high in the sky, though the odd cloud was drifting in from the west. But it remained warm and hard to imagine the place as a crime scene. Yet, here they were.

'What have we got?'

Povey appeared in the doorway. 'Nothing that helps directly. No evidence of any criminal activity, though the content of Gittings's wardrobe is offensive enough.'

'You mean his clothes, I presume?'

'Don't think he's thrown anything away since the nineties,' she replied curtly. 'But we've found something that might interest you.'

'Lead the way.'

Povey gestured towards the living room, where a non-CSI officer stood looking bewildered. On the coffee table sat a package about the size of a brick wrapped in brown paper.

'What's that?' Warlow asked, already suspecting the answer.

'I got them to re-wrap it as it was found,' Povey said. 'For you to see.' She smiled. 'Go on, PC Finlay. Give him the blow-by-blow.'

Finlay, a twenty-something Uniform in a black tactical shirt and a baseball cap, shrugged. 'We were sweeping the room. I was over by the fireplace.' He nodded towards a closed log burner in a bricked hearth. 'The log burner hasn't been used in a while, but it had been swept clean of any ashes. Then I saw some debris.'

'Debris?' Warlow asked.

'Yes, sir. A smattering of sand.' Finlay walked over to the fireplace. 'When I looked at the bricks, I could see a bit of a gap where the cement had fallen out, and …'

'Show the nice DCI,' Povey said by way of encouragement.

A gloved Finlay walked to the fireplace and used a screwdriver between two bricks, levering gently until one, or what appeared to be a part of one, came free.

'It's a brick slip, sir,' Finlay explained. 'Used for facing a wall when you don't want to use real bricks. They're twenty millimetres thick. When I took this one out, there was a hole, and inside the hole—'

'Was the parcel,' Povey finished the sentence.

Warlow walked across and peered into the gap. Behind the slip, a metal box had been cemented into the space. Large enough to accommodate several blocks the size of the one on the coffee table.

Povey unfolded the brown paper and took out the contents. 'Ten thousand pounds in used notes,' Povey said. 'The pile had a single elastic band around it.'

'This is a neat job.' Warlow still had eyes on the fireplace when he turned to the young PC. 'Great find.'

Finlay stood up. 'Thank you, sir.'

'We missed it the first time around,' Povey agreed. 'But why would a shamed politician need this kind of money stashed away?'

Warlow didn't answer immediately, letting the question hang in the air. The whole thing reeked of wrongdoing. Gittings may have been a liability in the Senedd, but this suggested something more sinister than just political misconduct.

'The more I find out about Mr Gittings, the less I like. Nothing else in the hidey-hole?'

'Thought you'd ask that.' Povey put the money down.

'The swab we took of the space has come up positive for cocaine on the DTK.'

Warlow interpreted DTK without effort. Drug Testing Kit. He huffed out a lungful of air.

Money and drugs – this shifted the investigation in a new direction altogether. Gittings's death, a car over a quarry cliff, the zip tie, all made the possibility of malice aforethought more likely at every turn.

'You think he was dealing?' Povey asked, almost rhetorically.

'Or laundering. Either way, it's dirty money. Anything else?'

'We've taken his laptop from the study. It's locked, but we'll get it open. No sign of his phone.'

'Gil's on that. We should already have his records from the provider.' Warlow ran his hand through his hair and massaged his neck.

Povey turned away and instructed her team to bag up the money. The notes, though not fresh, held secrets they'd soon try to unravel.

Warlow took a moment to survey the room, its rustic charm besmirched by this undercurrent of deceit. The beams and exposed stone were silent witnesses to a more sordid setup. What had happened in town – the boorishness, the bans – could be chalked up to the nature of the beast. But the secreted money and the manner of Gittings's death spoke of a different, more sinister world altogether.

'What the hell were you up to your neck in, Matt Gittings?' he muttered.

Povey got back to it, and Warlow stepped outside, needing a breath of fresh air. In the time it took to remove a brick slip, the investigation had taken a very dark turn. A bag of money wrapped in a brown paper bag was a symbol of corruption as obvious as a black sheep on a snowy hillside.

As he walked back to the Jeep, he glanced over his shoulder at St Fagos, now a pivotal point in their search for the truth. Though Gittings had left a grubby mark in London and Cardiff, Warlow couldn't shake the feeling that the genuine answers lay further west, in this chocolate-box harbour village. The irony wasn't lost on him.

But this was his patch. Even more so than the rest of the vast area Dyfed Powys policed, this western edge was where he had put down roots. The rugged landscape, the tight-knit communities, these were the things he cherished.

Gittings had chosen this area too, and on the surface, it seemed a reasonable choice. A quiet place to live, away from the hustle and scrutiny of Cardiff and London. But perhaps that was the point. Maybe Gittings's real motive for hiding away here was to escape the relentless press of the city for an altogether different reason.

———

ALL IN ALL, given what they'd come to expect, the house on Tabernacle Terrace wasn't in too much of a mess when Rhys and Gina got home around seven.

Sure, there were three coffee cups on the table, all dirty, none with coasters. The TV was still on, or at least a frozen image from *Lethal Unit 5*. The game Dan loved playing was still on the screen. And, naturally, there was no milk in the fridge. Luckily, Rhys had preempted that by buying a small half pint of semi-skimmed from the garage on the way home.

'You sort out the living room. I'll start supper,' Rhys said, shrugging off his jacket.

Gina sighed, a soft but definite sound of discontent. 'You still haven't told me why you were away for over an hour at lunchtime.'

'When I got back, Dan was here with two mates of his,' Rhys said, heading to the kitchen.

Gina's voice followed him, edged with suspicion. 'What mates?'

'Jared and Lowri,' he called back.

'Never heard of them.'

'Me neither.'

'He told me most of his mates had moved on.'

'They were young. God knows where he picks these people up from.'

'The pub, most likely,' Gina said, entering the room and crossing her arms.

'Yeah, well, that's where they were off to. But obviously, he's been back and gone out again, from the looks of it.' Rhys put some pasta on to boil and then emptied a defrosted tray of pre-made ragu he'd left in the sink at lunchtime into a saucepan. He'd done this in the certain knowledge that Dan would go nowhere near it; anything related to the sink was not in Gina's brother's wheelhouse.

'I'm going to get changed,' Gina announced, her tone clipped.

Alone in the kitchen, Rhys mulled over his reply about his lunchtime foray. He hadn't furnished Gina with the full truth, but he hadn't lied, either. He justified it to himself as a necessity – an omission rather than a deception.

Ten seconds later, Gina's yell from the top of the stairs made him dash from the kitchen.

She stood looking down at him, incredulous. 'Dan has locked his frigging door.'

'Yes, he told me he'd found a key.'

Gina's mouth dropped open in horror. 'But this is our house.'

'And that is Dan's room, temporarily. The fact that you want to go in there probably explains why he's locked it,' Rhys replied calmly.

'He's never locked it before. I'm putting a wash on,' Gina protested – the subtext clear; she was used to going into Dan's room, picking up his dirty laundry, and doing it for him.

'I don't have a spare key, Gina.'

'Bloody Dan. What is he hiding?'

'Perhaps you'd better ask him?' Rhys suggested, returning to the kitchen. 'Pasta'll be ready in ten.'

Gina stood fuming. Rhys left her to it, went back to the kitchen, and stirred the ragu, pondering the secretive habits that seemed to sprout like weeds in their lives. This house was becoming a battleground of hidden agendas and unspoken truths.

The pasta boiled away, with Rhys well aware they were tiptoeing around the edge of a bigger problem.

Gina might not have pursued her interrogation of Rhys's lunchtime detour, but the air between them crackled with tension. Dan, after all, was her problem, and at some point, she needed to know about his nasty little habits.

His nasty and illegal little habits.

And, though he did not want to freak her out with what he'd found, he could not allow the situation to continue. Both their careers were on the line. Dan knew that – and that, somehow, made it a hundred times worse. But would it change him? Rhys doubted he was capable of change.

Not without help.

As Gil was prone to say, 'There' more than one way to skin a banana. Though using your feet to do it on the bus on the way to work is just showing off.'

CHAPTER TWENTY-ONE

GITTINGS DOMINATED the news as Warlow drove in the following morning. He'd switched on the TV first thing, catching drone footage of the Middle Hill quarry and Povey's CSI snowmen still toiling where Gittings's car had careered over the edge.

Warlow recalled a time when such high-flying imagery was reserved for monumental events, requiring a network to shell out for a helicopter. Now, a £500 drone offered high-res images without guzzling fuel like it was going out of fashion.

The media was exaggerating the situation, highlighting all of Gittings's mistakes and controversies as potential motives, similar to Warlow's approach the previous day. They didn't need to try very hard to portray him as a polarising figure, laying on thick his most recent fall from grace at the Senedd as evidence. And though the national broadcasters had a remit of neutrality in all things political, when it came to accusations of predatory sexual misconduct, especially where a power dynamic had played a part, they pulled no punches. And the gloves had truly come off after #metoo.

For a while now, Warlow had clocked how obvious journos and presenters were with their biases – even on the news channels, for crying out loud. If you were unprofessional enough to let slip a smug grin or a snarky comment when someone you didn't agree with made a point, his take was you shouldn't be in that job. Keeping things impartial was one thing, but self-righteous virtue signalling was something else entirely. And it seemed like everyone and their dog was at it these days, both here and abroad.

But, as a police officer, Warlow was bound by rules of evidence and the law. His personal opinions on crimes and perpetrators had to remain secondary to his duty. Despite his disdain for Gittings, the man deserved justice. He might have been a creep, and a narcissist, but he was dead. Warlow's job was to find his killer.

He and Jess travelled to work separately, fully anticipating being at different locations by day's end.

At HQ, Warlow avoided the SIO room, dumped his briefcase on the nearest desk, and gathered the troops. Numbers had swelled, with more Uniforms and ancillary staff drafted in by Superintendent Sion Buchannan. But notably, the higher-ups had kept their distance, save for Buchannan, whom Warlow consulted almost daily.

The Gittings case *was* big news, the kind that'd normally have Warlow summoned to the Chief Super's office. But so far, nothing. Bleddyn Drinkwater had backed the wrong horse with Superintendent Goodey during Warlow's last big case, and now he seemed to be keeping his distance – probably to avoid another cock-up.

The Chief Constable, though, she'd been full of praise after Warlow cracked the Bowman case. She was also the only top brass, apart from Buchannan, who'd bothered to check on Gil while he was on the mend. Warlow had filed all that away in his mental scorecard.

For now, Warlow seemed invisible to the higher-ups—at least the meddling ones. He intended to make the most of it before the spell wore off.

Tea got made. Warlow called everyone to order. Jess and Gil were seated. Gina and Rhys stood off to one side, arms crossed, more space between them than usual.

Warlow wondered whether their defiant body language had anything to do with a ripple in the fabric of the domestic universe they occupied, or simply a need to get on with things.

Possibly a bit of both, he thought. Ah, well.

He cleared his throat to bring everyone to order. 'In case anyone missed my cryptic text, I'll spell it out.' He wrote on the board: FOLLOW THE MONEY, speaking as the words appeared. 'During a search of Gittings's property, a bundle of cash was found in a hidden compartment in his hearth. Forensics have confirmed that the notes were handled by Gittings.'

'How much, sir?' Rhys asked.

'Ten thousand pounds in used £50 notes. Raises questions about how and why a Member of the Senedd had this amount hidden.'

'No obvious legitimate source? Buying and selling antiques, or LPs?' Jess queried.

'None we've found,' Warlow replied.

'Either he was holding it for someone, or was paid for something he'd done, is my guess,' Gil stated.

'The question is which.' Warlow went on to detail his interviews from Solva's watering holes, which confirmed that Gittings was a liability after a few drinks. 'I also visited the old St David's airfield. Anyone know it?'

Blank looks were the response.

'Exactly. It's now an SSSI, and not much visited.'

'Could this be drug related?' Gina asked. A very good question, too.

'It may well be, Gina. Povey's tests on the box came back positive for cocaine and marijuana. Techs are examining his laptop.' Warlow threw Jess a glance. 'DI Allanby's been chasing known contacts with a grudge or some reason to despise Gittings.'

Jess shrugged in reply. 'It's drawn a blank so far. As, I suspect, the rest of you have, too? Or has anyone else found anything useful?'

'So far, no,' Gil said. 'I'm wading through his phone records. He had two, one personal, one for Senedd work. If we had his TwitteX access, it'd be revealing.'

'That's a thought,' Jess sat up. 'His PA might have access to his social media. I'll follow up via Tranter's PA.'

'What about the ex-girlfriend?' Warlow asked. 'Wilson?'

'No love lost there,' Gil replied.

'Where are we with CCTV?'

'We've got someone on it,' Rhys said. 'The pub's footage is better. I'll check in once we're done here.'

'I still need to eliminate the milkshake thrower. Waiting on a callback from his employer,' Gina added.

'Didn't someone offer him a job immediately after the incident?' Gil asked.

'A man who owns a chain of vaping shops,' Gina replied. 'The owner supports that method of protest. He thinks that showing your political disagreement by lobbing a volume of liquid at someone is perfectly acceptable.'

'Let's chase that up and all the other threads. Everyone has their tasks.' Warlow retreated to write up his conversations with pub owners, but an email alert from Bryers caught his eye:

Blood alcohol and Zolpinam levels on Gittings:

- Alcohol: 246 mgs/100ml blood
- Zolpinam: 0.21 mgs/100ml blood
- UK driving limit for alcohol is 80mgs/100ml. Zolpinam therapeutic levels are 0.01-0.02 mgs/100ml.

Bryers had added an addendum.

Values are three times the legal alcohol limit and ten times the therapeutic dose of Zolpinam.

He texted Bryers:

What state would he have been in?

Incapacitated if not unconscious.

Warlow sat back. Was this a suicide attempt after all? His musings were interrupted by Rhys knocking.

'CCTV from the Anchor Inn, sir. You need to see this.'

Warlow smiled. Rhys and Povey had the same taste for drama. He pushed back his chair and followed Rhys to the Incident Room.

The CCTV coordinator, a Uniform, Rhys addressed as 'Mike', played the footage as Rhys talked over it.

'Gittings sat and talked with Talbot for a long while. But then, at around ten, he went to the bar to order a round and someone walked in. Take a look.'

The footage ran. Gittings alive and animated. Cracking jokes with the staff. The woman who served him was perfunctory in response. And then, from the left, a man came into shot, walked to the bar and stood within a yard of Gittings. They exchanged words.

Initially, Gittings laughed. The second man got served, and the conversation continued. From the hand gestures, it looked very much as if Gittings had a lot to say. The second man took a step back, shaking his head in a negative gesture. Gittings reached out and grabbed the second man's jacket. He brushed it off and turned away, took his drink and walked out of shot. Gittings watched him go, flicking his hand as if to dismiss him, before turning away and rejoining Talbot at a table.

'There is no audio?' Warlow asked.

Mike shook his head. 'It's not the best view, sir. It's from behind. But there is another, better camera on the door monitoring people coming off the street. We've coordinated the timings. Just before that second man appears on screen, we have someone entering the pub.'

A second video appeared in a window on the screen showing a door. Mike blew it up. The door swung open, and a man entered. This time, the resolution looked better, and the man's face was clear as he stepped through the doorway.

Warlow caught his breath. 'Is that—'

'Piers Barber, sir,' Rhys said before Warlow could finish. 'I'd put money on it.'

Warlow made them replay the footage half a dozen times.

'Can you remember how long he said he was staying around?' he asked finally.

'He's delayed his return but he's driving back today, sir.' Rhys's eyes glittered with the promise of the chase.

'Right. Well, let's see if he'd be kind enough to call in and say hello on his way back to London, shall we?'

On his way to the SIO room, Jess caught Warlow's eye.

'You look … energised,' she said.

'CCTV from the Anchor. Our witness, Piers Barber, hasn't been totally honest with us. He and Gittings had a chat in the pub on Friday night.'

'What?' Jess's voice went up an octave.

'It looked like Gittings made a grab for him, too.'

'Oh, dear. Lovers' tiff?' Jess raised an eyebrow, her tone edged with sarcasm.

'A disagreement, definitely. Rhys is going to ask Barber in for a cup of tea.'

Jess smiled, but then her mouth flattened a little. 'Got a minute?'

She led him into the stairway of secrets. A dead space in the building where they wouldn't be heard. The walls, thick and silent, absorbed their whispered conversation.

'Did you notice Rhys and Gina this morning?' Jess's asked quietly

'Yes,' Warlow replied, leaning against the cool wall. 'Polite. Too polite.'

'The course of true love?' Jess said, her eyes narrowing.

'Is not helped by a feckless relative plonking himself in your two-up, two down.'

'Ah, so, you know?'

'Rhys is an open book,' Warlow replied with the slightest of shrugs.

'Gina usually keeps things close. Has she talked to you? Anything to be done?'

'No. Not unless they start a fight in the Incident Room,' Warlow said, trying to lighten the mood.

That should have been the end of it, but Jess didn't break eye contact. There was more to be said, obviously.

'Molly says she caught up with you. Chatted about Nina,' Jess ventured. Her voice had deepened, tinged with anxiety.

'She did.' He saw no need to lie or beat about the bush. 'She's anxious about it. Like you are.'

'What did you tell her?' Jess's gaze remained intense, seeking reassurance.

Warlow's smile hinted at an amused reluctance.

Jess read his hesitation. 'If you don't want to say, it's alright.'

'I have nothing to hide, Jess. I told her I respect her choices and that you do, too. I also said she should consider your understandable anxiety about the situation. But that it shouldn't stop her from following her instincts.'

Jess had her hands on her hips and now looked up at the space in the stairwell above her, not really seeing it. She found no answers there. 'I can't believe I'm so tense about this. It's so stupid.'

'It's family, Jess. The most important thing.' Warlow kept his voice even, offering a lifeline.

She softened, a small smile breaking through her worry. 'You're not running for the hills yet, then?'

'Not yet. I've got to sort this bloody case out first. And anyway, I want to meet Nina now.'

'So do I,' Jess admitted, her voice barely above a whisper.

'Montepulciano d'abruzzo doc,' Warlow said, breaking the tension with a familiar refrain.

Jess smiled and replied with, 'Rosso di Montalcino.'

Warlow grinned. 'See. We're fluent.'

They stood there for a moment longer, the silence now comfortable, before Warlow turned and walked back to the Incident Room.

Rhys was hunched over a computer. Gina was on the phone, her expression tight with concentration. Gil walked back in from wherever he'd been and saw, or perhaps felt, the change in atmosphere.

'We've got new footage from the Anchor,' Warlow explained as Jess moved out of earshot to join Gina. 'Gittings and Barber had a moment on Friday night. We need to dig a little deeper into Barber's background, I think. Find out if he's hiding something.'

Gil nodded, mouth downturned in appreciation of the progress. 'Looks like I should leave the room more often to relieve myself.'

'Too much tea?'

'No. This was a code brown.'

Warlow used his steepled fingers to support his head as it fell forwards and uttered a muted oath. 'Ooft. There is something to be said about being too candid.'

From three desks away, Rhys looked up and gazed at Gil. 'Code brown?'

'Freight offloaded,' Gil said, adding a pair of jaunty thumbs up.

'Where's all this come from?' Warlow looked aghast.

'My transverse colon, by the feel of it.'

Rhys giggled. It earned him a quelling glare from Warlow.

Gil explained, 'Rhys and I have been discussing water companies' profits and how to minimise them by not using too much water. Aka flushing. You know the drill; "If it's yellow, just mellow. If it's brown, flush it down." And, to be fair to Rhys, he's been the one most concerned with my well-being. He knew that some of the pain meds I've been on for the shoulder have a side effect of … verstopfung.'

'That's constipation in German, I take it?' Warlow asked, fearing the worst.

'It is. One of only a handful of words I remember from my German O'level. The others are—'

Warlow's voice went up a decibel or five. 'I don't want to know the others.' He turned to Rhys. 'Any joy with Barber?'

'Just passing Haverfordwest when I got hold of him. He's on the way in. He's dropping his wife and kids off in Neath station. I said we'd compromise and meet him in Llanelli, at the Hub.'

'*Wunderbar,*' Warlow said.

'That's not one of the German words I was thinking of,' Gil observed.

'No,' Warlow muttered. 'I bet it isn't.'

CHAPTER TWENTY-TWO

THE BARBER ARRANGEMENT ended up being convoluted because, though Jenny, Archie, and Paloma Barber had return tickets for the train, Jenny had refused to get on at Haverford-west, which added almost two hours onto her journey. And so, Warlow had agreed to let Barber drive his wife and children to Neath station for the three-hour train up to Paddington and drive back to Llanelli where they would meet him.

Warlow took Rhys along in the Jeep for the half-hour journey.

Llanelli formed the eastern border of the force area. Once across the Lougher River, pronounced with hard ch in lieu of the gh, since its original Welsh was *Llwchwr*, they'd be in South Wales Police's patch.

'Everything okay, Rhys?' Warlow asked as they sped along the A48 towards Cross Hands.

'All well, sir.'

Warlow, with his customary directness, saw no point in avoiding the pachyderm. 'How's Gina's brother getting on, uh, Dan, is it? Find some work yet?'

Rhys kept his eyes on the road. 'Not since Sunday, sir.'

'Is he looking?'

'Says he is.'

'Does he have a leaving date?'

'If he has, he hasn't told me.'

'Want to talk about it?'

'Not really, sir.'

'Fair enough.'

Only after they'd negotiated the Pont Abraham roundabout where the A48 became the M4 did Rhys break the silence.

'What was it like in your day, sir?'

Warlow glanced at him. 'What was what like?'

'Courting. Finding girls and that?'

'Before mobiles, you mean? We had dances. Rugby club socials. The chip shop.'

Rhys nodded. 'Not like that now, sir. Phones make everyone paranoid. Girls especially. They're scared to take a chance. Even talking to someone at a party can make you out to be a predator. It's mad.'

Warlow sighed. 'You met Gina at work, right?'

'Yes, sir. A lot of my mates, they'd rather not be in a relationship.' Rhys's grip tightened on the phone in his hand. 'They say it's too much work. Not the fun stuff, all the other stuff. They'd rather keep it casual. Situationships, they call it.'

'Sounds … bloody awful.'

'Like I say, I count myself lucky with Gina. She has her own mind.' Rhys's voice softened. 'She has a load of friends, but she doesn't buy into the relationship-by-TikTok stuff. A lot of girls do, though.'

Warlow read this for what it truly was: anxiety. 'Dan being a bit of a fly in the old ointment, is he?'

'Sort of, sir.' Rhys's shoulders slumped.

'You'll work it out, I'm sure.'

'I hope so.'

Warlow took the M4's Llanelli turnoff, heading in towards the newest addition to the Dyfed Powys Police estate. The Hub, or to give it its full name, The Carmarthenshire Custody Suite and Policing Hub. It had only been open a year. Another out-of-town construction in the Dafen industrial complex. It had eighteen cells and a lot of curves inside and out, silver steel Fort Knox doors, and a forensic medical exam room.

It still smelled new whenever Warlow went there. A much-needed resource and hailed as a revolutionary improvement. Prior to the build, custody had been shifted from the busy Llanelli and Carmarthen towns to Ammanford, with Brecon and Haverfordwest as overflow. A bloody nuisance for busy officers.

The Hub provided room for CID, crime scene investigators, and local response officers under the same roof. A vast improvement on the old town centre station. Bigger, better, lighter. It even had a gym and plenty of space for parking.

But it was out of town.

This trend was changing more than just where they worked – it was shifting the whole bloody focus. And Warlow, no matter how flash and handy the Hub seemed, couldn't shake the feeling it was just another load of red tape dressed up as progress.

They found a room. Warlow wanted it kept informal. Barber was not under arrest and the DCI made it plain to him when they sat down over a cup of tea. The chat would, though, be under caution.

Warlow led. 'Thanks for coming in, Pers.'

'Anything to help. But I've told you as much as I can.'

'Family safely on the train, I take it?'

Barber's wry smile looked appreciative. 'Bribed the kids with snacks. My wife is not so easily appeased, I'm afraid.'

Rhys had his laptop and opened it now so that they could all see the screen. 'We're not trying to catch you out, Mr Barber. That's not what this is about, but it's obvious to us you had met Mr Gittings before.'

'No, that's not true. I—'

The clip played on the small screen. Gittings at the bar, Barber arriving and ordering a drink. Warlow studied the expressions of surprise, followed by a dull, dawning horror on Barber's face.

'This is footage from the Anchor Inn on Friday evening,' Rhys explained.

'You told us you'd stayed in that night.'

Looking sick, Barber nodded. 'I did. I said that because I'm supposed to be off the booze. I'm supposed to be trying to lose weight. I told Jenny I would not drink.'

'But you went to the pub.'

Another nod.

'And while you were there, you met Gittings.'

'No, I … I've never met Gittings.'

Rhys pressed play again. The footage rolled on to show Barber ordering, then the exchange between the two men and the grabbed jacket.

'No, no … don't tell me that was him.'

'Don't you know?'

'No … I mean, I must have seen his face on the TV, but … this bloke, the one at the bar.' Realisation dawned slowly. 'That was Gittings?'

'Indeed, it was,' Warlow said. 'Care to tell us what happened?'

'I called in for a cheeky pint. That's all. I ordered my beer, and this bloke started up a conversation. Ordinary stuff. Where is that accent from? You're not local? Just visiting? I told him my dad used to have a place here, and that we grew up coming here for holidays and now it's mine. He asked me where I live now. I told him. Then he launched into some BS about London being unrecognisable now. About it being less English than ever and did I feel safe there? I mean, talk about baiting.'

'What did you say?'

'I told him I'd lived there for nearly twenty years and yes, I felt safe. He said something like, "Come on. You can tell me. No need to worry about any of that triggering crap around here. Tell me what you really think." I couldn't believe it. Last thing I expected to hear in a pub in Solva.'

'That sounds like Gittings for sure,' Warlow muttered.

'I wasn't interested. I got my pint and moved away, and the idiot grabbed my jacket and said I was a coward for betraying my British heritage.'

'What happened then?' Rhys asked.

'I shrugged off his hand and found somewhere else to drink my pint.'

'He didn't follow you?'

'No. I never saw him again. I mean, he was wearing a hat and had glasses on. He liked to be … different. He liked to stand out, or so I've heard since. I did not know it was him, and the only reason I didn't tell you about the pub and all this was because it didn't seem relevant. And I didn't want Jenny to know I'd been. I swear to God that's the truth.'

'Okay.' Warlow kept his voice measured. 'How did Gittings strike you?'

'In what way?'

'His manner. His speech. Was he drunk?'

Barber, bewildered, replied, 'No … I … No, not drunk. Not exactly sharp either, but—'

'Not depressed? Not morose?'

'Morose?' Barber baulked at the word. 'No. He seemed … full of himself. Downright cocky, I'd say. But I only wanted a quiet pint.' Barber hesitated and rephrased the sentence. 'I quickly figured out that he didn't simply want to chat. He was spoiling for an argument.'

Warlow let Rhys run the clip to show Barber moving out of shot before ending it. The DCI said nothing for a moment. What he'd learned tallied very much with what other people had said. Gittings loved winding people up. Probably why he chose politics in the first place and nothing about what Barber had told them rang any alarm bells in Warlow. But, and there always, always was a but, they'd also lifted the curtain to look at Barber's past and found a bone, if not a complete skeleton, rattling around in his cupboard.

'And if we were to search your car, Mr Barber, would we find anything you'd prefer us not to?'

Barber frowned. But didn't lose any colour. A mark in his favour in Warlow's book.

'What do you mean?'

'You were found guilty of being in possession of cannabis once, were you not?'

This time, the colour did drain away from Barber's face

like water down a plug hole. 'Oh, God, I was nineteen. I was still in Uni.' A note of protest caused his voice to rise.

'Does that mean you do not do that kind of thing anymore?'

'I've got kids now. So, no, I don't take drugs. And yes, search. Send a sniffer dog in, by all means. I hope it likes crisps.'

Warlow smiled. 'We'll do that if you don't mind and get you on your way.'

'Fine.' Barber's mouth became a razor line. 'All I bloody did was go for a jog in the quarry.'

Warlow nodded. 'And we appreciate that this is an ordeal. But we appreciate your cooperation more.'

Barber's downcast eyes looked up. 'Not a suicide, then?'

'Why do you ask?'

'You wouldn't be doing all of this if it was.'

Warlow didn't answer.

An hour later, Barber was back on the M4, heading to London older by a couple of hours. But none the wiser.

CHAPTER TWENTY-THREE

WHILE WARLOW DEALT WITH BARBER, Jess and Gina travelled east to chat with the woman embroiled in the improper behaviour accusation that led to Gittings being suspended from the Welsh government. It had not been easy to get the name. The standards committee was adamant that they did not want the woman involved exposed to the media, neither on social media nor in the press.

However, this was now a murder inquiry. As such, Jess had applied considerable pressure. A convoluted legal route involving warrants would only make the machinery of government look sluggish and obtuse.

In the end, someone from the Counsel General's office at the Senedd got in touch and provided a name. The woman worked from home three days a week, visiting the "petrol station on the west terrace" only once a week. Luckily, she lived in Radyr, a northern suburb of Cardiff accessible from the M4 with no need to go anywhere near the city.

Gina had rung ahead, and they'd agreed to meet at 2:30pm. They were halfway on a journey that Jess estimated should take just over an hour when Gina's phone rang. Jess caught the unbidden grimace that appeared on her junior colleague's face upon seeing the caller.

'Is it okay if I take this, ma'am? It's a neighbour.'

'Of course.' Jess flicked the volume down on the radio through the steering wheel control.

'Hi, Hakeem, you alright?'

They were in the confined space of Jess's Golf, and there was no escape. Though Jess could not hear what was being said by the other party, the voice sounded strident.

'Oh, God, Hakeem, I am so sorry.'

More loudness, the overall impression of an unhappy bunny. Gina mostly listened, offering the occasional 'okay' between long bursts of chatter.

'How long for? ... Okay ... okay ... Let me ring and see if I can do something ... I'm sorry, Hakeem, really ... Okay ... Thanks.'

Ending the call, Gina puffed out her cheeks and blew out air.

'Problems?'

'Nothing to do with work, ma'am. I am so sorry. That's my neighbour. My brother has the telly on loud again. He's probably forgotten and put earphones on.'

'How do you do that?'

'No idea. But he seems to be an expert at upsetting Hakeem. They're a nice family, too. Do you mind if I try to sort this?'

'Go ahead,' Jess said.

Gina found a contact and called a number. It rang ten times, but eventually, someone answered.

'Dan? Dan, what are you doing?'

A muted groan.

'Yeah, you have the TV on maximum. Again! Yeah, good. Yeah, it's a brilliant film, but why is it on at the same time as you're playing a game on my laptop?'

The reply, as muted and followed by a laugh, didn't please Gina as far as Jess could see.

'It's not funny, Dan. Hakeem ... Yes, our neighbour ... They have a baby. The noise ... Yeah, okay, turn it off ... No, but there is some cereal in the cupboard ... Okay ... okay ... Just keep the TV off if you're gaming, Dan.'

After she ended the call, she sat, phone in her lap, before turning to Jess again.

'That'll be Dan, then,' Jess said.

'He is doing my head in.'

'And the neighbour's by the sound of it.'

Gina nodded. It looked as if she might be on the verge of tears. 'He upset Rhys the other night.'

'Hmm, I wondered if something had caused a ripple in the romantic pond.'

Gina squeezed her eyes shut. 'Was it that obvious?'

'It was noticeable,' Jess said. 'Rhys would not do well at Poker.'

'No.' Gina laughed softly.

'Does Dan have a plan?'

Gina shook her head and rolled her eyes. 'His plan is to do what he wants to do. He's out when we get home. I hear him come in at two in the morning. He's in bed when we leave for work. It's not ideal. Though at least the pattern keeps him away from Rhys.'

'Sounds …'

'The words you're looking for are "messed up", ma'am.'

Jess's daughter was eight years younger than Gina. A sizeable gap in terms of world experience, but perhaps not such a gulf when it came to emotions.

'Are you worried more about Rhys or Dan?'

'Both, but more worried about Rhys. Scared of losing the one person I've really connected with.'

'You're still young, though.' She'd used that phrase with Molly more than once when boys had been a source of angst.

But Gina wasn't having it. 'Half the blokes my age are choosing to stay single and loads of girls too. A lot of them live their lives through social media. Insta is easy and quick, but not always great. I've got mates who spend all their time banging on about red flags and love bombing like it's the end of the world if someone shows a bit too much interest too soon. It's dead easy to get sucked into that and convince your-self it's safer not to get involved.'

Jess glanced across with a smile. 'I doubt you've had trouble getting involved.'

'You'd be surprised. A lot of men want nothing more than getting physical. All that rubbish about how empowering it is to be emotionally distant. They've bought into this idea that it's safer to not get attached.'

Jess gave a half snort, half laugh. 'You and Molly ought to have a chat. She hates all the mollycoddling. The safe spaces and safe-speech malarkey.'

Gina smiled, but it looked half-hearted. 'Rhys is the opposite of all that. He's willing to connect. Yeah, it means you can get hurt, but so what? I don't like living life in bubble wrap. And I don't mean babies.'

'I know what you mean.'

Gina sniffed. 'We shouldn't be talking about my issues.'

'Shouldn't we?'

After a beat, Gina caved. 'I don't know what to do.'

'Can I help?'

'No, thanks. I need to sort this out. But not now. Not at work.'

Gina was right, and it pleased Jess to hear her say it.

'Punch that address into Go-ogle and let's see if we can find it,' Jess said and turned the volume back up on the radio.

———

ADYA SATTI WAS a striking young woman of twenty-five. Her long, dark hair was pulled back into a neat ponytail, and her eyes reflected a mixture of anxiety and determination.

'Ms Satti?' Jess said, showing her badge as they stood on the doorstep of a neat, semi-detached house. 'Detective Inspector Jess Allanby, and this is Detective Constable Gina Mellings.'

Adya nodded, stepping aside to let them enter. They followed her into a small, bright living room where she gestured for them to sit.

'Can I get you anything? Tea? Coffee?' Adya offered, her voice steady but polite.

'No, thank you,' Gina replied with a smile. 'We appreciate you taking the time to speak with us.'

They settled into chairs, and Adya perched on the edge of the sofa, her hands clasped tightly in her lap.

'Ms Satti,' Jess began, 'we're here about your complaint against Matt Gittings. I presume you've heard or read in the news about what's happened?'

Adya nodded, her expression hardening slightly. 'When you phoned, I didn't know what to think. Is there some kind of connection?'

'No. Not directly. We're trying to build a picture of Mr Gittings. That's all this is,' Gina reassured her.

'I told the committee what happened,' she said, rubbing the back of one hand with her fingers as she spoke. 'But I didn't give them the full story.'

'What did you leave out?' Gina asked.

Adya took a deep breath, her eyes glued to the coffee table. 'It kicked off with dodgy comments. He'd say these suggestive things when we were alone in the office. This was after Covid, when they were pushing us to come back in. At first, I put up with it. We, us secretaries, all knew what sort of bloke he was, but it just got worse and worse. I started changing how I dressed – kept my hair up, cut down on makeup. Anything to make myself less noticeable.'

Jess leaned in a bit, her voice gentle. 'Can you give us an example?'

Adya's voice shook. 'He'd go on about how I looked, saying I was "tempting" and "hard to resist". Made my skin crawl, but I didn't know how to tell him off without risking my job.'

'And what about the night it all kicked off?' Gina asked, treading carefully.

Adya went pale, but she pushed on. 'He was a bit pissed. We all were, but it was a big group, so I thought nothing of it. Then he vanished for about fifteen minutes. When he came back …' Her eyebrows shot up as she remembered. 'We'd moved on to the pub. There was a DJ. He danced with me and a few of the other girls. I could see he looked different, wired somehow. When the song finished, he followed me to the toilet. I didn't notice until … Before I could get in, he tried to grab me. I shoved him off. Lucky for me, some bloke came out of the gents and asked if I was alright. Matt mumbled something and legged it. I was bricking it. Still am if I'm honest.'

'You did the right thing coming forward,' Jess assured her. 'It's important we get a full picture of his behaviour. Did he ever make any threats or suggest there would be consequences if you didn't comply?'

Adya shook her head, her eyes welling up. 'He never came out and said it, but the threat was there, you know? Made me feel like I was cornered. Like I had no choice. Like it was all my fault somehow.'

Gina gave Adya's arm a gentle squeeze. 'We believe you, Adya. You're not on your own here.' She caught Jess's eye, and something unspoken passed between them.

'I reckon we've all had our fair share of blokes trying it on throughout our lives. Flirting is one thing, what you've experienced is something else altogether.'

Jess nodded. Gina, as usual, was spot on. But she wanted to ask about something Adya had said. 'You say he disappeared for ten or fifteen minutes and came back "wired"?'

Anya nodded again. 'I could see it. So could others. If I had to guess, I'd say he'd taken something.'

Jess offered a tight-lipped smile. Her mind recalled images of a hidey-hole behind brick slips in the hearth of Gittings's house in Solva. 'That's really useful, Adya. Is there anything else you remember?'

Adya took a moment, her eyes closing briefly as she gathered her thoughts. 'I've talked about it since with some of the other women. No one felt comfortable around him. But no one else has come forward.'

Or had the guts to, Jess thought.

'Thank you for telling us,' she said softly. 'Now that he's no longer around, perhaps they will. Just know that we're on your side.'

As they stood to leave, Adya looked up. 'Thank you for

listening. I just want this nightmare to end. What worries me more is the press finding out.'

'They won't from us,' Gina assured her. 'What you've told us isn't directly relevant to the case. But it's extremely helpful.'

Outside, the detectives exchanged a glance. The gravity of Adya's words needed no embellishments. But Jess couldn't help herself.

'This man sounds like a monster.'

'Makes you want to say that he deserved what he got, ma'am.'

'As a woman, I would. As a DI, I think the more we learn about Gittings, the more it looks like he was targeted.'

CHAPTER TWENTY-FOUR

WARLOW, Rhys, and Gil sat eating a late sandwich lunch. With Barber released, they turned their attention to other leads.

'Gina asked me to chase up on Milkshake man, sir.' Rhys, unlike Gil and Warlow who were scanning the chaotic-looking boards, kept his eyes on a screen.

'I'll call his employer today to confirm he was at work last Friday, but I've also found out that there is an online group calling themselves the Shakeshifters.'

'Really?' Gil asked.

'Lots of posts about politicians and the usual targets. Anyone against the current trends, identity politics, racism, Islamophobia, et cetera. It's like a hit list of transgressors and a timetable of when and where they'll be. In public, that is.'

'Is Gittings's name down there?'

'It is, but it has a big red cross through it.' Rhys turned the screen for them to see.

'*Argwlydd mawr*, how the hell do these people get away with it?' Gil asked.

'Our Milkshake attacker, Tyler Collins, is a bit of a hero, of course.'

'Any suggestions as to preferred flavours?' Gil asked.

'No. But there are details about how to make sure the lid

is loose before it is launched and to remove the straw which can affect trajectory.'

Warlow grunted. 'But no one had Gittings appearing in the Anchor pub at 9pm last Friday on the schedule?'

'No, sir. In fact, he has no public appearances scheduled on this list. Not since he was suspended.'

'Chase up our Milkshake man's alibi,' Warlow suggested. 'In the meantime, I'm heading back to Solva – one more pub to check. I've spoken to the manager, and the bar staff involved in the latest of Gittings's infractions is at work this afternoon.'

'Alright for some,' Gil muttered, but with no real rancour. 'You're not going back to that airfield, are you?'

Warlow noticed a wicked glint in his eye.

'No, why would I?'

'Perhaps you've got a thing for snakes. I knew a magician once who used them in his act.'

Warlow guessed that Gil was lining up some dreadful pun to relieve the tension. All he had to do was wait.

'Like a snake charmer?' Rhys asked.

'No, he used to produce them from his top hat.'

'Like rabbits?'

'No, like snakes. He'd put his hand in and pull out a snake. After he'd said the magic words, of course.'

'Dare we ask?' Warlow rumbled out the question.

'Adder cadabra.'

'Now I'm definitely leaving.' Warlow got up and threaded his way to the SIO room to pick up his keys.

He needed to get out to dispel his increasing frustration. Not with Gil. He was way past that. But he'd thought that perhaps Barber might have been the answer, the little nugget of information they'd prised out of the dirt that may have helped and pointed them in the right direction. It still could, but Warlow didn't get the tingle that came with knowing they were knocking at the right door, even if what was behind that door remained hidden.

Barber wasn't off their radar, but neither did the man set off any early warning alarms. Warlow couldn't stay cooped up in the office for another four hours.. He needed some time to think.

––––––

THE PRESELI ARMS, just off the main road north of Solva, was a large pub with a reputation for food and rooms. Reputations were precious. There were other pubs, so it was sink or swim.

The afternoon stayed warm with a few bruised-looking clouds edging their way across from the distant west. Warlow glanced up at them as he exited the Jeep and thought that with a bit of luck, they might miss this little corner of tranquillity for a while.

After the sticky ride down in the car – no matter how much aircon he had on, he always got a wet spot in the small of his back this time of year – he walked through to the bar and ordered a drink. After announcing his presence, he took his very innocent lime and soda with ice outside to sit on a bench under an umbrella and enjoy the sea breeze.

Five minutes later, two people approached him. The first introduced himself as the duty manager and the other, a younger woman in her early twenties, was introduced as Iona Stevens. She stood in front of him, about five foot two, with an anxious, serious face that did not detract from her attractive features. She wore a Preseli Arms apron over a black T-shirt, black skinny jeans, and trainers. But she looked flushed. Whether from work or nerves, standing before a DCI clearly rattled her. He tended to have that effect.

After a stilted introduction in which he quickly realised his role had ended, the duty manager left. Iona declined Warlow's offer of a drink with a shake of her head. But she sat when he suggested it, hands together on her lap under the bench.

She was yet to smile, and the reason became obvious in her first words.

'Am I in trouble?'

Warlow smiled. 'What for?'

'For what happened to him? Matt Gittings.'

'Why would you be in trouble, Iona?'

'Because I'm the one who complained about him. I'm the one—'

Warlow raised a hand to stop her there. Gently but firmly, he said, 'Iona, you are not the only one. In fact, you are one of many people who have good cause to complain about Gittings.'

'But—'

'No buts. I'm not here to get you into trouble. I'm here to find out what Matt Gittings was up to. And from what I've heard so far, he was up to all sorts and none of it good.'

She smiled. A toothless flicker of relief.

'And if you'd rather not speak to me, I can arrange for a female officer to—'

Her turn to interrupt him. 'No, it's okay. I know who you are. It's been all over the news. In fact, some people in the pub today were in Solva because they want to find out where it happened. It's sick. But my dad said that if you're on the case, it will be sorted. *Ma dad yn ffan.*'

She switched to Welsh seamlessly, explaining that her father was a fan. Many of the locals were natural Welsh speakers, but with so many people having moved into the town over the years, it struggled a little to keep a foothold. But those who spoke it, spoke it well. Warlow smiled and answered. Self-deprecatingly, in the same language. *'S'gen i ddim llawer o genfnogwyr.'*

It was true. He did not have many fans.

Iona's smile this time was genuine and transformational. She carried a scent of flowers and fresh pastries. Her eyes bunched, her teeth showed white and even, and Warlow knew they were going to be fine. This time, he continued in Welsh to her.

'I've had the story from Julian, the owner, but I'd like it if you told me, please. None of it needs to go any further than us two. But it will all help.'

Iona nodded, and he saw her visibly relax.

Most of what she told him followed a depressingly

familiar pattern. Gittings liked to hold court and, over the winter, had come in to eat regularly on weekends. At the beginning, he'd been generous with tips, chatty, interested to learn that she'd taken a year off after her degree to help her dad out on the farm before going on to a master's. Somehow, he'd got her phone number – not from her – and started messaging her. He'd eat on his own and ask that she serve him. When the pub refused, he upped the messaging game, and she thought she'd seen his car following her home once.

The messages got more frequent. Lots and lots of them. She had told no one. She never replied to them.

'One night, Gittings got really drunk, or hyper, I couldn't tell which. But it was nasty. In front of people in the restaurant, he said he had a ton of money and that he had girls lining up and that I was a little tart. Julian threw him out and told him never to come back.'

'But I'm guessing he didn't stop hassling you?'

Iona's head dropped. 'If anything, it got worse. Texts, like hundreds of texts. From different numbers, so it was hard to block them. And photos.'

'Of?'

She shook her head again, not wanting to talk about it, but knowing she had to.

'Do you mean… inappropriate pictures?' Warlow prompted.

'Of one kind. The male kind. I stopped looking and deleted everything as soon as it arrived if it came from a number I didn't recognise. Just swept it away without opening it.'

Warlow's anger smouldered as Iona recounted her ordeal. The pattern was depressingly familiar: Gittings, starting off as charming and generous, turning into a relentless stalker.

'I wish I knew how he got my number,' Iona said, her voice trembling.

Warlow's jaw clenched. 'Did you tell anyone?'

Iona's eyes glistened. 'I couldn't tell my parents. I just couldn't.'

'A boyfriend? A friend?'

'There's no one serious,' she whispered. 'I did tell a friend at first, but after a while I lied and said it had stopped.'

Warlow leaned forward, his concern palpable. 'What happened next?'

Iona's voice quavered. 'I went to see him.'

Warlow's heart plummeted. 'To his house?'

She nodded, wringing her hands. 'About a month ago. I had some friends come and pick me up to go to Tenby for a drink. I said I had something I needed to drop off, so I had them with me. They sat outside in the car, and I nipped to his house. I could hear the music from the car. It gave me confidence. I wanted to tell him to stop, to threaten going to the police. But he wasn't there.

'His neighbour saw me and told me Gittings had gone out. He was nice, the neighbour. A Mr Talbot. He didn't look well. I've never seen him in the pub, but I have about town on a bike.'

She paused, her face drawn. 'I don't know how it happened. All he did was ask if he could help ...' Another little shake of her head. 'He must have thought I was stark raving mad.' Her composure cracked as she recalled breaking down in front of the stranger. 'I stood there on one side of a gate with this poor man listening to me tell him that Gittings was sending me disgusting photos and messages and begging him to ask Gittings to stop. I mean ... it wasn't Mr Talbot's fault. He had nothing to do with it. I realised after five minutes what I was doing and stopped and apologised. He was really, really nice,' she said, her voice barely above a whisper.

Warlow's expression softened. 'Did Gittings stop after that?'

Iona shook her head, a miserable tear escaping down her cheek. 'No. The texts kept coming. I ... I deleted them without looking.'

Gently, Warlow asked, 'Do you have any of the messages?'

She hesitated, then pulled out her phone with trembling fingers.. What she showed Warlow made his stomach churn.

As he took screenshots, Iona's voice broke. 'I should have told someone, shouldn't I?'

Warlow looked up. 'You're telling someone now, Iona. That's what matters. And this is how people like Gittings work. They make you feel guilty for something you have no control over. You kept it to yourself and dealt with it. That's incredibly brave.'

'Thank you.' Her voice was small and on the point of breaking. She found a tissue and brought it up to her face.

'Other officers will be in touch. For a chat like we've had now. A DI Allanby and a DC Mellings. You'll like them. And remember, you're not in any trouble at all. But they will want to hear what you've told me. They'll interview you because I think you need to tell this story to other people and it'll make you feel a lot better. No one else will know. Is that okay?'

Iona, eyes red from the quiet tears, nodded again.

'He's out of your life, Iona. For good.'

'What really happened to him?'

'We're still trying to find out.'

Iona's lower lip trembled afresh. 'I wish I was sad, but I'm not.'

'If it's any consolation, few people are.'

CHAPTER TWENTY-FIVE

ONCE AGAIN, Warlow saw no point in getting the team back for vespers. When he reached his car in the harbour car park, some reporter was doing a piece to camera on the beach in front of the Inn, soaking up the atmosphere. No doubt they'd be interviewing staff or punters from all over the town, but he'd told Iona to stay well away and given Julian at The Preseli the same message. He couldn't stop the press, no one could. But they could be a bloody nuisance.

He sent a message through to Gil for another early start the next day, adding that he hoped they'd have something a bit more concrete to work with.

'Hope springs eternal,' Gil said when he called him back. 'Rhys is still here doing some Internet chasing. Jess and Gina are finished in Cardiff and on the way back.'

They'd be a good hour at this time of day.

'How about you? Had enough of gadding about the pubs of Solva?'

'I have. The hyenas are arriving, already sniffing around the corpse.' Warlow didn't need to explain. Gil knew full well who the hyenas were.

'On that note, I had a call from our pet hyena, Lucy Sanders.'

'What did she want?'

'Checking on progress; her words.'

Warlow uttered an oath under his breath.

Gil stifled a laugh. 'You're dancing with the devil there.'

'Bad enough when the higher-ups were breathing down our necks. We've swapped that out for a journalist who can smell the advance now that Gittings's death has upped the interest stakes.'

The three seconds of silence that followed told Warlow that there was more to come.

'What?' he growled.

'She was asking about you?'

'Me?'

'Not directly. She was probing. Asking how well you'd adapted after your return to work from an early retirement.'

'And?'

'I spilled the beans, of course I did. Told her all about your existential crisis. Denise's illness, your HIV contracted from a spiked needle kindly donated by a junkie in Llanelli.'

'You did not.' Warlow couldn't help sounding irked.

'Of course, I did not. I'm saving all that for my memoirs. Point is, she is digging, grubbing around like a truffle pig. She's going to want to make you, or us, a part of her truth.'

'Don't use that combination of words in my presence. The only truth is the truth.'

He could almost hear Gil's grin. 'As I say, a samba with Satan. Oh, and I have further analysis of Gittings's phone records. Want it now or shall I share it with everyone tomorrow?'

Warlow sighed. The day's travelling and the heat were sapping his energy. 'Tomorrow.'

But first, there was an evening to get through.

Warlow returned to Nevern and picked up Cadi on the way. When he got out of the car, just for a moment, he felt the world spin. The second time that had happened. Nothing much, just a momentary dislocation of time and space. He needed to drink more water. At least, that was what he told himself.

At home, he watered some plants and cut his patch of

lawn while the dog flip-flopped from sun to shadow, waiting for Jess to return. Several times, Warlow heard the reassuring lapping of water from a bowl as the dog slaked her thirst. He found the sound calming.

And a good reminder to do the same.

Jess came back, they ate, drank only water, and swapped stories of Gittings the serial offender. How he was a coarse, lewd, predatory nuisance who got worse the more he drank … or sniffed.

Iona and Adya's stories were similar enough to tell Warlow that there were likely other young women who had been victims of his unwanted attention along the way. And it said something about why Gittings had chosen politics. A job that came with power, and one that brought him into contact with many young people.

'Is getting put upon enough of a motive for murder, though?' Warlow asked, aware there'd be no answer.

'If he did something like that to Molly, I wonder how I'd feel,' Jess said.

Warlow did not reply.

———

Gina and Rhys had a late supper, again without Dan. Gina told him about Adya. Rhys told her about how he'd spent the late afternoon looking through deaths on smart motorways.

'Sounds like you had even less fun than me,' Gina said.

'It's like everything to do with Gittings and this case is, what's the word, tainted? Everything he touched seems to end up worse off.'

'Some people are like that.' She thought about telling him that Hakeem had phoned her, but she didn't. Dan was out, and she wanted to sit down on the sofa with Rhys and watch some mind-numbing TV. Not think about Dan, or Adya, or dangerous motorways. She rarely felt like this, but tonight she did.

Gina's mind drifted to her phone conversation with Dan that afternoon when she'd finally tried pinning him down as regards plans. He'd let slip fragments of his life in Cambodia. The bombshell: he'd got a girl pregnant. That's why he'd fled back home, he'd said. Needed time to "think it through".

Her response had been razor-sharp: 'What's there to think through?'

'I'm not ready for that shit, Geen,' he'd mumbled.

Her laugh had been sharp, bitter. He was just a scared boy running from responsibility.

'What about work?' she'd demanded, her anger flaring. 'You said you needed money.'

'I do. I've got feelers out, Geen. Any day now.' His voice pleaded with her. 'I need a base. Once I get work, I can find some proper digs, yeah?'

She'd wanted to tell him he had a week to clear out – the house was too small for three of them. But the words had stuck in her throat. That baby, real or imagined, had thrown her. Even now, she couldn't decide if she should be furious or sympathetic. If any of it was even true.

Gina pushed the thoughts away, focusing on the warmth of Rhys's body next to her on the couch. She held a tissue to her nose and blew.

'Got a cold coming?' Rhys asked.

'Just sniffles,' she'd said.

But in truth, she was holding back tears of frustration.

The night promised a quiet respite, a chance for Rhys and Gina to reset. But at 2am, Dan's return shattered that illusion. The door creaked open, his unsteady footsteps echoing through the flat, a feckless reminder of the complications that had invaded their lives.

————

MEANWHILE, miles away, Evan Warlow and his partner Jess found their own rest abruptly cut short a bit later. At 4:30am, the shrill ring of a phone pierced the pre-dawn silence. The duty sergeant's voice on the other end, tense and urgent, meant only one thing: the case that had consumed their waking hours was about to take another dark turn.

Two households, separated by distance but united in their disrupted night, braced themselves for whatever grim developments the early morning would bring.

———

THREE HOURS LATER, Barry Talbot stood at his door, leaning heavily on a walking stick, his face creased with worry and fatigue. Warlow, dressed in a well-worn but tidy suit – the lightest he possessed to accommodate the weather – approached with a purposeful stride. He had slept little since the early morning call but had waited until 7am before setting off. He was here to get the details firsthand.

'Mr Talbot,' Warlow greeted, extending a hand. 'We meet again.'

Warlow had come through via St Fagos, where another response vehicle had parked at the entrance to keep away prying eyes. And there were more of these already. A CSI vehicle also pulled in as Warlow crossed to the gate leading to Talbot's house.

They moved into the living room. Talbot lowered himself into a chair with a wince, placing his stick within arm's reach.

'I suppose you want a blow-by-blow?' Talbot asked.

'If I could,' Warlow replied.

'It was around 3am,' Talbot began, his voice raspy. 'I don't sleep well these days. It was a warm night, so I had the windows open. I heard noises – rustling, a thud, then the security lights came on.'

Warlow took out his phone. 'I'm going to record this if it's alright?'

Talbot shrugged. 'I got out of bed. That takes a good couple of minutes these days. I grabbed my torch and made my way downstairs. That's when I heard a window smash. I knew it must be coming from next door.' He paused, taking a deep breath.

Warlow noticed pain lines etched into the old man's face.

'I went outside,' Talbot continued, almost apologetically. 'I saw them straight away in the light – two dark shapes, trying to break in. I shouted that I'd called the police. They shouted something unpleasant back. But they'd been thrown by the lights and ran off. I walked across and saw they'd smashed a pane of glass at the back door but they didn't get in.'

Warlow shook his head. 'You understand how stupid that was? Things could have got much worse.'

'I was being curious, that's all.'

Warlow thought about mentioning what could happen to cats but refrained … with difficulty. 'Did you get a look at them?'

'They were quick, and I was too far away. Just shadows, really.'

'And you're sure they didn't get inside?'

'Positive. I checked as best I could without going in myself. The door is still locked. I had a walk around, but I'm not as spry as I used to be.'

Warlow glanced up, a hint of a smile on his lips. 'None of us are, Barry. It's a toss-up between foolish and brave to have gone out there, but next time, please stay inside and let us handle it.'

Talbot sighed, his shoulders slumping. 'I know. It's just … living alone, you feel like you have to take charge. And with Gittings gone, someone has to watch the place.'

'I understand,' Warlow said gently. 'But your safety is more important. There are all sorts of people around now. Journalists, chancers, urban bloody explorers. This is exactly the sort of thing they'd get up to for their YouTube channel. But please, leave the dangerous stuff to us. How are you feeling otherwise?'

Talbot hesitated, then shrugged. 'I get by. The nights are the worst. Pain keeps me up, and the mind wanders, you know?'

'You're not alone in that,' Warlow replied. 'I know what it's like to lie there, eyes open in the dark. Especially when I'm on a case.'

They shared a brief moment of silence. Someone else would take a detailed statement. Someone else would examine the damage to St Fagos. But Warlow had wanted to see Talbot, make sure he was okay. Satisfied now that he'd been frightened but not damaged, Warlow stood to leave, offering a reassuring smile. 'We'll keep an extra eye on the area, Mr Talbot. And please, ring us if you notice anything at all untoward.'

Talbot nodded, looking more haggard than ever.

'Thank you. I appreciate it.' He made to get up, trying to balance his stick with one hand on the chair arm.

'I can see myself out, Barry,' Warlow said. 'Honestly.'

As Warlow stepped outside, a car pulled up, and two people dressed in scrubs emerged. They carried medical bags and moved with the practiced efficiency of healthcare professionals. Warlow intercepted them, showing his badge.

'Good morning,' he said. 'I'm DCI Warlow. I was just speaking with Mr Talbot about an incident last night. Did he call you?'

The news elicited shocked expressions. 'Is he okay?'

'He interrupted a break-in next door.' He glanced back. Talbot's front door remained closed. He turned back and caught the badges on both women's chests. Warlow frowned. 'Palliative care?'

'We're the Palliative Care Community Pathway, Care At Home team. Bit of a mouthful, I know.'

Warlow swallowed some saliva. 'Mind if I have a word?'

The two exchanged glances before one of them nodded. 'How can we help?'

Warlow's eyes softened. 'Palliative … I didn't realise. He didn't mention …'

The nurse sighed. 'He has CNS and bone secondaries from a liver primary. It's terminal. He's declined more chemo and radiation therapy. We're here to manage his symptoms and provide support as much as we can.'

'CNS?'

'Brain.'

Warlow's own brain did the maths. 'He said he'd had a seizure?'

'That's how he presented. Unusual, but …' She shrugged.

'How long?' Warlow asked, his voice low.

'Another two months at most. He's had three rounds of treatment but he doesn't want anymore. We're trying to get him to visit the hospice once a week, but he is a stubborn man.' Her smile had an edge of fondness to it.

Warlow took a moment, processing this. 'He wants to stay here?'

'For as long as possible. And why not? A Marie Curie nurse calls twice a week, too. We're here for pain and symptom control and general support.'

The second nurse added, 'And chats about getting things arranged.'

Things arranged. Warlow felt stunned. 'He's a stoical old bird.'

'Barry is that, amongst other things,' the nurse said with another smile.

'How will this pan out?'

'Eventually, he will go to the hospice or hospital when the pain gets too much to manage here, or he starts fitting. In the meantime, we'll support him as long as possible.'

'Thank you for letting me know.' Warlow turned away but then had a Columbo moment. 'Medication wise, he tells me he can't sleep.'

'It is hard. He's on a cocktail of stuff.'

'Not Zolpinam by any chance?'

'No. He's on something else at night. Why do you ask?'

'It's one I've heard of, that's all.' Warlow slipped out the obfuscation as easy as breathing. Gleaning information indirectly and remaining truthful about it in the process was an art.

He had indeed heard of Zolpinam, but these good people didn't need to know from where and why. Good question, though. Why *had* he asked that?

Because he would not have put it past Gittings to have stolen them from Talbot.

'And morphine?'

'Small dosages. Orally for now.'

He watched as the nurses headed inside, feeling a pang of sorrow for Barry Talbot. Living alone and dying.

Christ.

As he walked back to his car, he pondered whether to return and offer more words of comfort but decided against it. Talbot was in good hands, and his presence would only add to the burden. He'd toyed with quizzing the old man about Iona and to get his take but now was not the time. It would keep.

Warlow drove away, on the one hand satisfied that Talbot had come to no harm, but troubled too with what he'd learned. And though he'd been truthful in saying that someone breaking in could have been troublemakers, there were other possibilities which made him wonder about the wisdom of having an invalid living next door to the property.

He'd need to talk to someone about setting up cameras at St Fagos to keep an eye on things. Talbot deserved that, at the very least.

CHAPTER TWENTY-SIX

WARLOW ARRIVED at the Incident Room to find a full complement awaiting him. They all turned to look at him as he breezed through the door. It was not a morning for pleasantries. Rhys spoke for them all when he asked, 'How's the neighbour?'

That gave the DCI pause. Some questions were like footballs – round and easy to kick away. Others more rugby-ball shaped – not as easy to catch, and the bounce could take you anywhere.

'He's a Bond cocktail. Shaken but not stirred. Looks like his security lights did most of the spooking. A window got smashed at the rear of the property. He didn't actually challenge them, thank God. CSI is there now, but once the scene is released, it would be good to get some kind of surveillance set up.'

Gil wrote something down on a pad.

'What do you think they were after, sir?' Gina asked.

Warlow considered this. 'I have some theories.' He repeated the notions he'd given to Talbot. 'Whoever it was may be back, and we can't have the neighbour as our watchdog.'

He spotted a mug of tea with "Foxtrot Foxtrot Sierra" written on it. His mug.

'As ordered, sir,' Rhys said, noting the DCI eyeing the tea.

'Buchannan wants a catch-up, but I've put it off until we go through what we've got.' Warlow picked up his mug and sipped while turning to the boards. 'My visit to the third pub, The Preseli, felt like a scene from Groundhog Day. Gittings often ate there alone, mainly to ogle one of the servers. A young woman named Iona. To be fair to the management, they protected her, and when Gittings became objectionable and hacked off that they kept Iona away, they banned him. But that didn't stop him hassling this poor girl. I've seen some texts he sent. Fawning and suggestive to start, later on down-right lewd. Offering gifts for … favours. She blocked him. But he used different numbers to pester her in the worst way possible.'

'She didn't tell anyone?' Rhys asked.

'No,' Warlow replied.

Gina spoke up. 'That's so often the way. The victim feels they're to blame somehow.'

'It culminated in her visiting him to beg him to stop. Luckily, he wasn't at home, but she spoke to Talbot, the neighbour, and asked him to intervene. I'm yet to talk to him about that. But he's not well and today wasn't the time. My point is, she's yet another one of his victims.'

'And it's a long list,' Jess agreed. She outlined their visit to Adya.

Warlow listened as did Gil. In his peripheral vision, Warlow took in the burly sergeant's silent attention and the hardening of his eyes. There were no jokes here.

'He liked to target younger women, then,' Rhys said.

'He did, but neither Adya, nor the miffed ex-girlfriend that triggered the Westminster scandal strike me as capable of overpowering Gittings and making him drive off a cliff,' Jess said. 'And their alibis check out.'

'I don't see Iona as a murderer, either,' Warlow declared. 'She wouldn't be able to overpower Gittings and there doesn't seem to be a significant other that might have championed her distress.'

Gil spoke for the first time in a while. 'Spoken to her dad?'

'She asked me not to. She doesn't want her parents involved.'

'What if he found out?' Gil asked.

Warlow threw him a glance.

'I know how I'd react, that's all,' Gil explained.

'Okay, we'll keep Iona on our witness list. But she did not come across as someone hiding anything. What else? Rhys?'

'Smart Motorways, sir. There is a petition that's got three hundred thousand plus signatures.'

'That's more than enough to trigger a parliamentary debate, right?'

'It is, sir. There are websites, too. Often run by victims' families or support groups. Gittings's name features as their most wanted, but it's all legitimate. They've stopped building them, these Smart Motorways. Now it's a question of trying to get those that are running removed.'

Warlow sighed.

There were so many people in Gittings's life with a reason to despise him. But nothing concrete yet. Nothing to sink their teeth into.

'Then there is Milkshake man, Tyler Collins,' Rhys said.

'What about him?'

'There's a bit more to him than meets the eye. He's part of a group. They call themselves the Shakeshifters. And I still did not get any kind of sense from Mr Collins. He's not cooperating. Despite telling Gina he was at a friend's house and was supposed to give details of that friend to his community work supervisor. He still has not done so.'

'Deliberately?' Jess asked.

Rhys shrugged.

Warlow shook his head. 'Is he one of those?'

They all understood what the DCI meant: someone who believed they had the right to be antisocial in the name of a cause – whatever that cause happened to be. A moveable feast if ever there was one. And for some, refusing to cooperate with the police was often seen as a tactical weapon, ready to be used whenever the chance presented itself

'I think he *is* one of those, sir,' Rhys said.

'Tidy. Shall we bring him in?' Gil asked.

'A trip up to Brecon, sir?' Rhys sounded hopeful.

Warlow made a face.

Gil changed tack. 'While you ponder that, I have news on Gittings's active text life.'

Gina gave him a lopsided smile as he slid over the floor in his chair and retrieved a sheaf of paper from his desk. 'We still haven't accessed his work phone. That has to go through some governmental gymnastics because of the likelihood it contains sensitive information.'

'That'll take forever,' Jess said. 'I once worked on a case involving an MP and it took weeks, if not months, before we got in.'

'What I can tell you from going over his private records is that he ate a lot of takeaways. There's Mrs Will the Fish on there and somewhere on Main Street in Solva seems to have a standing order on certain nights.'

'Not a chef, then, Mr Gittings?' Jess posed the question.

'I would say no. We've chased down a lot of regular numbers. His ex-wife, his kids, one or two other SMs. But, of particular interest is a list of PAYG numbers. Ten of them.'

Warlow frowned. 'What's unusual about them?'

'I didn't spot it, but one of the digital forensic techs picked it up right away.' He handed Warlow some sheets, three in total, each with four highlighted streaks in yellow. 'The same number appears four times in a given month. Always the same day and time. A Wednesday. Then the number changes and that new number appears again four times.'

Warlow tensed. 'A burner phone?'

'I'd say so. Swapped out every month.'

Gina looked confused. 'Is that significant?'

'It's a definite pattern,' Warlow explained. 'The kind of pattern you might see if someone had arranged for a regular … appointment.'

'And not with a dental hygienist,' Jess added drily.

Gina's brows knitted. 'What, then? Was he having an affair?'

'I wouldn't put it past him,' Gil agreed. 'But I'm thinking of something far less romantic.'

Rhys looked like he wanted to say something, but Warlow sent him a glance that told him to let Gina answer. 'An arrangement of some sorts, obviously.'

'Follow the money, Gina,' Warlow said, gently.

Gina's eyes widened as the suggestion clicked into place. 'Oh, God, you think it may be drug related?'

'There's enough evidence to suggest Gittings had some involvement. The cash. The hidey-hole. The drug traces. As I say, follow the money.'

'How much does a Senedd Member earn?' Jess asked.

Rhys consulted his phone. After a few seconds, he looked up. 'Nearly seventy thousand. Not bad. And I expect he'd been suspended on full pay.'

'But it's likely that money would come to an end come the next election. Even if he stood, it's not likely he'd get in, right?' Warlow asked with a look at Gil.

'You never know,' the sergeant replied, 'not these days. But the kind of transgression he's been suspended for does not sit well with people. He's weed on his chips once too often.'

'So, he'll need a different source of income,' Gina said with a slow nod. 'What can he do? Did he have any skills before politics?'

'I read somewhere he worked in the City,' Rhys answered her question.

'He's too old for that game,' Warlow muttered.

'But drugs?' Rhys looked sceptical. 'I mean … he's an ex-MP and a current representative of a national government.'

'Well, that doesn't stop him from being a creep,' Jess said with a degree of finality. 'And how big a step is it from being a predatory weirdo to being caught up in something messy, like drugs?'

Silence descended like a thick fog.

Warlow leaned back in his chair, brow furrowed as he tried to connect the dots. A serving member of the Welsh Parliament involved in drug trafficking. It wasn't just tabloid fodder – this had the makings of a political earthquake that could shake Cardiff Bay to its core. If word got out before they had solid evidence, the entire investigation could go tits up in a heartbeat.

Gil broke the silence. 'We need more than just theories. We need hard evidence.'

'I agree,' Warlow said, his voice steady but firm. 'Gina, I want you to dig deeper into those PAYG numbers. Trace every call, every text. See if we can find a link to any known dealers. Have a chat with Dai Vetch at Cardigan.'

Gina had determination etched on her face. 'I'll get on it right away, sir.'

'And Rhys,' Warlow continued, 'we need to put pressure on Collins. If he's a cog in a bigger wheel, we need to know who the others are and if any are active down here. So, Brecon it is.'

'On it,' Rhys replied, already reaching for his phone.

The room buzzed with renewed activity.

Warlow took a deep breath, trying to calm the storm inside him.

Jess walked over. 'Are we getting any closer?'

He sighed. 'Closer, yes. But closer to what, I'm not sure. Every new lead we follow seems to open up a dozen more. It's like we're kids chasing bubbles that burst every time we get close.'

'We'll get there,' Jess said, her voice resolute. 'We always do.'

Warlow gave her a small, weary smile.

But, as the team continued their work, a feeling of unease settled over him.

Gittings had been a man with many enemies, but the nature of his death suggested something more sinister than a simple act of revenge. And the drug world was full of all kinds of horrifying acts perpetrated in the name of vengeance, or as internecine warnings. A darkness lurked under the surface here.

He glanced at the board, at the photos and notes that

seemed to mock their efforts. Somewhere in this tangled web, the truth lay hidden.

He swallowed another mouthful of now tepid tea and set the mug down with a decisive thud. 'Okay,' he said, his voice cutting through the hum of activity behind them. 'Let's get to work. I need to talk to Superintendent Buchannan.'

'I forgot to tell you. Someone's popping in to see you at nine-thirty.' Gil studied his watch. 'In three minutes' time.'

Something about Gil's politeness rang an alarm bell. 'Who?'

'Our good friend, Lucy Sanders.'

Warlow closed his eyes for a couple of beats, then opened them as slits and slid his gaze over to Gil in a scathing glance. 'You could have told me earlier.'

'I wanted it to be a surprise.'

'Sanders is no Kinder Egg.'

'No, you're right. More of a slug-in-the-lettuce kind of surprise.'

'Nice.'

'But before you meet her again, I, too, have been doing some digging. Have a read of this.' Gil handed over another printed sheet for Warlow to look at.

He took it, glanced at it, and then read it again, this time giving it his full attention.

CHAPTER TWENTY-SEVEN

LUCY SANDERS still wore her trademark baseball boots and carpenter's jeans. He wondered if she ever wore anything else. Was it in defiance of the tyranny of fashion, or out of comfort? She was young enough for fashion still to be important in her life. But then, he knew nothing about her personally.

They met in the same conference room. No tea this time, or water. This was business.

'I thought that the easiest way to do this might be to arrange regular meetups.' She wasn't wearing glasses this time.

Contacts, Warlow supposed from the way she blinked a little too often. Her naked face made her look older somehow. She exuded an air of authority, relishing that he had agreed to the meeting, enjoying the fact that she held the aces.

Warlow remained impassive. 'Does that mean you have information to share with us?'

'A little.' She hesitated before asking, 'So, me first, is it?'

'You asked for the meeting.'

She held his gaze for a couple of beats before speaking. 'The press are thinking it isn't suicide. They're angling towards a revenge killing.'

'Really?' Warlow leaned back in his chair.

The conference room was silent except for the single tick of the second hand of an electric clock as it moved around the face, each tick a reminder of the balance of power between them.

'Oh, come on,' she said, her voice cutting through the silence he'd left. 'You as much as acknowledged it wasn't suicide last time.'

'I said we're looking at all angles.' Warlow kept his voice steady, but his eyes narrowed slightly.

'Enemies. Yes, I remember. So, how is that going?'

'You know I can't discuss any of this with you in the middle of an investigation.'

Sanders's grin widened, a predatory gleam in her eye. 'That works both ways.'

'No, it doesn't.' Warlow's tone was ice cold. 'We agreed that we would allow you to interview us if and when there is enough information to decide if this was anything other than suicide. Once we had enough for the case to go to court. An exclusive.'

'I'm still waiting,' she said, crossing her arms and leaning back, mirroring his posture.

'It's been all of two days.' Warlow's exasperation seeped through despite his best efforts to remain composed.

'Things move fast,' Sanders countered.

'Do they?' Warlow's voice dropped an octave. 'Can I remind you that whereas us discussing anything with you is at our discretion, you withholding relevant information from us is called obstructing the course of justice?'

Sanders shrugged, her eyes darting around the room. 'I had a chat with Geraint Lane.'

Warlow stiffened. 'Why?'

'He has a book coming out.'

'We are aware of that,' he replied, his jaw tightening.

'He says there are some home truths which might not make for comfortable reading.'

'I'd be very careful of taking anything Lane tells you other than with a great big dollop of salt.'

Sanders' eyes were bright with challenge. 'It's a great

story, though. His involvement with Hunt. But he devotes a chapter on the main actors, as well as spotlighting one of your own. Catrin Richards.'

Warlow's pulse quickened, throbbing at his temples. He remained silent, letting her words float.

'There's a bit about the rest of you, too. What motivates you all. The crack team who stopped Hunt the first time, but who failed the second time. I mean, you only managed to extricate yourselves from *beaucoup de merde* by finding Richards, yes? And the dog with a starring role?'

Warlow's pulse had gone up a notch. He let her words sink in, reducing days of worry and heartache over the search for a kidnapped Catrin to a throwaway sentence that sounded like a bloody Disney film. Sanders hadn't finished though.

'But he's had a rummage around in the teams' past, too. To make it interesting. The uncomfortable, but juicy sub plots. First, a pregnant Catrin Richards, guaranteed to stir top interest. Then the DI running away from a messy divorce in Manchester. Ladle in a craggy old sergeant named Jones, scarred from being tied up with Operation Alice. And you, divorced, early retirement, an alcoholic wife. God, I'm spoilt for choice when it comes to who I want to interview.'

'Keep on the way you're going, and you can forget it,' Warlow said, a thin smile that stopped an inch above his lips his response.

'But I spun the bottle and it ended up pointing at you. Because there's a piece of the puzzle that's missing in you, Chief Inspector. And I'd like to find out what it is.'

Warlow placed his hands on the table and made to stand. 'All very interesting and full of air. We won't be having any more of these meetings. If we get some information that fits with what we agreed, I may consider letting you discuss the case, and nothing else, with me or one of the team. Until then, much as I have enjoyed our little chat—'

Sanders made no effort to leave. 'Gittings was not a complicated man. He liked women, and he liked money and power. Politics was a natural feeding ground for a predator like him. We both know he did not know the meaning of the

ONE LESS SNAKE   193

word altruism. Everything he did, he expected something in return. That was why I couldn't figure out why he came down here. It isn't exactly sophistication central, right?'

Warlow paused, his hand hovering over the chair. 'That's the very reason people come here. It's a choice.'

'I get that. But Gittings? Really?'

'What are you saying?'

'I'm saying that he was unsophisticated, too. Certain things drove him. Power, women, and money. He fed his power craving by dabbling in the Senedd. He couldn't help himself and, of course, he had a platform already as an MP. Women … he was a menace. But he fed that desire with the other two.'

Warlow frowned, leaning in slightly. 'What do you mean?'

'He told me he had a girlfriend in Birmingham. Saw her once a week. Combined business with pleasure. His words.'

Warlow's interest piqued. He sat forward. 'You have a name?'

'Not yet. I'm working on it. And then there's the third driver. Money.'

Warlow's gaze sharpened. *Follow the money.* He'd had the same thoughts. 'And?'

'And it remained the one thing he never talked about. The divorce stripped him bare. He kept the house in Solva in the settlement, but that's about all. The Senedd job gave him an income, but he couldn't keep his hands to himself, so that blew up in his face. Even the book was out of desperation, the one I'm supposedly writing. He agreed to a small share of the royalties for allowing me to interview him. That's between him and the publisher.'

'But that won't be much, right?'

'No, it won't.'

'You suspect he had another source of income?'

Sanders nodded. 'Once or twice, when I interviewed him, after a couple of glasses of wine …' She paused and added an aside, 'I always got rid of half of mine in the sink and topped up with water whenever he went to the loo. Oil up the punter, but stay sober yourself. Old journalist trick. Anyway, he'd mention investments, but with a funny look on his face. At first, I wondered if he'd stashed money away offshore to avoid it being part of the divorce settlement. Just the kind of thing he'd do. But he always had that smirk. And then I remembered the Tonhill fiasco.'

Warlow arched an eyebrow. 'Remind me?'

'A donor for his election campaign as an MP turned out to have been a demolition business owned by a woman accused, but never charged, with being a money launderer with links to crime.'

Warlow's eyes widened slightly. 'What?'

'He denied knowing the link at the time. But there's no doubt she was part of the Tonhill Farm syndicate.'

Warlow's mind raced. He knew the name. A Midlands-based organised crime firm.

Sanders kept talking. 'There's always been talk that Gittings was wild. Liked to sniff some of the white stuff and smoke a bit of pot. That was the rumour and some of his staff witnessed it, but if they blew the whistle, they'd never get another job. I never got one to say it on record.'

'It's an interesting thought,' Warlow said, 'but where's the evidence?'

Sanders smiled, leaning in. 'Don't tell me it hadn't occurred to you?'

'I'd forgotten about the scandal. What was the headline again?'

'Politicians for Sale in Peaky Blinders Donor Scandal.'

Warlow groaned inwardly, rubbing his temples.

Sanders continued, enjoying herself now, 'It got swept under the carpet. She'd given something to every political party, but they all gave it back. At least, that's what was said. Though I suspect not all the money found its way home.'

'You have proof?'

'Of course not. But we're here in West Wales. It's on the white stripe route. From Birmingham to the ferries to Ireland and the rest of Europe, the sneaky way.'

Warlow weighed up her theory, his eyes narrowing. White stripe referred to hard drugs. Follow the money, he'd said, and there was one path the money could lead them down. 'Nice theory, but lacking in proof,' he said.

'Really? What about last night's shenanigans at Gittings's property, then? Was it a foot soldier looking for cash? Or milk and coffee, white or brown, whatever "food" they're missing?'

'No one broke in,' Warlow replied, his voice a low growl, irked by her use of street terms for drugs. The "food" that gangs so often liked to use as euphemisms.

'But someone tried to, right?' Sanders shot back, her eyes gleaming with triumph.

'Fascinating as all of this is, we work with evidence, not hearsay.' Warlow wasn't prepared to let on that his thoughts had already begun to turn in the same direction as an option. Finally, he spoke. 'We've been doing some background checks, too. And it turns out that you have an arrest record.'

Sanders exhaled through her nose and shaped her lips into a mirthless smile. 'I was young.'

'That's not much of an excuse for attacking a police officer.'

'It was an anticapitalism demonstration. It had a load of different supporting groups. I got caught up in something I regret. They were arresting a demonstrator. I went to help.'

'A demonstrator who suggested that politicians who did not back a no-borders approach to immigration should be shot?'

'He was just a kid. Nineteen.'

'So was the Boston bomber. And let's not mention the sniper at a certain political rally in Pennsylvania. You were arrested, charged, and found guilty.'

Sanders' laugh sounded shrill when she let it out. 'Are you suggesting I killed Gittings?'

'Did you? Have you rolled back on all your anticapitalism beliefs?'

'I was young.'

'You've already said that. And all this organised crime information is very interesting. We'll look into it. But in the meantime, do not come back here unless you have some actual proof. We'll be in touch. And beware of Lane, unless you enjoy trading yodels in an echo chamber.' Warlow got up.

Once again, the room swam for an instant. He half turned away to hide it.

'Were you there when your wife died?'

The question from Sanders cracked the air like a gunshot. A blind, knee-jerk need to wound from a woman who'd lost a round of a game she was used to winning.

'It's been a pleasure,' Warlow said without turning back as he walked to the door. 'Someone will be along to let you out … this time.'

CHAPTER TWENTY-EIGHT

WARLOW RETURNED to the Incident Room after his chat with Sanders and put his head around the door, wearing an expression like a ginger'd horse. Jess said as much. His meeting with Buchannan had now been escalated to include Chief Superintendent Drinkwater and the force press officer with a view to some sort of formal press conference. Warlow's least favourite subject and something he avoided, like cold soup and open-toed sandals.

Of course, once the DCI had left to go to his meeting, Gil had dissected Jess's turn of phrase. '*Mam fach*, I haven't heard that one in a while. Face like a gingered horse.' He shook his head with a smile.

'No clue what that means.' Rhys, honest as always, looked from Jess to Gil.

'A complex metaphor if ever there was one,' Gil said. 'A face like a horse implies length and indeed, DCI Warlow did not look happy. But the gingering adds a certain panache.'

Rhys turned to Jess, and she obliged. 'It's a thing, a cruel thing, some breeders – or formerly, the odd jockey – used to do it. Apply a little ginger to the horse's perineal region and it encourages it to raise its tail, which, in horse shows, is something people look for.'

'And in races, is meant to make them go faster,' Gil said.

'It's banned almost everywhere,' Jess added, witnessing the look of shock on Rhys's face.

'But, given the combination of despondency and manic intensity we just witnessed in DCI Warlow's expression, smack on, if I may say so,' Gil explained. 'Which, I suspect, is also one way of applying the ginger.'

'That's horrible,' Gina said, mimicking Rhys's distaste.

'It is indeed,' Gil agreed with a degree of mock serious-ness that immediately had everyone on high alert, apart from Gina.

'It's cruel and unforgivable, and jokes about animals are not at all funny,' Gil continued. 'And the universe is always willing to get its revenge. At Christmas time, one of our neigh-bours had the grandchildren visit and bought some farmyard Christmas crackers. Old Mal Jenkins pulled one, and two little plastic horses flew out, and he bloody swallowed them.'

'Oh, my God,' Gina said.

Jess opened her mouth in warning, but not soon enough to stop Gil from delivering his punchline. 'Yes – ended up in hospital. Of course, we went to see him the next day. Once he was stable.'

The expression of horror on Gina's face faded as she shut her eyes and muttered, 'When am I going to learn?'

But it meant the trip to Brecon to visit Collins, the "Shakeshifter,"'had defaulted to Jess and Rhys. Gina had set up a call with Vetch, the drugs officer, and Gil remained chained to the office, still under the doctor's orders. Said doctor being Evan Warlow.

Collins pleaded poverty and so had been brought in from north of Builth Wells by a response vehicle and was awaiting their presence in Brecon nick when Jess and Rhys arrived.

Tyler Collins wore a "Dead Inside" black T-shirt over green cargo shorts. He sat with arms crossed, legs wide, his unruly curls hanging over wire-framed glasses, which, along with his stubble, contrasted with his pale skin. He watched, unmoving, as Rhys and Jess sat opposite him in the interview room, surveying them with scrutiny and disdain.

Rhys made the introductions and thanked him for his time.

'Huh, as if I had a choice.'

'You had a choice not to throw that milkshake over a sitting member of government,' Jess countered. She'd already decided that trying to establish a relationship would not be worth the effort.

The job brought you into contact with people like Collins – those who did not do well in a given system and therefore took the easy way out by becoming victims. Anyone who did well, or who represented that system, were, by definition, oppressors. Once that situation became established, it gave the victims carte blanche to hitch their wagon to almost any cause where the establishment held sway. Collins fitted right into that category.

He shifted in his seat and smirked. 'Felt good, though.'

'Why have you not provided us with your whereabouts last Friday night?' Jess asked.

'Thought I was at a mate's, but I wasn't. I was out and about. I can't remember where I was every minute, can I?'

Jess smiled. 'I can. So can Sergeant Harries. Is your social life such a whirl that you're unable to recall where you were for twelve hours?'

'Yeah, well, not all of us bow to the fascist flag and the clock. Besides, I don't have a car.'

'How do you get about?' Rhys asked.

'Walk. Or a bike. I board, too.'

'No skateboard park in Builth, is there?'

'No. We make do.'

'So, you were not in Solva last Friday?'

Collins made a sound with his lips that implied derision. 'Why would I go to that shithole?'

'It's where Gittings lived.'

Collins's smirk blossomed into a smile showing a row of teeth with a missing premolar. 'Not anymore, he don't.'

Jess placed a printout of a screenshot Rhys had taken of the Shakeshifters website with a photograph of Collins's trademark smirk in full view, being led away by police after his milkshake attack on Gittings.

Collins smiled warmly at her. 'I'm a hero, see?'

'A hero with a criminal record,' Jess said, her tone cutting.

Collins's smirk slipped.

'Are you active in this Shakeshifter group?'

'Nah. I mean, we don't know who's in the group. S'just names, yeah?'

'Are there any active members in the Solva area?'

'They got eyes everywhere, man.'

'Did they have eyes on Gittings?'

Collins, arms folded, nodded. 'Bound to.'

'Do you have any information that might be useful to us in our investigation, Mr Collins?' Rhys asked.

Collins sniffed, considering. 'What's in it for me?'

Jess read the calculating light in Collins's eyes. 'We could speak to the probation service. There are several kinds of unpaid work. Some easier than others. I could see if a couple of hours in a charity shop might better suit you.'

Collins chewed his cheek.

'You'd have to not turn up looking like an extra from some skater video game,' Jess added.

'That's your opinion.'

'Are there people in and around the Pembrokeshire coast who had been watching Gittings?' Jess asked bluntly.

'Yeah. They know his movements. Know which pubs he uses. Know he likes chasing women. Know he goes up to the airfield to do some dogging.'

'Dogging?' Rhys asked, taken by surprise.

'And you are sure about that?' Jess asked.

'The doggin'? Why else? Every Thursday, regular as clockwork. The bloke was a perv, yeah?'

Jess sat up, frowning. 'And you know all this? How?'

'WhatsApp group. Encrypted. But I'm not giving you my phone. I'm just giving you the info, yeah?'

They probably would need his phone, but he needn't know all that yet. 'Okay, Tyler. We need you to write all of that down. And exactly where you were last Friday night with people we can actually talk to who will confirm it.'

'You'll speak to the probation officer?'

'I will.'

'Sweet. Give me a pen.'

'Why didn't you just tell us all this before?' Rhys asked.

Collins looked bemused, the pen poised.

'You're the enemy, man.' And he said it in a way that made it sound as if this were the most obvious thing in the world.

———

Warlow was not back by midday. Gil glanced at his watch and got up.

'Right, I'm out of here for an hour,' he said to Gina. 'You have the conn.'

'What's a conn?'

'Not a Star Trek fan, Gina?'

'Not really my thing.'

'No connections with the navy?'

Gina shook her head.

'Then conning tower is going to mean not much to you. Let's start again. You're in charge until I come back.'

'Okay.' She beamed at him. 'Going out for lunch?'

'Meeting up with an old friend. But I'll be back by one.'

Gina waved him off. 'Have fun.'

He gave her a thumbs up and hurried out.

Lunchtime and the Incident Room had fallen oddly quiet. She tried Vetch again and this time, the call connected. He was a veteran drugs officer who'd worked with Warlow and his team on several cases but had not spoken directly with Gina before.

'Sergeant Richards still off, then, is she?' Vetch asked after she'd introduced herself.

'She is,' Gina confirmed. 'DCI Warlow asked me to give you a ring.'

'Always ominous when Warlow wants my input. What have you got?' His voice was clipped and efficient sounding.

Gina took a deep breath. 'It's the Gittings's case.'

'Gittings? The politician?' The line hissed as Vetch weighed up the request and made a quick assumption. 'Not a suicide, then?'

'We don't think so.' She hesitated, choosing her words carefully. 'When we searched his property, we found a stash of money. Exactly ten thousand wrapped in a brown paper bag in a hidden spot in his hearth. We found no drugs as such, but swabs of that same spot have come back positive for marijuana and cocaine. Mr Warlow wants me to ask if you ever had Gittings on your radar.'

'Honest answer, no.'

Gina quelled a pang of frustration. She needed more. 'There has been some suggestion of him having taken drugs in the past.'

'Many people have,' Vetch said, his tone dismissive. 'But why the cash?'

'We were hoping you might tell us.'

Another silent beat as Vetch considered what Gina had told him. 'No need for me to explain county lines operations to you, is there, Detective Constable?'

Gina nodded to herself, recalling the briefings. It had always struck her as ironic that such an innocuous term was used for drug running and organised crime. 'I know it involved drug trafficking from the bigger cities into rural areas. I know they use phones as lines of communication for ordering and that.'

'Spot on. That's what it says in the manual. And they do target kids or other vulnerable people who see it as easy money to act as their mules. We look for patterns of behaviour in young people. Kids who turn up with new trainers or labelled clothing all of a sudden. Who take time off school and end up where they shouldn't be. Lots of unusual texts, that kind of thing.'

'Challenging to enforce, then?' The complexity of it all made her head spin.

'Not easy. This time of year, we have tourists flooding the area already and ten times more in July. From Liverpool and Manchester in the north, Birmingham in the middle. And down south, it's three and a bit hours from Swansea to London on a train. Not to mention the coast. All those lovely beaches and inlets for boats to bring in whatever the hell they like from Ireland, and, of course, there are the ferries.'

Gina's mind raced. She hadn't considered the geographic implications as Vetch continued. 'But it isn't always kids. Crime gangs want consistency. A steady supply of regular shipments. I'm not sure how Gittings fits into all of that.'

'We've found no links between him and Ireland,' Gina said, feeling a bit out of her depth.

'I won't lie to you. Of course, there's a local problem. Not big and maybe not in somewhere like Solva, but we have to consider supply chains.'

'Can you explain that, sarge?' She needed to understand every angle.

'Drugs coming in from Europe and dumped on the coast, for distribution elsewhere. I don't need to remind you of Hopper, right?'

A cold shiver seized her breath for a moment. Of course, she remembered Hopper. A rogue officer who'd murdered a fellow officer and staged a discovery of a drugs shipment whilst helping himself to some of the spoils. A man who had also tried to inveigle himself into Gina's life and who'd shot at her and Warlow in a fit of vengeance.

He'd missed. But not by much.

'We're talking transport back to the cities. The opposite of the typical county lines pattern,' Vetch explained.

Silence bloomed as she took all this in.

'Am I being a help or a hindrance?' Vetch asked when the silence grew.

'A help, sarge. Mr Warlow will want to know all of this.'

'I'm sure he will. You have my number if you need me.'

Gina ended the call and sat back. She spoke to herself as she muttered, 'Oh, Mr Gittings … what were you up to?'

CHAPTER TWENTY-NINE

Gil's "old" friend sat in her car on Tabernacle Terrace a good forty yards from Gina and Rhys's house. Gil parked somewhere else and walked the two blocks to the street, opened the car door and got in. In the driver's seat, Sergeant Catrin Richards smiled as her colleague slid in.

'Where's the little one?'

'With my mother,' Catrin replied.

'*Mamgu* time.'

Catrin nodded. 'Dry run for when I come back.'

'Tidy. When is that again?'

'Couple of months.'

'And here you are, on a busman's lunch. Any sign of him?'

Catrin glanced at her phone. 'Rhys says he leaves between a quarter and half past twelve, usually. We have five minutes.'

'Lights, action it is, then.'

Gil opened his door and groaned with the effort of getting out, walked back up the street to a corner, and waited while Catrin got out. She walked in the opposite direction, past Gina and Rhys's house to the property next door – Hakeem's house – where she knocked. The door opened, and Hakeem, whom neither Catrin nor Gil had ever met, spoke to Catrin.

Meanwhile, Gil began walking slowly up the street towards her. He'd gone twenty yards when the door to Rhys and Catrin's opened and a man emerged. Medium height, hair a tad longer than the current fashion, in T-shirt, shorts and flip-flops, a backpack slung over one shoulder. The man started on seeing Catrin talking to his neighbour but turned quickly without acknowledging either her or the neighbour, and headed towards Gil. When he was about to pass him, Gil spoke.

'Did I see you coming out of Number 8, there?'

Startled, Dan stepped off the pavement, eyeing up the older man.

'Who wants to know?'

Gil had his credentials on a lanyard, and he flashed them now. 'Sergeant Gil Jones.' He wore a big smile. 'Ah, yes, I can see the resemblance now. Dan, isn't it? I work with your sister in Dyfed Powys. She said you were staying with her and Rhys.'

Dan blinked but recovered enough to realise he could not walk away without seeming weird and a bit rude.

'Oh, right.' A nervous smile flickered over his features.

'Bit of luck for you, me catching you like this, though. Sergeant Richards was going to knock on your door next.' He nodded beyond to where Catrin was chatting to Hakeem.

'What's going on?' Dan asked. A normal enough question but delivered with jittery glances up and down the street.

'We're canvassing the neighbourhood. This and another couple of streets. House to house. We've had reports of some … unpleasantness in the area. Most likely yobs, though we can't rule out people selling drugs.' Gil paused before asking, 'Haven't noticed anything yourself, have you?'

'No,' Dan replied, a tad too nonchalantly.

'Oh, well, if you do, you're spoilt for choice to report it.' Gil let out a theatrical laugh. 'What with your sister and Rhys living with you.'

Dan's reciprocating smile looked nowhere near as amused.

'Gina says you're visiting from Vietnam, was it?'

'Cambodia.'

'Bit warmer there than here, I bet.' Gil was full of bonhomie.

'A bit.'

The small backpack on Dan's shoulder seemed to have a life of its own. Or rather, kept shifting as he moved his weight from one foot to the other. Finally, he slid it off and let it drop to the floor between his legs.

'Straps are unequal,' he mumbled.

'Yeah, always fancied the Far East but never got around to it,' Gil said, ignoring the backpack. 'Gina said you work out there?'

'Yeah.'

'Nice to come back?'

'Nothing much has changed,' Dan muttered.

'Too right. Well, this is simply a heads up. There'll be an extra presence around here. Maybe the odd sniffer dog. I've warned Gina, better get rid of all that drug stuff or you'll be for it.' He laughed uproariously at that, but reined it in on seeing Dan's unamused look. 'Not that she or Rhys would ever … I mean, *Arglwydd*, we have a zero-tolerance policy on that one. They hang us coppers out to dry if we take one too many bloody aspirin. Face in the papers and everything. Anyway, not to worry if you see the odd K9 sniffing about. It's a show of strength.' Gil looked him over. 'Off to the beach?'

'No, just meeting up with a few friends for a chat.'

'Well, don't let me keep you.' Gil grinned and held out his hand. 'Lovely to meet you, Dan.'

For a frozen moment, Dan stared at the hand as if it had sprouted fangs. But he held out his own and shook.

'Yeah, good to meet you, uh …'

'Gil. Gil Jones. Tidy. Hi-ho.' Gil stood back as Dan hoisted the backpack in one hand and, smiling like someone who's spotted the banana skin seconds before treading on it, hurried by.

He didn't turn around, but later, Catrin told Gil that Dan had done a quick step up the street once their conversation had ended.

Catrin said goodbye to Hakeem, and the door closed as Gil reached her.

'What did you tell the neighbour?'

'We're doing a survey. Asking people their thoughts on the police.'

'And?'

Catrin dropped her chin. 'He thinks we should all have tasers that shoot out of our chests.'

'Nice thought. They probably do where he comes from.'

'Done?'

'Yep. Let's hope that's enough to put the wind up him. My guess is he had something in that backpack. It kept moving about like it was on fire.'

'I saw that.'

'Yes, well, we'll never know. Right, Y Pantri. They do excellent coffee.'

'Don't mind if I do.' Catrin gave Gil a jaunty smile.

'And you can tell me all about *Betsi fach*.'

———

THE DRIVE back from Brecon was lovely, but long. On the outskirts of Llandovery, Jess's phone rang.

'Molly, I'm in the car with Rhys.'

'This isn't on the car's speaker, is it?'

'No. But in case you decide to scream or blaspheme. You remember how sensitive Rhys is.'

Next to her, Rhys screwed his face up, shooting Jess a bemused look that implied this was news to him.

'He can't hear me, Mum,' Molly pointed out.

'No. I'm teasing.'

'Where've you been?'

'Brecon,' Jess explained, her voice growing more serious. 'Everything okay your end?'

'Fine. Nina's excited to come.' The sound of a kettle whistling in the background punctuated her words. 'I have a shift at Gelatojoy until eight, but I'm meeting her at Swansea station at nine. She said she'd Uber it, but I wanted to meet her.'

'Uber? That's a good one. You can tell she's a big city girl. No Uber in Swansea, is there?'

'There is now. Since March.'

'Wow.'

'Yeah, It's great.'

'You excited about Nina coming?'

'Yeah,' Molly answered, then hesitated before asking, 'How about you, Mum?'

A simple question that writhed with all kinds of serpentine implications.

Warlow had told her to be honest.

'Mixed feelings. I mean, you and Nina are far removed from the family trauma. I was, too, to an extent. But your gran felt it so much, and I did as well. So, yes, I'm anxious, I won't lie. I'm not sure how I'll react when I see Nina.' She waited for Molly to dismiss her concerns with the brash candour of youth. But she didn't.

'I think she's pretty nervous, too,' Molly said softly, her voice filled with understanding beyond her years. 'It's okay to be anxious. But we can't keep running from the past.'

A lump formed in Jess's throat as she listened to her teenage daughter's wisdom. They'd been through so much as a family already, and now this spectre from the past had come out of the blue to haunt them.

'I know, love, but it isn't always easy,' Jess replied. 'I just don't want you to be hurt.' She almost added "again," but bit it back.

'Mum, it's fine. She's a cousin from Italy, and I would like to reach out. It's a bit of our history neither of us knows much about. And Nina coming here is great. Look at it as a sign that things could get better for all of us.'

'You're probably right. Anyway, let me know how it goes, and I'll see you both on the weekend.'

The quiet hum of the car and the low tinkle of music from the radio Rhys had turned way down were the only sounds as mother and daughter seemed to reach an unspoken agreement.

After a brief pause for them both to reset, Molly steered the conversation around to Jess's work. 'Are you and Rhys still on this Gittings's thing?'

'We are.'

'Was he as bad as what the newspapers are saying about him?'

Jess let out a weary sigh.

'He was. Worse even,' she admitted quietly.

'They're saying he got what he deserved.'

'Newspapers and the press are very good at being judge and jury.' Jess's gaze drifted to the horizon. 'Who knows if he got what he deserved? Sometimes, the world has a way of protecting those who don't deserve it.'

'That's deep, Mum.'

'Isn't it just? I think I need some lunch.'

'Me too. Okay, I'm not working Sunday, so it'll probably be then we come across, okay?'

'Alright, love. Talk to you soon.'

Jess hung up and glanced at Rhys. 'I don't think I've seen a straighter face, Rhys.'

He chuckled. 'Just trying to give you some privacy. So, how's Molly?'

'She has a cousin coming to visit who I have never met for a whole host of complicated reasons. I'm worried, and Molly's being very much the grownup.'

'Good to hear.'

There was a brief pause before Jess shifted in her seat. 'Speaking of people coming over, how's your brother-in-law's situation?'

Rhys sighed, rubbing the back of his neck momentarily before getting both hands back on the wheel when he realised what he was doing. 'Still here.'

She read that as meaning both the brother-in-law and the problems associated with him. 'How so?'

'Gina had a chat with him. The neighbours have

complained. I'm staying out of it. It's a brother and sister thing. She's had words, but … Dan has a very thick skin.'

Jess raised an eyebrow. 'Gina strikes me as someone who can be persuasive.'

'You have no idea. She's tough when she needs to be. But she's too soft with Dan. Or has been …'

'Oh, dear. Well, I hope you get it sorted.'

'Me too. Anyway, I was thinking about lunch. There's a couple of good cafés in Llandeilo.'

Jess rolled her eyes. 'Always thinking with your stomach, Rhys.'

'Too right. But I heard you say you needed lunch too,' he retorted with a grin.

'I did. But we need to get back to HQ. We've got a lot to go over.'

'Fine, fine. But one of these days, you are going to have to try a Llandeilo custard slice.'

'We'll see about that.'

As they drove on, the tension from Jess's earlier conversation with Molly eased.

Custard slices.

'Does Evan like them?' Jess asked.

'Gil makes sure there's always one at Chez Jones whenever we call in, ma'am.'

'It wouldn't do any harm to stop off for five minutes, would it?' she whispered.

'You will not regret it, ma'am.' Rhys had an ear-to-ear smile.

CHAPTER THIRTY

WARLOW'S MEETING turned into a marathon, which should have been a sprint or, at the most, a four-hundred-metre race. Drinkwater, obviously conscious of his position after his exposure as having almost let the Bowman slip through their grasp by backing Superintendent Goodey, a protégé of his, over Warlow in a recent high-profile case, wanted to make sure that the "optics" looked good on this one.

Warlow hated that word.

It featured on a list that seemed to get longer every day. Jess called them "Warlow's whiny words".

Both he and Buchannan listened as Drinkwater outlined a campaign driven by the press officer. They still had boots on the ground in Middle Hill and the quarry to stop the hyenas and inquisitive tourists from getting in the way. And careful handling of the impending press conference became the main agenda. An agenda that Drinkwater clearly saw as a way of redeeming himself in the eyes of the Chief Constable, having already blotted his copybook. The fact that none of it directly involved Warlow remained the only saving grace of the whole ninety-minute drone-fest. A text from Povey came just at the right time, and he excused himself despite the disparaging glance from Buchannan, who obviously wished that text had been for him.

When he met the crime scene investigator in an office in Digital Forensics, she eyed his smile warily. 'What's up with you?'

'Nothing. Reminding myself of how lucky I am to have such great colleagues, that's all.'

Povey tilted her head. 'My text get you out of some dozy meeting, did it?'

'Are you from a future where they can read minds?'

'I wish,' Povey said and swivelled a screen around for Warlow to peer over her shoulder. 'Digital forensics got into Gittings's laptop. Nothing startling. A little pornography, but nothing illegal. Want to know what floated his boat?'

'My guess is females and of the younger variety.'

'Yes. But all models look over eighteen. Few over thirty.'

Warlow nodded. 'Fits the pattern. But that's not why you brought me here.'

'No. We've been able to access his emails. Again, some interesting stuff there. Some things he sent to a few targets expressing admiration who, after a short time, tell him to stop bothering them. My guess is that they are, or were, work colleagues, and he would not have wanted to email them on a government computer.'

'Get me a list of the email addresses and we'll take a glance.'

'Already on the local network. But the interesting threads are to an email address at a company email: kat@hiltnt.net. There are at least fifty of them. The person he addresses is called Kat.'

'And?'

'It's an address linked to a domain name for a company that specialises in demolition. Linked to the Tonhill family. Kat is Kathryn Tonhill.'

A bell rang in Warlow's head. 'Isn't that the company that caused that donation scandal?'

'Yep. And Kathryn Tonhill is the CEO.'

'Were they having an affair, her and Gittings?'

'No. The emails are innocuous. The dates, especially from

when Gittings moved down here, imply that he might have been doing some work for her.'

'What kind of work?'

'The word transport is mentioned quite a lot.'

'That's not illegal.'

'No. But you asked us to fish. This is what we caught.'

Warlow let things percolate. 'This on the network, too?'

'As of an hour ago.'

He thanked Povey and walked away with more unanswered questions. Sometimes, if there'd been some kind of breakthrough, they went with that. More commonly, as now, the old IIE adage applied.

Identify, interview, eliminate.

It was after 4.30pm when the team got together for vespers at HQ with fresh tea and with the Human Tissue for Transplant box open. Jess provided a précis of their visit to Collins, who she described as an anti-establishment activist.

'But they had eyes on Gittings locally?' Warlow asked.

'So it seems. It backs up your information of him visiting the airfield regularly. Of course, if they were planning another milkshake attack on him, they'd want that to happen openly for maximum humiliation and embarrassment.'

'Still, it's useful information for us,' Warlow mused.

'How can going dogging every Thursday be a help to us?' Rhys asked.

Gil answered. 'It's part of the pattern the techs found. Calls came through always on a Wednesday, the day before his visits to the airfield.'

'Dogging confirmation?'

'Now that's a religious act I'd like to see the brochure for,' Gil murmured.

After a long and uncomfortable pause in which Gil grinned, and the others all had to deal with a panoply of dubious ecclesiastic imagery marching through their brains, Gina outlined her chat with Vetch.

'Gittings has not been on Vetch's radar, sir,' she explained. 'But he mentioned the word conduit. The reverse of county lines. How the OCGs get drugs from the ferries and the coast to the cities. Regular transport.'

Transport.

Warlow quickly told them all about his chat with Povey. More evidence of Gittings's links to organised crime.

'Weak link, though, sir,' Rhys said.

And it was. 'That's why we need to go over everything that Povey has sent us. Gil, have a word with Vetch about these Pay As You Go numbers that contacted Gittings. See if any of them mean anything to him.'

'Will do.'

Warlow reached for another biscuit. 'Everyone okay with another hour of digging? AOS?'

He got nods back from Rhys, Jess, and Gil, then got up and hurried to the SIO room to fire up his computer and have a look through Digital Forensics curated emails from Gittings's computer. He barely heard the whispered question that Gina breathed to Rhys.

'AOS?'

It didn't need explaining. He knew AOS meant the nitty gritty of all investigative work.

Arse on seat.

———

LATER, after the AOS session that stretched well beyond 6pm, the team retired to fight another day. Warlow had found nothing startling in the emails. Nothing lurid or lascivious to suggest a sexual element. Nothing like the insidious emails Gittings sent to some of his colleagues at their private addresses. They followed the same pattern as the texts he sent. Flattering and encouraging, picking up on some minor triumph at work and then escalating to be suggestive, about how he could help in a career. Finally, suggesting a meeting outside of work over a drink or coffee.

Reading them made Warlow's skin crawl. They'd made Jess's crawl too when they discussed it later. He dared not imagine what they were doing to Gil, who had two daughters and three granddaughters.

The more they dug into Gittings' chaotic existence, the more unpleasantness they unearthed. If the man had any saving graces, he'd managed, over years of boorishness and slime, to bury them deep.

———

BARRY TALBOT LEFT the Anchor pub just after 10.15pm, the warm night air doing little to alleviate the stiffness in his joints. But the beer he'd consumed had helped. He couldn't forget his predicament, but he could dampen his feelings and steer them towards pleasant reminiscences. Of times he'd spent with Marlene and old friends. Better times.

The alcohol and the morphine worked in tandem to ease the pain throughout his body, and the E-bike he rode was his lifeline. He made sure it was always fully charged, and it had enough juice to get him uphill to Upper Solva. He'd never make it under his own steam. Not anymore.

Soon, he'd probably have to give this up, too. He could feel the cancer clawing at him, but it hadn't sunk its talons all the way in.

Not yet.

Solva's narrow streets were quiet as he navigated the familiar route home. The night sky was clear, stars winking down at him, but Barry's mind was focused on reaching his bed and the relief of a hot water bottle. It helped. Even though it was now June. And how the hell had that happened? Time had become a slippery eel sliding through his fingers.

As he turned onto Whitchurch Street, Barry immediately noted the dark vehicle idling by the kerb. He squinted at the car as he passed. Through the tinted windows, he could vaguely distinguish a figure with a camera, its lens pointed at his house and the shared entranceway to St Fagos.

His heart rate quickened, a mixture of fear and indignation surging through him, a bravado fed and watered by the alcohol in his veins.

What were they doing?

He rode past slowly, trying to catch a better glimpse without drawing attention to himself. The figure in the car remained fixated on their task, seemingly oblivious to Barry's presence.

Anger flared up, eclipsing his usual caution. He manoeuvred his bike around in a turning circle, the motor whining softly as he faced the BMW saloon. The car's headlights flared into life, blinding him as he finished his turn. Undaunted, Barry drove onto the wrong side of the road towards the car. He stopped thirty feet away, squinting against the halogen lights as he took a deep breath.

'What the hell do you think you're doing?' he called out, his voice firm despite the tremor in his hands.

The response was immediate and violent. The engine roared to life, tyres screeching against the asphalt as the car lurched forward.

In a split second, Barry's world exploded into a blur of motion and sound.

The front of the car smashed into man and bike, sending Barry sprawling onto the pavement, before the BMW crunched over the bike's back wheel, jerking forward.

On the ground, pain searing through his left leg, Barry's vision blurred as shock numbed his senses.

He tried to move, but his limbs felt heavy, unresponsive.

The car screeched to a halt, and then backed up slightly, positioning itself for another strike. The sound of the engine revving filled the night, drowning out Barry's gasps for breath.

He looked up at the car, its brake lights like burning eyes, and tried to make out a number plate, but pain brought tears to his eyes and everything blurred just as as another car's headlights lit up the road. The BMW's gears crashed, and it sped off before the oncoming car was in full view.

He lay motionless as this second vehicle slowed and stopped. He heard car doors opening and incoherent shouts mingling with his own whimpers until, at last, the stars above blinked out, and Barry lost consciousness.

CHAPTER THIRTY-ONE

1.15AM.

Warlow stood at the nurse's station at Glangwili Hospital speaking with a registrar named Bohai. He introduced himself as a shortened, 'Bo,' and spoke with a Cardiff accent. He did not wear a white coat or have a stethoscope hanging around his neck. Bo had long outgrown those.

'It sounds American, but it's easier than my whole name. Not so unusual in Beijing which is where the 'rents are from.' He smiled with no show of teeth before going on. 'Mr Talbot has a spiral fracture of his left femur and a mild concussion, but he's awake.'

'What's the plan for him?'

'He'll need surgical fixation. Probably an IMN—'

Warlow stopped him there. 'My son's a surgeon, I'm not.'

'Sorry. An intramedullary nailing. A rod that goes inside the femoral shaft, fixed in place with screws. Allows the bone to heal without displacement.'

'Will that be soon?'

'Ideally, within the first forty-eight hours. Obviously, we've considered the option of conservative treatment, but on balance, we think it would be better to fix and at least try to get him mobile for the rest of his time. I presume you're aware of his other diagnosis?'

Warlow swallowed audibly but managed a nod.

The rest of his time.

'Will he need to be transferred to get it done?'

Bo shook his head. 'We are a trauma centre. Trouble is, there's a lot of it. I can't give you a time yet.'

'I need to speak to him.' Warlow looked over to where Rhys was talking to one of the nursing staff.

'You can do that. We have him comfortable for now. He's immobile, of course, and we have to take everything else into consideration.'

'The arthritis and the cancer, you mean?'

'It's not a perilous operation,' Bo explained. 'But there are risks such as pulmonary complications and infection, especially in a compromised patient like Mr Talbot. The anaesthetists will assess him tomorrow, decide if it's general or a spinal.'

'I'll keep it brief.'

Across the ward, Rhys gave Warlow a thumbs up.

Talbot lay in a four-bedded unit with drapes drawn around him. He sat propped up, looking frail and pale, his left leg supported by an arrangement of pillows, a drip running into his arm, his face bruised and swollen. Stark evidence of face-pavement contact.

'Barry. Up to talking a bit?' Warlow asked, keeping his voice as low as he could.

Someone snored on a bed opposite. Machines hummed. A side light lit the inside of a cocoon of drapes so as not to disturb the other patients.

'Good meds. I can barely feel the pain.' Talbot's words were slightly slurred.

Warlow suspected it was the medication, not what he'd consumed in the Anchor Inn.

'Can you tell me what happened?'

Talbot's voice lacked animation and sounded croaky, but the details were clear enough. 'I was on the way home after a couple of pints. All the talk in the pub was about Matt. Speculation. No one knows anything. And I kept quiet. Anyway, I saw the black BMW as I crested the hill. I didn't get the number plate before you ask. I think they'd blurred it somehow with muck.'

'Doesn't matter. Just tell me what happened,' Warlow pressed.

Talbot recounted the events shakily. He'd noticed a camera and assumed it was a journalist. Emboldened by the evening's alcohol, he decided to confront the person. He couldn't specify the individual's gender, but remembered a baseball cap. He felt certain they'd been watching St Fagos.

'I know there've been some extra patrol vehicles about and all that. But seeing that car there made me see red. So I shouted at them,' Talbot admitted.

Warlow eyed the man in the bed with restrained frustration. 'Probably not the smartest of moves. Do you recollect anything else about the car?'

'Not much. It was all black, that's all. I mean, even the grille in the front was black, not silver. A saloon, not an SUV. The other car, the people that stopped for me, they might have seen more.'

'We'll speak with them,' Warlow assured him, though Rhys had already done so. The witnesses had only glimpsed taillights speeding away, distracted by Talbot and his overturned eBike.

Talbot changed tack suddenly. 'They want to operate, but I'm not sure.'

'People are mobile within days. You could be home in a week,' Warlow countered.

'Yes. That would be good. I still have a few things left undone.'

'I mean, they get people up on their feet within a day of surgery.'

'Normal people, maybe.'

'They know what they're doing,' Warlow insisted. 'We criticise the NHS, sometimes rightly so – and my son would know because he's one of them. But when it works, it's a blessing.'

'Your son is a doctor?'

'He is.'

'That's something for you to be proud of.'

It was. When he thought about what both the boys had done with their lives, despite the obstacles that he and Jeez Denise had thrown in their paths, it seemed nothing short of a miracle. 'Yes, he's done alright.'

'Sorry to drag you out of bed,' Talbot apologised.

Warlow shrugged.

'This isn't my first rodeo with this leg,' Talbot revealed. 'The X-ray showed the old break. Happened in the army. Shrapnel from a landmine. Nearly lost the sodding thing.'

'Where was that?'

'Afghanistan. '87. Training Mujahideen to fight the Russians. Ironic, eh? The Russkies got a bloody nose there, I can tell you.'

'You're a tough old nut, then.' Warlow smiled. 'I'll come back once they've done the surgery. If you remember anything else, tell the nurses or the doctors. They'll contact me.'

————

HE DIDN'T BOTHER GOING BACK to Nevern after visiting Talbot. There seemed little point. He could have gone up to Gil's in Llandeilo, just twenty minutes away on an open invitation, but he told Rhys to go home and took himself to the SIO room at HQ. Not the first time he'd bedded down on the floor in there, and he had a method.

He took a few seat cushions from the visitor's chairs downstairs, used his coat as a pillow, and texted Jess to bring him in a clean shirt for the morning. She'd get that when she woke up.

It took him a while to get to sleep. Unfamiliar noises came to him from the building. The odd whistle, the banging of doors. But he filtered them all out and drifted off, thinking about a black BMW and the sort of person would run down an old man on a bicycle.

Five hours later, he awoke from a horrifying nightmare. And it was, in Rhys's vernacular, a brammer.

He found himself at the edge of the quarry, its dark, yawning mouth beckoning him. The moonlight cast eerie shadows, transforming the jagged rocks into monstrous silhouettes. Out of the shadows, and with no warning, as was the way of nightmares, Gittings stood before him, burnt and blackened, his eyes hollow.

'You think you know the truth?' the dead man rasped.

Around them, snakes slithered, their scales glinting under the pale light, hissing accusations. Warlow tried to speak, but his words were swallowed by the suffocating silence. The politician began to laugh, a sound that morphed into the grinding of metal, reminiscent of the car's fatal plunge.

The ground beneath Warlow's feet crumbled. He teetered on the brink, staring into the abyss below, a pit of writhing serpents and shattered glass.

Gittings reached out a charred hand, pulling Warlow closer.

'I can help you. Come on, Evan.' A soft sibilant hiss followed his name, and Warlow felt himself being dragged into the void. He fell, and the world twisted into a kaleidoscope of faces, the dead and the living merging into a grotesque tapestry.

He woke with a start, brought back from the fall by a knock on the door. His heart pounded, each beat a hammering reminder of a ticking clock, and the gnawing fear that he was missing something crucial.

He stood up in his socks and stepped clumsily into his trousers, muzzy from sleep. When he opened the door, Jess stood there, fresh as newly cut hay, and smelling even better. In her hand, she held a paper bag, and Warlow breathed in the aroma of breakfast rolls and coffee.

'My God. Are you an angel?' he croaked.

'I am many things, but not one of those. You look like you've just awoken from a terrible dream.'

'That would be about right.'

Jess held up a rucksack. 'Shirt, socks, underwear, and shoes.'

'Brilliant.' He leant forward and kissed her on the cheek.

'You could do with a shower,' she said. 'Make yourself presentable, and I'll lay the table.'

'What time is it?'

'7.30.'

'You're early.'

'I want a rundown before the troops arrive.'

'Right, give me ten.'

They had a shower and changing facilities at HQ. Warlow was as good as his word and came back to the SIO office looking and smelling a lot better than when he'd left. He wolfed down the roll and the coffee and told Jess about Talbot.

'Poor bloke,' she said.

Outside, the rumblings of arrivals grew in volume. Secretarial staff, indexers, the usual. At eight, they heard the deep bass laugh of one Gil Jones. Warlow peered out to see him already busy at his desk with Gina and Rhys logging in, too.

When they both emerged from the SIO room a minute later, they did so to grins of surprise.

'We're thinking of offering it on Airbnb,' Jess said, pre-empting any comments. But her pithy aphorism was the only attempt at jocularity that morning.

Warlow quickly filled them in on what had happened to Talbot, and the sergeant listened with his head low, throwing in the odd shake when the detail of the sick man's injuries emerged.

'*Iesu bach*, what the hell was he thinking?'

'He'd had a drink or two,' Rhys said. 'Some of his old army bravado must have bubbled to the surface.'

'Anything come through on the bush telegraph since last night?' Warlow asked.

Gil redirected his attention to his screen. 'I've had an email from my BFF in Digital Forensics – hang on.' Gil's keyboard clicked, and he slid down his glasses from above his forehead onto his nose. 'Right, here it is.'

He made noises as he speed-read the text. Not words as such, mumbles that sounded like words. A noise that ended abruptly as he looked across at Warlow, with all trace of the jovial Gil suddenly evaporating as he blinked.

'What?' the DCI demanded.

'I'd sit down if I were you.'

'Come on, man. If this is a wind up, I'll—'

'No wind up. She's gone back through Gittings's records. Looking for patterns, cross-referencing these PAYG numbers. She found a couple from years ago. One of them is linked to a phone found at Penmor Farm.'

Warlow stared at him. But then he sat, without speaking, because it felt like his legs might give way from under him.

No one else spoke either, since they all had the same frozen-into-silence look on their faces.

All except Gina, who asked in all innocence, 'Penmor Farm. Is that significant?'

'It is,' Rhys explained, his voice a whisper. 'It's from a case we were all involved in a couple of years ago. Down on the coastal path in Cardigan.'

Warlow's voice cut across the explanation. 'Where was the phone found?'

Gil turned back to the email and read out. 'The phone was found in Ben Gower's bedroom. They also found a load of unused sims in the same location, but this number was the number of the sim in the phone.'

Silence again.

Gina looked confused. Jess put her out of her misery. 'It's the first case we, as a team, bar Gil and you, worked together. The Pickerings, a couple that had gone missing years before were found where they'd been buried, after a landslip. It became a complex investigation during which one of our colleagues, Sergeant Mel Lewis, jumped to his death off the cliffs near Mwnt in Cardiganshire. The reason he jumped is that he'd become entangled in a drug-running operation in which a marijuana farm had been set up under an old, abandoned Engine House on a headland. The land there was owned by some farmers, Ryland Gower and his son, Ben.'

'And this phone number links Gittings to that case?' Gina asked.

The obvious question to ask. And yet, it seemed to lance through Warlow's brain. A brain that had suddenly turned to thick porridge.

He shot Gina a look that made the young DC flinch.

'Yes,' he said after a while. 'It does. And now it means I need to go and talk to Ben Gower after I'd hoped I'd never have to look the sod in the eye ever again.'

The food in his stomach felt suddenly leaden as bitter memories surfaced.

'We'll go together,' Jess said.

Warlow didn't argue.

CHAPTER THIRTY-TWO

SWANSEA PRISON. A grey Victorian pile sitting as a reminder of a past resistant to change, despite all the money spent on regenerating the Maritime quarter nearby.

Hitler had attempted his own murderous reconstruction between 1940 and 43, flattening the centre of the town. But the jail had survived the Luftwaffe raids. Some people, many if not all of HM Prison's residents included, probably wished it had not.

Ben Gower was fetched from the cell he shared with a thief from Port Talbot.

The latter, a criminal mastermind according to him and him alone, whispered as Gower was led away, 'Don't forget smokes, Ben.'

They met in a shabby, soulless interview room that smelled of disinfectant. The industrial kind that still didn't quite mask the stink of sour sweat and stale vomit that years of use had tainted the atmosphere with. The walls were a drab grey. Three blue plastic chairs sat in a two and one arrangement on either side of a metal-legged table with a dark Formica top.

An easily wipeable Formica top.

Gower looked thinner than when Warlow had last seen him. Still burly, like his father, but the ruddy farmer's complexion had faded, replaced by an indoor pallor that made him look sickly. He'd shaved his head and sat slumped and unsmiling, arms folded, dressed in standard grey prison joggers and sweatshirt. His gaze flitted between Jess and Warlow, but lingered on the former, a trademark smirk on his lips in the sickly fluorescent light.

'Know why we're here, Ben?' Warlow asked after introductions were made.

'Catch up on old times?' Gower chuckled in condescension. He kept his eyes on Jess.

'Do you watch the news, Ben?' she asked.

'Nah. Watch a bit of Love Island for the girls. Top Gear reruns. That's about all.'

Warlow clenched his jaw. He did not like Gower. When the judge had given him thirty years for drug offences and human trafficking, Warlow had celebrated in the pub and bought the team a round.

'Matt Gittings,' Warlow said.

The name didn't faze Gower. He let his eyes drift to the ceiling. 'Never heard of him.'

. Jess leant in, calm but firm. 'We found a PAYG number linked to you from his phone.'

Gower grinned. 'You think I kept track of every number that contacted me then? I was very popular.'

Warlow's mind flew back to the horrific conditions Gower had kept workers in at gunpoint under the Engine House. Men, women, and children trafficked for slave labour. He felt his patience fraying. 'Gittings was found dead. You want to add murder to your resume?'

Gower's eyes snapped to Warlow, a dangerous glint of temper flashing there. 'You think threatening me will get you anywhere? I'm already doing thirty years, thanks to you.'

Jess put a hand on Warlow's arm. She turned her attention to Gower, her tone softer but no less authoritative. 'Ben, we're not here to make threats. We just need to understand the connection. This could benefit you.'

Gower sneered, but behind the bravado, cogs were meshing. 'I'm listening.'

'Gittings,' Jess continued, 'was involved in a possible laundering operation. We know he had connections with some unsavoury characters. If you help us piece this together, maybe we can talk about helping you.'

Gower's eyebrows raised slightly, the first sign of interest. 'Helping me? How? Two weeks in Marbs, all-inclusive?'

'I hear your mother isn't that well,' Warlow said.

'You bastard.' Gower's face soured.

'Yep. That's right.' Warlow never took his eyes from Gower's. 'The same bastard who got the CPS to drop the trafficking charges on your mother.'

Gower's expression hardened.

'Heart failure,' Gower muttered. 'And my dad's got something wrong with his chest. He's in and out of hospital too.'

Ryland Gower was also in prison. But not in Swansea.

'If you can give us something useful on Gittings, we could talk to the Governor about letting your mother visit more frequently.'

'I've tried,' Gower said, his face suddenly flushed.

'Yeah, well. You're not exactly keeping your nose clean in here, are you?' Warlow asked. Petty squabbles and fights were Gower's track record since going down.

'It's a jungle. Eat or get eaten.'

Jess kept her voice even. 'Okay, well, like I say. A word from us might go a long way. But there is no free lunch here.'

Gower pulled his legs back and sat up, but kept his arms folded. 'You realise what you're asking. If anyone found out I named names …'

'That's not what we're asking. We want to know if Gittings had ties to the marijuana farm. You haven't told us anything about who was behind it.'

For now, Gower was holding up his end of the organised crime bargain. He'd kept his mouth shut. Witness protection had been offered, but he'd declined as had his father. They would get nothing directly from Gower, who preferred to at least live safely in prison and come out an older man, than risk a sharpened toothbrush handle in the liver inside.

'So, what are you asking?'

'Let's assume he was involved,' Jess said. 'Give us a direction and we'll do the rest.'

'Oh, yeah.' Gower's smile dripped with derision. 'And after our little chat, suddenly my mother comes twice a week. How the fuck is that going to look?'

Optics, Warlow thought and suppressed an inner smile. But he already had an answer. 'We'll get the Governor to revoke your privileges for a couple of weeks because you pissed us off. And we'll make it known why. Make it look like you would not cooperate with us. After that, your privileges return—more than before. Drip by drip.'

Gower's small eyes flicked between the officers. Finally, he spoke. 'We needed someone to get the closure order on the Engine House. Gittings was one of those Senedd Member pricks. He pressed some buttons, and it happened. Before that, we had tourists clambering all over it.'

Warlow nodded.

Of course. Gittings would never dirty his hands directly, but he would be useful behind the scenes, exerting his influence. Closing off the listed building for years to allow the Gowers free rein to set up the power and water needed to grow and harvest marijuana. To farm it in the tunnels and storage areas hewn out of the rocks for when lime had been transported by sea a century before.

In the twentieth century, metalled roads required hard stone and the local dolerite, a finer grained stone than granite, was ideal. The Engine House was used to transport dolerite in drams on a tramway from a nearby quarry to the cliff top. From there, it was crushed, and the winches lowered the drams to the base of the cliff through curved tunnels, to the narrow inlet below for loading on a jetty. But the quarrying ended, and the Gowers, with the Engine House on the edge of their land, had diversified in the worst and most sickening way.

For that, they'd needed Gittings the politician oiling the wheels for the machinery of misery. There'd be a paper trail.

Warlow got up. He didn't thank Gower. Forgive and forget did not apply to this monster. It was why he'd brought Jess.

'You'll sort it, yeah?' Gower said as they both walked to the door. 'For my mother?'

'I'll speak with the Governor,' Jess said. On the table, she left a packet of two hundred cigarettes.

Warlow walked away without looking back.

————

GIL WAS ALL SMILES. Tea had been made, *biscuits*, pronounced the French way, offered.

'Mr Warlow sends his apologies, but wanted me to keep you in the loop.'

Lucy Sanders had declined the refreshments. 'I know about the neighbour and his eBike.'

'Everyone in Solva does, by now.' Gil was congeniality personified. 'You staying locally?'

'I'm in an Airbnb in St David's.'

'Ah, the cathedral town near the sea. 1181—that's when they started it. But it goes back further to Dewi Sant. That's Welsh for St David. He was there in the sixth century and he became something of a cult. Links to Ireland and Brittany. If you get a chance, you ought to pop in.'

'Not really my thing,' Sanders said.

'Just you in the Airbnb, is it?'

'Yes. Why?'

'Only asking.' Gil dunked a biscuit and expertly transferred the moist "tropical with a hint of coconut" baked item to his mouth without fracture.

Next to him, Gina sat shuffling papers. It was she who spoke next. 'Mr Warlow wanted us to make sure you knew that Mr Talbot's accident was no accident.'

Sanders' eyes narrowed. 'Hit and run?'

Neither of the officers spoke.

'Well?'

'We were wondering if you had any information for us in that regard?' Gina asked.

Sanders bristled. 'What do you mean?'

Gil transferred the un-dunked section of biscuit to

between thumb and index finger for the dangerous second half of the procedure.

'Do you have to do that?' Sanders said.

'I am so sorry.' Even though he apologised, Gil followed through and made the biscuit disappear into his mouth, chewed, swallowed, and waved a hand to emphasise the apology.

'Old habits,' Gina said, speaking for her sergeant.

'That's a nun's charity shop, right?' Gil grinned after a quick sip of tea to wash the biscuit down.

Sanders sighed. 'Geraint Lane warned me you were a bit of an unfunny joker.'

Gil's grin didn't slip. 'He is an expert on that topic.'

'You have a paragraph or two in his book.'

'Only a paragraph? I'd have expected a chapter.'

'Don't flatter yourself.'

Gina studied the exchange, amused at how quickly Sanders was to take a dislike to people. 'And how did you get down to Solva, Ms Sanders?'

'What?' Sanders frowned. 'By car, of course.' She sat up, glancing suspiciously at the two officers. 'What is this?'

'Make?'

'I have a Mazda—' At last the penny dropped. 'Are you two interrogating me?'

'No, only ensuring that you are up to speed,' Gil said.

'Whoever struck Mr Talbot left the scene,' Gina explained. 'He tells us he saw someone taking photographs from a car and stopped to challenge them.'

'You think that was me?' Sanders got up out of her chair, anger bringing a flush to her face.

'No,' Gina said. 'You drive a Mazda. It wasn't a Mazda.'

'Then …'

'You're a journalist, and it isn't beyond reason to think you might have wanted some photos,' Gil said.

'You shits.' Sanders spat out the word.

'That's not nice,' Gil said. 'Now that you've told us what you drive, we can eliminate you from our investigation. Unless you hired someone …'

'Piss off.' Sanders, already on her feet, turned away towards the door.

'Don't fancy a selfie?' Gil threw the remark out to her departing back. When she did not respond, he added. 'No, nor me. I try and keep people who take selfies at arm's length.'

'That's terrible,' Gina said as the door closed behind the journalist. 'Do you think we were too hard on her?'

'I offered her tea.' Gil sounded put out. 'And DCI Warlow told us to find out what car she drove.'

'I'll go out to the car park just to be certain, shall I?' Gina offered.

'Good idea. Fancy this last one on the plate?'

'No, sarge. It has your name on it.'

Gil picked it up and read the stamped letters, took a bite, shut his eyes, and murmured, 'Nice.'

CHAPTER THIRTY-THREE

BACK FROM SWANSEA, Warlow let Jess explain how the meeting with Gower had gone. About how Gittings had been involved, if only superficially, with setting up the drugs operation at the Engine House near Mwnt by steering through a Health and Safety ban on public access to the listed building.

They'd got one of the secretaries to wade through some council records that confirmed the common name that appeared through all the layers of bureaucracy.

Matt Gittings. Senedd Member.

Warlow sat back and said nothing while she spoke, unable to block out the unpleasant recollection that he'd tried to compartmentalise.

Seeing Gower and hearing him speak had brought all of those memories back in glorious technicolour. The squalor of the conditions Gower had kept the workers in. Mel Lewis's expression as he stepped off the cliff just feet away from Warlow. Gower threatening Jess with a shotgun.

'Is that our direction of travel now?' Gil asked, one eye on all the extra information that had gathered on the Gallery and Job Centre.

Jess threw Warlow a glance.

He pushed off the desk where he'd been perched. 'Any number of people had good reasons to dislike Gittings. But we have to consider which amongst them is capable of this level of violence. To drug a man, immobilise him, tie him or otherwise confine him to a car, and then drive it off a cliff.'

'Sounds more and more like gang related when you put it like that, sir,' Rhys said.

Warlow nodded. 'We have Gittings linked to the Tonhills who run a demolition company which, to all intents and purposes, is a front for organised crime in the Midlands. Someone who thought it an ironic cosmic joke to donate money to all political parties in the run up to the last but one election.'

'One way of laundering a bit of money,' Jess said.

Warlow continued, 'One way of also covering their tracks. After Gittings blots his copybook in London and ruins his marriage, he moves here and decides he can still be a politician, albeit on a smaller scale. But it's not much money for a man with his tastes. However, he knows Tonhill.'

Jess followed Warlow's train of thought and added, 'And he has a good reason for travelling to and from the Midlands once a week. To see his kids.'

'Didn't someone say he had a girlfriend there, too?' Gina asked.

'They did,' Warlow agreed. 'So, where did he go? We know he didn't go to the family home. Where did he stay on his trips?'

'We can look at his credit card payments, sir,' Rhys said.

Warlow smiled. 'My guess is he will have used cash where he could, but Gittings hasn't struck me as the most careful of blokes. Let's get on to that. And check with his wife again, see if she knows.'

Gina looked puzzled. 'I'm not sure I follow, sir.'

Warlow's smile was devoid of any amusement. 'There are a lot of twos and twos that need to add up to four here. But Gower has confirmed that Gittings was a cog in the wheel. We derailed Gower's little scheme, but getting rid of one rats' nest doesn't mean there aren't more.'

'But all we found is a bundle of money and evidence that

there had been some drugs in that secret space of his.' Gina remained confused.

Gil provided her with the answer. 'Part of what Vetch and the other drugs units do is look for patterns. They use ANPR to look for, and track, vehicles coming in and out of areas. Which is why crime gangs use county lines. Kids travelling on trains that can't be tracked. Mothers with prams. That kind of sly and insidious thing. Someone who does regular, legitimate journeys to and from a city is a godsend to them. And Gittings, though he didn't have diplomatic immunity, and he wasn't Harry bloody Lime—'

'Who, sarge?' Rhys asked.

'Graham Greene, *The Third Man*. Worth a read, or a watch,' Jess said.

'No one is going to question him because he's been doing it for years, and he has a reason,' Gil continued. 'Divorced dad visiting his kids on a specific day of the week. An OCG would jump on that.'

'Do you think he was being forced to do it?' Gina asked. 'Threatened?'

Warlow looked doubtful. 'Knowing what we do about Gittings, I suspect he was very much in bed with them as a consenting adult.'

Gina waved vaguely at the boards. 'So, all that stuff—' She sounded disheartened.

'Tells us that Gittings was not a good man,' Jess interrupted her. 'It tells us he is more than capable of what we're proposing.'

'But how do we prove it? How do we catch who did it?'

Warlow listened to his team teasing it out, massaging the little tuft of stubble out of habit. A move that meant all the gears were whirring inside his head.

'Patterns,' he muttered.

They all turned to stare. 'That's what Vetch said he looks for. Patterns. So, what do we know about Gittings's patterns besides his weekly visits to the Midlands?'

'He drank in the pubs regularly,' Gina mused.

Warlow nodded briefly. 'Anything else?'

Rhys looked up. 'The airfield?'

'Exactly.' Warlow walked over to the Job Centre. 'We've had that from two sources. One from the pub manager at the Coopers and from Collins and his Shakeshifters. They'd seen him there on a Thursday. The day before he'd go to the Midlands.'

'You think he might have been there to meet someone? Not dogging?'

'Now I do.'

'A drop-off?' Jess asked.

Warlow felt the stirrings of something. Ideas gelling. 'Gil, those PAYG numbers that he'd contacted. Isn't there a pattern there, too?'

Gil turned to his desk and found the printouts while Warlow stared at the Job Centre, not seeing what they'd already posted, but looking for what wasn't there.

'Yes,' Gil said. 'There is. They're always on a Wednesday, those calls.'

Warlow took that and ran with it. 'Right. So, he gets a text that he replies to on a Wednesday. Goes to the airfield on Thursday night, then goes up to the Midlands on a Friday, comes back either the same day or on a Sunday.'

'What are you thinking, sir?' Rhys stood behind Warlow, looking over his head – as he did with most people – at the boards, and seeing nothing except Gittings's death and his trail of misery.

'I'm thinking that perhaps Gittings might not have been the only person visiting that airfield on a Thursday evening,' Warlow muttered.

'Hang on. Are you suggesting a visit?' Gil arched an eyebrow bushy enough to almost rustle. 'Surely, if there was some kind of exchange of drugs or money going on there, they would have heard of Gittings's death?'

Warlow swivelled to reply, his eyes now alive with possibility.

'They might. But Vetch tells me that in many cases, names are not used. Safer that way. The people delivering the goods might not know Gittings from Adam. And what if they were delivering more than one package to more than one collector?'

'Lot of "what ifs" there, Mr Warlow,' Gil observed.

'One way to find out.' Warlow smiled. 'Let's double-check everything. Find out where Gittings stayed when he visited Birmingham. Find out if he stopped on the way. Double-check that it was Thursdays he went to the airfield. Let's get digging.'

And they did. Jess spoke to Gittings's wife to confirm that he did not stay in the marital home when he visited. That those visits were once a fortnight, not weekly, and that she had no idea where he stayed and didn't bloody care ... though he'd once mentioned the Maisonbleu Hotel.

A call to the hotel chain in Birmingham confirmed that Mr Gittings was a regular guest and used the same room almost every weekend. She told the manager that someone from the West Midlands force would probably be along to sort through CCTV footage of Gittings's last visit. She wasn't hopeful. In a city as big as Birmingham, clandestine meetings would be easy. And out of sight of CCTV.

Rhys rang the Coopers Arms and spoke to John there, and quickly confirmed what Warlow had thought. That Gittings had been seen parked at the airfield on Thursday evenings. By the time vespers came around, the atmosphere in the Incident Room was crackling.

'Patterns confirmed,' Jess said. 'But that's all they are for now. We need some confirmation that Gittings was actively engaged.'

'And how do you propose to do that?' Gil asked.

Warlow chewed his cheek. The team recognised it as an indicator that a plan might be hatching.

Gil looked at Jess, who returned his gaze by lowering her chin.

Still, Warlow didn't speak.

'This is worse than waiting in the doctor's office for a jab,' Gina muttered out of the side of her mouth to Gil.

'You know they're training dogs to do all kinds of doctors'

work these days,' Gil said in one of his lightening-the-mood moments,

'Not to give injections, surely,' Gina scoffed.

'No. But they can smell cancers and certain types of infection. Pretty soon, it'll be an appointment with Rover, not the GP. The only thing they are not good at, apparently, is broken bones.'

Jess waited for the inevitable. Rhys had already started smiling. Warlow was lost in his own thoughts.

'Yes,' Gil continued airily. 'Their one drawback is that they can't read X-rays or MRIs.' A timed beat followed before he added, 'Whereas of course, Cats can.'

Rhys grinned. 'Good one—' His delight ended abruptly when Warlow looked up as if seeing the team for the first time, and they looked back at him, all with arms folded, waiting and grinning.

'Did I miss something?' he asked.

'Absolutely nothing, sir,' Gina replied, pretending to be annoyed that she'd been taken in again.

'Good. Today is Thursday. Gina, I am going to have to borrow Rhys for the evening.'

'Are we going somewhere, sir?' Rhys's grin morphed into one of puzzlement.

'We are. We're off for a game of snakes and ladders. And it's likely we'll need sandwiches and a flask.'

———

GINA GOT BACK to the house on Tabernacle Terrace at around seven to find a note on the kitchen table and a bottle of wine from Aldi. The note was on the back of an already opened envelope that she'd put in the bin that morning. The pencil that had been used to write the note sat next to the bottle of wine.

HEY GEEN,
   Sorry, but I had to shoot off. A mate of mine's got a job going up in

Scotland stacking logs on a big estate. Good money for a couple of weeks and then I am flying back to Ko Kong. Thanks for having me and for letting me use the place. Once I'm back, I'll send some pics of Choum, the girl I told you about.

If we do ever get hitched, it'll be on a beach out here, and you and Greasy will be on the list.

PS. I took £20 I found under that stupid ornament near the telly. I know you said it was for the window cleaner if he called, but I checked the windows and they look fine to me.

PS2. I checked the wine and it's an okay one.

I'll text you.

Dan

GINA NOW SAW that the wine was a quarter empty. On the one hand, Dan had stolen money and done a bunk. On the other, he'd at least left a note. There'd been no text from her brother. But then, his phone was not on contract, and he was forever cadging money to top it up.

She put her bag on a chair and hurried upstairs. Dan's bedroom door stood ajar, the key in the door. Inside, it looked as if it had been burgled with the bed unmade and the sheets crumpled, the duvet a lump on one side. The bureau drawers were all open. She shook her head, surprised at how angry she was.

He could have at least stripped the bed.

Gina was hungry and tired, but she couldn't leave the room in that state.

Sighing, she bustled downstairs for the hoover, dusters, and spray bottles full of disinfectant and cleansing agents, parked the hoover on the landing, and stripped the bed and piled all the bedclothes outside the door.

She did the drawers first, spraying and wiping inside and out. She attacked the floor with the hoover. On pushing the bed itself over by a foot to get at underneath, she stopped and stared at something on the floor,

At first, she wondered if it was a rolled-up sock or piece of paper. But one sniff told her what it really was.

'Oh, Dan.' She breathed out the words, her pulse pounding in her throat.

Panic seized her. Shoving the bed a whole yard over, she found two more rolled-up joints and a single white tablet. She stood there and squeezed her eyes shut, ran downstairs for a plastic bag, and threw in the drugs. She spent another ten minutes searching the room for more, without success, and then walked outside to under the window where she found two smoked butts.

She put all into the bag and burned the lot on their tiny barbecue in the garden, not daring to imagine what Rhys would say if he ever found out.

Being found with drugs was a sackable offence. Ridicule, dismissal, an end to their careers. She growled at the sky.

'Dan, you total arse.'

From over the fence, she heard Hakeem ask, 'You okay, Gina? Funny smell. You burning something?'

Gina put on a Wallace and Gromit grimace. Hakeem couldn't see her, thank God. 'Yeah. Some mouldy old books. Sorry, it won't be long.'

'No worries. I like it. Your brother gone, has he?'

'Yeah. Thanks, Hakeem.'

Gina squeezed her eyes shut again. Torn, as always, between loyalty to her feckless brother and her love for Rhys.

Thank God he had not seen what she had. When the fire had burned to nothing, she dug a small hole and buried the ashes. It felt, somewhat, as if she'd just cremated Dan, and it surprised her how satisfying it felt.

Then she went back inside and texted Rhys.

CHAPTER THIRTY-FOUR

As so often with observation jobs, Warlow had no proper plan for how long they'd stay at the airfield. But for this, he was willing to let his gut rule the roost. Dusk seemed as good an endpoint as any, simply because the area had no lighting. At night, you'd need a torch to get around, and torchlight would draw attention. At this time of year, the sun set around 9.20 and dusk could linger for another sixty minutes, depending on the weather.

Alone in the Jeep, he looked out to the west to see a bank of clouds receding and the sun poking through underneath. A clear, cool night had been forecast, with a risk of more sea mist. Ah, well. They had another hour and a half at most, by his reckoning.

The airfield proved a tricky place to monitor. The two established parking areas were small. At the southwest corner, perhaps fifteen cars at a push. Much less in the lay-by type parking area at the northeast corner. But Warlow was after stealth. They'd compromised with the DCI parking the Jeep beside a caravan on a patch of ground opposite the last bungalow in the hamlet of Fachelich after a quick word with the owner. A mere stone's throw from the airfield and the larger car park, but well out of sight.

Jess, meanwhile, had parked her Golf in a field opposite

the lay-by parking area in the north-east, behind a hedge. There, she could observe any comings and goings. Ironically, less than half a mile to the east of where she was positioned stood the quarry where Gittings had come to a sticky end.

It all made a kind of sense to Warlow when he'd thought it through.

He would patrol the western side of the airfield, casually walking in from his car and back to it intermittently. Jess's only task was to stay in her vehicle to watch for any activity, and Rhys would cross the area from west to east along the paths to meet up with Jess, and then walk back to Warlow, with an eye on the other pedestrian access ways.

Traffic had been light for the last half hour. Three cars had passed Warlow on the A487. The car park on his side had three vehicles in it.

None a black BMW.

On foot, he reached the entrance from the car park where the lurid orange adder warning signs made sure people, and their dogs, were aware of the risk.

He rang the WhatsApp group they'd set up.

'Rhys, are you with DI Allanby?'

'He is,' Jess replied. 'He's just having a quick drink of water.'

'Sounds like you have Cadi in the car,' Warlow said.

'I heard that,' Rhys's voice joined in and added a, 'woof.'

Warlow looked up. Ahead, a woman with two Labradoodles neared the gate. They exchanged smiles as she passed him, and he walked on along the path he'd taken on his previous visit. With earbuds in and phone out of sight, he continued the conversation.

'I'm setting off now through the snake gate. I'll walk up the main concrete strip and then loop south to join the road.'

'Got you, sir. I'll head back in and walk back to you along the path north of the strip. It took me twenty-five minutes the first couple of times.'

'Watch out for snakes.'

The evening had stayed warm. But as Warlow reached the concrete apron, now crisscrossed with grass growing between the rectangular slabs, heading east, he glanced north and saw, as before, the mist gathering above Abereiddy.

'Damn,' he muttered.

Still, there were worse places to be on an almost summer's night.

As he walked to the middle of the landing strip, he wondered how pilots must have felt eighty years before when they saw that mist creeping in. Much the same as him, he suspected. They'd probably sworn under their breath.

Half a mile along, he hit the second concrete diagonal that crossed the central runway and found a path flanked by hedges that took him south.

He saw no one. Heard no one. When he emerged onto the roadway opposite some farm buildings and headed back towards Fachelich, not one vehicle passed him. No wonder Gittings and whoever it was he met up with had chosen this spot.

He reached the southwest car park just as Rhys came through the snake warning gate on his return leg. Warlow kept walking a hundred yards to the Fachelich turnoff. Rhys, five minutes behind him, got to the car. Warlow leaned against the bonnet as the young officer joined him.

'Nice evening for a walk, sir,' Rhys said, unscrewing the top of a water bottle and drinking thirstily. His eyes darted nervously towards the horizon, avoiding Warlow's gaze.

'I think one more sweep in reverse and that's it. It'll be dark by then.' Warlow's voice was calm, but he sensed his fellow officer's unease.

'No cars in the car park this time, sir.'

'No. Maybe Gittings was up here just for the exercise after all.' Warlow's tone was flat, but his brow furrowed slightly.

'Really, sir?'

'No.' Warlow shook his head slowly. 'I don't believe that.'

Rhys took another gulp and arched his long back, the tension clear in his posture. 'Can I ask you something, sir?'

'That's why I'm here, Rhys.'

'Hypothetically, we're duty-bound to report a crime if we

see something, but … is there any discretion?' Rhys's voice wavered, and he studied his feet.

'We need some context there. Undercover officers see crimes committed all the time, but they wouldn't act if it hampered the bigger goal,' Warlow said.

Rhys nodded, fiddling with the cap of his water bottle. 'I get that, sir. But let's say someone found some drugs in someone's bedroom.'

'By someone, do you mean a relative, like a son or a brother or sister?' Warlow raised one eyebrow.

'Yes, along those lines.' Rhys's hands clenched the bottle tightly.

'Then it depends. Are you talking about a kilo of heroin or a small joint of cannabis? In the first example, there'd be no choice, and you'd be complicit if you did not act. In the second instance, personal use means there is leeway.'

'Leeway. Right. So, you wouldn't have to actually report it?' Rhys's eyes flicked up to meet Warlow's, seeking reassurance.

'No.' Warlow waited, watching Rhys closely. When he stayed quiet, Warlow probed, 'I presume this is all to do with your sergeant's exams?'

'Just asking for a friend, sir.' Rhys shifted uncomfortably.

'Always tricky when it's a relative, though. And it makes you wonder. If that relative knows they are living with a police officer, why would they be so stupid as to put themselves, and the officer, at risk?'

'I suppose it takes all sorts, sir.' Rhys's voice was low, and he glanced away to avoid meeting Warlow's gaze.

'It does. But remember, a quiet word is sometimes more effective than a big stick.'

'That's my way of thinking, too, sir.' Rhys managed a small nod.

'And that quiet word doesn't have to involve a wagging finger, either.' Warlow's smile offered what he hoped was encouragement.

'Again, I agree.' Rhys's posture relaxed slightly.

'Good. How is your brother-in-law?'

'Sir, I—' Rhys began, but Warlow cut him off with a knowing smile.

'I don't need to know anything more than what you've already said. Is it Gina who is anxious?'

'I may have asked Catrin to have that quiet word, sir,' Rhys admitted, his voice trembling.

'And?' Warlow prompted gently.

'Gina texted me. Dan has gone. She found some stuff under his bed. She burned it all and now she's feeling guilty because if she hadn't found it, Dan could have buggered it all up for both of us. She's confessed that to me, and now I feel bad because she thinks I didn't know.' Rhys's voice cracked, eyes downcast, shame flickering across his face.

'Sounds a mess,' Warlow said.

'I can't keep lying to her, sir.' Rhys's shoulders slumped.

'Then don't. Pick at a boil and it will fester. My advice, lance the bugger. Now, let's do this one last time and we can all go home, okay?' Warlow said firmly, but his eyes conveyed understanding.

Rhys looked unconvinced, his brow furrowed with worry.

'Listen. What you two have will survive Dan, the hippie brother-in-law. Did I ever tell you she's a keeper?'

'It must be those extra-large gloves she wears, sir,' Rhys said with a half-smile, a glimmer of relief in his eyes.

'That must be a Gil-ism?' Warlow muttered.

Rhys nodded, the tension easing from his shoulders.

'We'll reconvene in half an hour. Off you go.' Warlow watched as Rhys walked away, noticing his slightly heavier footsteps, as if weighed down by the thought of a tough conversation to come.

———

RHYS WALKED BACK the way he came. The evening light had softened, but not enough for gloom. That adjective applied only to his mood.

Something yellow and black lay curled up on the floor just off the path. Rhys stopped and stared. It was not moving. He took a small stride closer. The adder looked dead. Something had run over it and, judging by the smudged tyre mark, appeared to be a bicycle. He hadn't noticed it before, but then he had not been looking too hard. The smudges had dried. This was not new.

He photographed it and sent it to Gina with the caption, 'One less snake.' Though even as he did it, felt a pang of regret. He hadn't meant to sound gleeful. The snake had every right to be in this sanctuary. It was the cyclists that were the interlopers. He took out his phone and dialled Gina's number.

She answered after a couple of rings. 'Thanks for the photo.'

'Sorry. Bad taste.'

'I've taken everything out of Dan's bedroom. Oh, my God, I'm sorry, Rhys. You warned me. I'm such an idiot—'

'Gina,' Rhys cut her off. 'I knew.'

'What?' She breathed out the question.

'When I went back to change my shirt that lunchtime, I caught him with two of his friends, if you can call them friends. The place stank of weed and there were two butt ends under his window. I knew.'

'Why didn't you say?'

'Because … because he's your brother. Because he'd deny it. Because he might twist it to make it look like I was making it up just to get rid of him. I can think of a dozen ways he might wriggle to get between you and me.'

'Oh, God, Rhys.' The horror in her words came over loud and clear.

'So, I did something else. Full disclosure, I spoke to Catrin about it. She told me to do nothing and that she would sort it. And now you say Dan's left?'

Gina's breath sounded ragged. 'You told Catrin?'

'I panicked. Smoking dope is one thing, but I wouldn't have put it past him to be selling the stuff. If he was caught doing that and he was holding drugs at home with us in his locked bloody bedroom …'

Gina stayed silent.

Rhys ploughed on, 'I'm your partner and I'm a copper and I needed to talk to someone. I didn't want you to get into trouble. I …' His words ran out of steam.

'I can't believe any of this.'

Rhys's phone chirped. A WhatsApp message from DI Allanby:

> Cyclist entered from my end. And fog rolling in as I text. Are we in a B horror movie?

Rhys swivelled.

The mist was rolling in about a hundred and fifty yards north of where he was.

'Gina, I have to go. I'm sorry. I should have told you. It's shit to find out about things this way, but things are happening here.'

'Okay.' Her voice was small and though he searched, Rhys found no hint of forgiveness in it. He felt the throbbing of an imaginary boil. He wanted to say a lot more, but a second message appeared. This time from Warlow:

> Cyclist entering from the south path.

'Gina, I have to go.' He ended the call there and ducked down behind the hedge as another cyclist appeared on the path.

When it passed, Rhys sent his own message:

> Cyclist in via snake gate

He stepped back onto the path and jogged in the direction the cyclist had taken.

CHAPTER THIRTY-FIVE

RHYS JOGGED, patches of fog rolling around him and carrying the faint taste of salt.

Where the hell had it all come from all of a sudden?

The sounds of the evening had all but disappeared into the dampening mist, leaving only the soft whirr and hiss of the bicycle ahead. His mind bounced erratically between the difficult conversation he'd had with Gina about her feckless brother and the abrupt silence that followed when he ended the call as the cyclist first came into sight.

Her voice had tightened with emotion, choking into silence when he cut her off. There was more to be said. But not now.

Now he needed to work.

He focused on recalling the layout of the airfield, which he'd walked several times today on reconnaissance.

The path veered right, heading east and passing four diamond-shaped concrete footings where buildings once stood. He ran faster, using the bike's noise as a guide, seeing it and its rider ahead and then losing them as a denser patch of sea mist obscured his view. Scrubby bushes loomed, dark and indistinct shapes that seemed to shift and move as he passed. His mind flickered back to the conversation with Gina, her voice echoing in his ears even as he tried to concentrate on the path ahead.

Even now, Dan could be such a bloody pain in the arse.

Rhys banished thoughts of Gina's brother and envisioned the airfield's layout: the main runway to his right, a field in between.

Halfway along, DCI Warlow would circle back if he'd seen a cyclist heading this way. Directly ahead was DI Allanby parked in her Golf.

'Anyone emerged your end, ma'am?' Rhys huffed out the words into his phone, breathless.

'Negative.'

'Same here,' Warlow said. 'They're up your end, Rhys.'

'Okay.' Rhys slowed.

Up his end meant this length of the northern perimeter of the airfield and the diamonds of concrete on the ground. There was nothing else up here except … He grunted out an oath and instantly regretted it. People were listening. 'There's a Gorsedd circle up here, sir.'

'A what?' DI Allanby asked.

But Rhys didn't answer. There'd be time later to explain about the Eisteddfod that had once been held and its tradition of setting a circle of stones.

Rhys closed the gap, coming within sight of the stones. Twelve small monoliths stood in a rough circle, one repositioned so it was no longer symmetrical. At the centre lay a larger, flatter stone, now slick with condensation. But that was not all. Four cyclists had congregated there, their silhouettes barely discernible through the mist. One of them looked up and saw Rhys.

Not walking. No dog. Running hard.

From the south, Rhys heard Warlow shout a warning.

The cyclists panicked, their movements quick and frantic. All of them wore rucksacks, masks, and goggles. Whatever they were doing ended as they shouldered their bags.

Three of them turned east, the quickest route out, but one headed off north.

Rhys turned to intercept, angling his run towards where

the bike was trying to outflank him along one arm of the concreted diamond.

As a flanker for his rugby club, tracking diagonally across a field to wipe out a runner was his job in that game. As such, he'd become a great judge of angle and pace. And the arms of the diamonds of solid ground were at ninety degrees to one another, so not strictly diamonds, but diamond-shaped none the less. Upon reaching the apex of one, the cyclist had to cross grass in order to continue to the next bit of hard ground. And at the very last diamond – which Rhys had already passed – there was a point at which it rejoined the path. That would be where the cyclist was aiming for.

No need to inform anyone of the plan here. Rhys simply ran. He'd worn bone-conducting headphones which, since getting them, he'd found a godsend. They looped over his ears and did not block out the extraneous noise of traffic or, in this instance, bicycles, but still let him hear whatever his phone's Bluetooth transmitted.

Now it was transmitting Warlow's shouts as the cyclists sped past him.

But Rhys kept running.

He caught up with the bike just as the last diamond of concrete met the path back to the snake-warning gate. Or rather, Rhys's desperate kick caught the bike's wheel and sent it wobbling.

Brakes were applied with a rubbery squeal, and machine and rider wobbled.

Rhys kicked again, and this time, the rider fell off. He looked fit and young.

Rhys had to scramble over the bike's wheel to grab at him. But the light was disappearing quickly, and, in the mist, Rhys miscalculated and felt a foot hit his chest, sending him off balance.

But he was bigger and recovered quickly.

'Stop!' he yelled as the cyclist started running.

Rhys caught him by his arm, and they both fell, rolling off the path into the coarse bushes. Rhys felt wiry muscle and bone under the jacket in his hand.

'Piss off,' the cyclist yelled.

Another kick. This time, it missed.

Rhys was on top now, grabbing at hands. Stopping them from getting a hold of a weapon, glad, as always, of the stab vest he wore whenever out and about with Warlow.

Movement on the path caught his eye. Another figure wearing a dark watch cap coming out of the mist.

'I can help.' He didn't recognise the voice.

'No,' Rhys said. 'I've got this under—'

He heard the spray before he felt it. He saw it shoot out towards the masked and goggled cyclist who bucked and jolted Rhys awkwardly so that whatever it was the "helper" was spraying caught him, too.

Full in the face.

The pain was immediate and incapacitating.

There was nothing Rhys could do but roll away, both hands to his eyes as the stinging sent his lids into spasm. He heard, rather than saw, the helper squeal, the noise of someone falling into the undergrowth and then the hiss of tyres as the cyclist, protected by his facial covering from whatever had been sprayed, shot off.

'Shit,' Rhys said. 'What the hell!'

More footsteps on the path and, this time, a familiar voice.

'Rhys? Rhys?' Warlow's voice.

'Sprayed, sir.'

'Keep still.'

Rhys couldn't open his eyes. He'd also inhaled some of the stuff and he was now coughing uncontrollably. Warlow's instruction to keep still seemed a tad unnecessary.

Above him, through a fog that was now his own blinded sense, he heard Warlow step away and then another question, not for him.

'Are you okay?'

A muffled answer in response, 'Yes, I'm fine. I'm—'

'You!' Warlow roared out the word as an accusation.

'Sir?' Rhys asked,

'Stay where you are, Rhys. Jess, Rhys has been sprayed in the face.'

'Another one?' Jess exclaimed.

In a moment of clarity through the agony his eyes were poleaxing him with, Rhys realised he still had his earphones on. He knew what DI Allanby was talking about.

Catrin has also been sprayed in the eyes once. Just like this.

'Is that Rhys groaning?' Jess asked.

'Yep. Can you bring some water?'

'I will.'

'Sorry,' Rhys hissed and tried to keep his moaning to a minimum.

'I also have a suspect under detention,' Warlow said.

'You caught the cyclist?' Jess asked.

'No. I caught the person who sprayed Rhys in the face.'

'It was an accident. I was trying to help. I was trying to spray the bloke with the bike,' a whining voice objected.

'Who the hell is that?'

'A not-so-innocent bloody bystander. I don't think you've had the pleasure of meeting Lucy sodding Sanders.'

'The journalist?' Jess said.

'The supposed journalist,' Warlow said.

'Oh, God,' Rhys said as a fresh bout of coughing racked his chest.

'This is being recorded,' Warlow was addressing Sanders. 'Two questions. Why do you have a canister of PAVA spray which is illegal unless operated by a police officer? And, more importantly, why and how are you here?'

A long pause followed.

'Can you hear me?' Warlow yelled.

'The PAVA spray was given to me by a friend.'

'He or she is in trouble, then.'

'They are not police. Not anymore.'

'I wonder bloody why.'

Another pause. Warlow filled the space with a slow and angry repetition of his questions. 'What are you doing here?'

'I followed you. I've been keeping tabs.'

'You'd better not have a tracker on any of our vehicles.'

'No, I don't. I followed you, that's all. To this airfield. I saw you and DS Harries walk it five times. I guessed since it was getting dark, this would be the last time, so I came in on foot after I saw the cyclist enter wearing masks and goggles. They looked pretty suspicious. I saw your sergeant go for the cyclist. I … I thought I could help.'

'I hope you're a better bloody journalist than you are a Samaritan,' Warlow ground out the words.

'Am I under arrest?'

'You could be. Obstruction. Assault on an officer.'

'I was trying to help. I was … I'm sorry.'

'I don't have time for this now. I expect to see you at 8.30 tomorrow morning. If not, we'll issue a warrant. You're lucky that I have an injured officer to deal with, otherwise I'd put you in handcuffs.'

'Can I help?'

'Do you have any water?'

Rhys moaned.

Sanders answered, 'No.'

'Then, I think you've helped quite enough for one evening.'

Rhys heard shuffling and then footsteps as Sanders left.

'Looks like we need to add goggles and mask to that stab vest when we're on a case, Rhys,' Warlow said. 'Jess is on the way. We'll wash as much off and get you to the hospital. Get you checked out.'

'I'll be fine in half an—' A bout of coughing cut off his reply.

'I know, but it's standard procedure. Get a look at the cyclist?'

'No, sir, But I think I saw one of them drop something.'

Warlow moved slightly. 'Jess, swing by that stone circle on your way. See if you can find anything.'

Jess answered three minutes later, 'Guess what, there's a nice little brick of something wrapped in plastic on the floor near the centre stone of this ring which I still don't know the reason for.'

'Keep your eye open for druids,' Warlow said. And then, more softly, said to Rhys, 'At least we were right. Definitely a drop site. My guess is Gittings came in after they all left for his exchange. I can't see him on a bike myself. Probably picked up payment and a new delivery in one move.'

'I almost had one, sir.'

'I know. You did well. We'll get you washed off and back to Glangwili.'

'PAVA spray stings like hell, sir.'

'I can see Jess. She's almost here. Then we'll get some water on you.'

'I'm happy to answer questions, sir.'

Warlow blew out a dry laugh. 'Keeping a sense of humour, sergeant. I'm impressed.'

'Will you ring Gina for me, sir?'

'I will. One way of getting her to forget about desperate Dan for a while, right?'

'As distraction techniques go, sir, I don't think I can recommend a face full of that stuff.' His words ended in a paroxysm of coughing that lasted until Jess gave him some water to drink and then emptied the rest of the bottle over his face as Warlow did his best to prise his eyes open.

'My car's closer,' Jess said as they helped him to his feet and Warlow slid his arm around the bigger man's waist.

'I don't think I like your version of snakes and ladders, sir,' Rhys said, wincing involuntarily.

'No. It's tiddlywinks for us from now on, Rhys. I promise.'

CHAPTER THIRTY-SIX

AT THE HOSPITAL, they irrigated Rhys's eyes a lot more. A doctor applied anaesthetic drops with fluorescent stain to check for any permanent damage. There was none. He emerged from the exam room with some residual yellow stain around his red and sore eyes, but they were open.

'I can see,' he said, a hint of relief in his voice.

Gina, who'd been sitting with Warlow while waiting for Rhys, leapt up and crossed the room in three swift steps, grabbing him in a hug.

Rhys hesitated for a moment, appearing unsure of what kind of reception he might get, but then he returned the hug, squeezing her tightly.

'Why is it always you?' she muttered into his chest, her voice muffled but raw with concern.

'I almost had him, Gina. Bloody PAVA spray,' Rhys replied, his frustration obvious.

She pulled back, looking up at him. 'Did it hurt?'

Rhys let his shoulders sag, the memory still fresh. 'You can't do anything. It's all you can think about. The pain.'

Warlow, who had been observing the two of them, stood up quietly and moved towards the door. 'I can see you're in capable hands now, Rhys. I'll leave you to it. See how you feel in the morning. We'll need to write up a full report on this evening's little escapade. But only when you feel up to it.'

'I'm sure I'll be fine by tom—'

'I spoke to Gil.' Gina's sudden statement cut across Rhys's response. She pulled back further, looking directly at him. 'About Dan,' she added, her voice tight.

'We can talk about this at home, Gina,' Rhys said, a nervous, tentative smile flickering over his lips.

Gina shook her head. 'No. I can't. He's my brother. If there's any comeback, it has to be on me.' She swivelled to address Warlow. 'That's why you should hear this too, sir.'

Warlow's brows bunched, but he kept his voice neutral. 'Hear what? That your brother was using drugs at your house?'

Gina's eyes flew open. 'How do you know?'

Rhys looked equally bemused. 'How did Gil know? I spoke to Catrin about it to get her advice, but …'

'Is No. 8 Tabernacle Terrace a crack den now?' Warlow asked. He said it drily, trying to keep things light and in perspective.

But Gina was too wound up, and it backfired.

'No,' she objected in a wail of denial. 'But when I cleared up after Dan, I found some roll-ups under the bed.'

'Destroyed?' Warlow asked.

'Yes, sir. But I still don't know how you know.'

'Rhys and I had a tutorial. The sort of thing you need to know about if you take your sergeant's exams. Hypothetical scenarios. Because these sergeants can be devious sods.'

Rhys's confusion hadn't abated. He glared at Gina. 'What did Gil tell you, exactly?'

'That he'd happened to bump into Dan. They'd had a chat about his work situation and the world in general.'

'I'm sure they did,' Rhys said sarcastically. He shook his head in despair. 'Catrin must have spoken to Gil.'

'They both visited Tabernacle Terrace, apparently,' Gina explained.

Warlow smiled at their confusion. 'As I said, sergeants

have a way of doing things. Not all of it comes from a manual.'

'My God, Rhys. Is this going to be on the ten o'clock news?' Gina's lip wobbled, her eyes filling with unshed tears.

'You say you found the drugs when you were cleaning up? Does that mean your brother's gone?' Warlow asked.

Gina nodded.

Warlow tilted his head. 'And Gil said he'd bumped into him?'

Gina nodded again. 'But he doesn't know Dan.'

'I suspect Dan now knows Gil,' Warlow said. 'And that's something he'll never forget.'

'But the drugs, sir?' Gina's voice sounded on the verge of breaking.

'Are not there now, are they?' Warlow's repetitive tone was firm.

She shook her head.

'And they did not involve you or Rhys?'

She shook her head again. 'I had no idea.' She glared at Rhys. 'But you did. And you didn't tell me.' Her voice had risen but her anger was half-hearted, muted by misery.

'Then you ought to tell Dan you found them and issue a warning to him. That's all you need to do. That's the law.' Warlow smiled. 'That way, you've done your duty and cannot be held responsible. If you did that and he repeated the offence, then he could be charged with possession. But he's gone, so that does not apply.'

'But what if he'd been doing something worse at our house? Dealing or … what if it had come back on us?' Gina's voice trembled with fear and frustration.

Warlow nodded thoughtfully. 'You want my opinion? There seems little point in dwelling on it. Sounds like your brother needed a wake-up call, and I can think of no better alarm clock than the wake-up call that is Gil Jones and Catrin Richards. Has Dan expressed any regrets? Admitted to anything?'

Gina shook her head, her expression miserable.

'Then issue the warning. And the next time he comes

looking for somewhere to stay, I suggest you lay out some "one-strike" ground rules,' Warlow said.

'I'll lay them out if you'll let me,' Rhys said, his voice steady. 'I know he's your brother, and he's older than you, but he needs to grow up.'

Gina sighed deeply. 'I'm so sorry.' She looked from Rhys to Warlow and then back again, guilt etched on her face.

'I know I've told you all to leave your dirty laundry at the Incident Room door when you come to work. But it isn't always that easy, is it? Families are … complicated.' Warlow grinned.

'Thank you, sir,' Gina murmured. She stepped across the room and quickly hugged her boss.

Rhys looked on with a relieved smile.

Warlow disengaged and glanced at his watch. Five minutes to midnight. 'Go home, you two, and get some sleep.'

'And you, sir,' Gina said.

'Yep. My own bed tonight.' He left them to it, though there was one thing left to do at the hospital. He wandered up to the orthopaedic ward, found a nurse, and flashed his badge.

'Any news on Barry Talbot?'

'First on the list tomorrow. I can see if he's awake if you like. He hasn't been sleeping too well,' the nurse offered.

'No. I was here anyway. Thought I'd check to see if the op had been done. But if it's tomorrow … I'll ring mid-day.' Warlow turned and left.

Jess had already gone back to Nevern. Tomorrow would bring more questions, and hopefully, a step closer to some real answers. But for now, he needed rest. The night outside was still warm and, as he stepped into the quiet, he let out a long breath, feeling the tension slowly ebb away from what had been an eventful evening. Full of action, but low on entertainment and *nil points* for satisfaction.

DESPITE HALF THE team getting to bed late the previous night, a full complement gathered at eight the next morning. Gil listened with horrified disbelief as Jess described the events that led to Rhys ending up in hospital.

She'd posted up a blown-up image of the airfield on the Gallery.

'And you saw no sign of the cyclists who headed back towards you?' Gil asked Jess.

She pointed towards the stone circle and traced the path back towards the exit where she'd parked. But the path itself turned south at the corner towards at least one more pedestrian access at the south-eastern corner.

'My guess is they went that-a-way,' she said.

'They were electric bikes,' Rhys explained. 'In and out in a matter of minutes on one of those things.'

'An effective method,' Warlow said. 'They wait until dusk, where there'd be a minimum number of people in an unlit area. As Rhys says, in and out in minutes. Gittings would have been the rogue participant. My guess is he didn't bother with a bike. Just sat in his car and probably had one cyclist deliver to him.'

'And the dropped package?' Gil asked.

'Identical to the brown paper brick we found at Gittings's house but with an extra layer of black plastic.' Jess showed them a photo. 'Povey has it. They're putting it through the forensic wringer, but she's confirmed it's a £10,000 bundle.'

'That means someone has lost twenty grand,' Gil murmured.

'It might explain the black BMW, sir.' Gina had said little that morning, and so Warlow was pleased to hear this contribution from her. She also looked a lot better than she had eight hours ago.

'As in?' he asked for clarification.

'As in, perhaps they were scoping out Gittings's place to check on activity with a view to getting in and trying to find their cash.'

It was a good point.

'Haven't they tried already, though?' Gil said.

Gina shrugged. 'If at first you don't succeed, be smarter about it the second time?'

Warlow made a mental note of that. Though that first attempt thwarted by Barry Talbot had seemed crass.

'What about the journalist?' Gil asked.

Warlow allowed himself a smile. 'What about her, indeed? She should be downstairs by half eight.'

Rhys glanced up. His eyes still looked puffy. 'She's there already.'

Warlow grinned a plotter's grin. 'Right. Jess, how about you and Gil have a chat with her?'

'Are we charging her?' Jess asked.

'Let's see what she has to say for herself first.'

———

THIS TIME, they used the interview room.

'Do I need a solicitor?' Sanders asked as soon as Jess and Gil walked in.

'That's up to you. You are not under arrest. You're here voluntarily.'

'I wouldn't put it quite like that. But I can leave anytime I want?'

'You could,' Gil said. 'But then we probably would arrest you. Just to make everyone's life easier.' He smiled at her.

She did not smile back. Both officers remembered Warlow explaining how cocky she'd been. Of how much delight she'd had in telling him she'd 'consulted' with Geraint Lane on their backgrounds. But she was not cocky this morning. And Gil was disinclined to let her off the hook.

'How is Sergeant Harries?' she asked.

'Let's just say he's not taking part in sniper training today.'

'I am so sorry. I'd like to tell him that myself.'

Jess ignored her request. 'Shall we talk about the pepper spray?'

'As I explained, I found it—'

Jess interrupted. 'That is not as you explained. You said, and I quote, "The PAVA spray was given to me by a friend".'

'I did. But that friend lives abroad. I smuggled it home in some luggage from France. My friend lives there.'

'Very convenient,' Gil said. 'But still a prohibited weapon in this country.'

'How did you come to be at the airfield, Ms Sanders?' Jess sat back and folded her arms.

Sanders sighed heavily. 'I followed DCI Warlow's car.'

'And you've been following him on a regular basis?'

'For a while, yes. Nothing illegal about that.'

'No. But it is illegal when that activity leads to interfering in an investigation.'

'I was trying to help.'

Gil nodded sagely at her reply.

'I saw the sergeant grappling with that cyclist and—'

'If you hadn't interfered, we'd be interviewing that cyclist now.'

'Are they involved? The cyclists? Is this a gang-related thing?' Sanders' excitement level went up a notch. 'Matt Gittings had some very unsavoury acquaintances. And you know I've been very cooperative.'

'Some might say you cooperated with the man who Sergeant Harries was trying to apprehend.' Gil let the words out slowly.

'That's unfair. I was trying to help.'

'Yes, tell us how that went again?' Jess asked.

Sanders didn't answer. Instead, she whined out a complaint. 'We had a deal about interviewing DCI Warlow.'

Jess slapped her hand on the table. 'What is wrong with you? A man is dead, an officer injured, another man severely injured by a car ramming into his bicycle—'

'The neighbour. I wondered—'

'And all you can do is ponder how all this fits into your story?'

'People need to hear—'

'My God,' Jess whispered. 'You sound like him.'

'Who?'

'Lane. A so-called journalist with about as much integrity as a toadstool. But then, you know that.'

'Lane is—' Sanders didn't finish.

'Yeah. A vulture,' Gil said. 'Scouring the carcass of society for the juiciest, most scandalous scraps to feed his craving for attention. He rips out people's emotions, splatters them across headlines. Not to spark change or promote good, but to satisfy his own lust for fifteen bloody minutes of fame. All he does is twist human suffering into a spectacle for the sake of titillation and personal glory.'

Jess had turned to look at Gil with a slightly shocked look of admiration.

Sanders could only blink.

Jess turned back to her. 'What he said.'

'Look. I did not know those people were going to be there.'

'Then you're no help to us,' Jess said.

'Tidy.' Gil grinned. 'Have you got your own solicitor or should we get you one?'

'Wait. You're charging me?'

'Lesser charge of possession of a prohibited weapon. Probably be a fine and costs. Lucky for you, Sergeant Harries does not want to press charges for assault. I tell you, that boy is too forgiving for his own good.'

Sanders twisted in her chair. 'But I was only trying to help.'

'Then tell us what you know about Gittings's trips to Birmingham.'

The journalist went pale.

Gil stood up. 'We'll get the duty solicitor. That work for you?'

'Wait!' Sanders shouted. 'I followed him several times—to the Maisonbleu in Birmingham. He'd meet a woman there. On the way up or back, he'd always stop at the Cardiff West service station to grab a bite. But that only happened every other week.'

'What do you mean? He didn't always go to Birmingham?'

'No,' Sanders replied. 'It alternated. Every week, he'd stop at the service station. One week, he'd just grab something to eat and head straight back to Pembrokeshire. The other weeks, he'd continue on to the Midlands and come home on Sundays.'

'So, the common factor is the service station,' Gil said.

'We need dates. Have any photos?' Jess asked.

'A few.'

'*Wel i mynuffernu,*' Gil sat down. 'Now we really are cooking with gas.'

CHAPTER THIRTY-SEVEN

BASED on their failed attempt to capture the cyclists at St David's airfield and Gittings's enigmatic weekend travels, the focus of the murder investigation had shifted. That Gittings had been involved in some kind of illegal activity seemed now to be obvious. And logic argued that his demise, rather than being the act of one of the many individuals he'd upset along the way, might have more to do with gang-related rivalry or even internecine violence of the type more common in cities like Manchester, London, and Birmingham.

Warlow was no expert. In fact, Jess had more experience than anyone else. But finding names and links would be a huge challenge.

By definition, organised crime ignored police force borders. As such, ROCUs – Regional Organised Crime Units – working with local officers had oversight. In South and West Wales, that meant *Tarian* – a Welsh word for shield – overseen by South Wales Police but funded centrally and by all three of the South Wales forces: Gwent, South Wales Police, and Dyfed Powys.

The team got stuck into more AOS work.

A lot more AOS work.

Contacting the service station on the M4 to pore over footage of Gittings that might link him to known OCG contacts. Because that was how it looked. Gittings used the service station to transfer drugs or money. Waiting on Povey's forensic assessment of the money brick from the airfield. Ringing West Midlands police for any information they had on Gittings. Liaising with the Maisonbleu Hotel in Birmingham for similar access. The golden hours after the event were already beginning to lose some of their glitter.

Warlow lost a whole day in meetings with Buchannan and other interested agencies like drugs, economic crime, the National Crime Agency, and UK Border Force now that possible links to drug smuggling had been thrown into the pot.

His, Jess, and Rhys's fishing trip to the airfield had opened a door into a whole new world. But he kept reminding himself, and one or two others, that his job was to investigate the possible murder of Matthew Gittings. He only managed to get away in time for vespers.

No one had anything groundbreaking to report, and the day's frustrations were eased only by the appearance of Sergeant Catrin Richards, together with her husband Craig and baby Betsi.

'Probably not a good time,' Catrin apologised as she put her head around the door to find the team drinking tea and discussing ANPR requests and how long the Maisonbleu held on to their tapes for.

'I can't think of a better time,' Warlow said as Craig began unfastening the baby carrier he wore on his chest to reveal a six-month-old Betsi, who immediately became the centre of attention.

And, of course, work was never the right place for a child, but that Friday afternoon, it was also exactly the right place.

Betsi, a chubby smiler who grinned at everyone, ended up first in Gina's, then in Jess's arms being shown around the Incident Room, fascinated mainly by the computer screens and bright ceiling lights. Craig played the proud father as if born to it and traded friendly insults with Rhys.

Warlow and Gil sat back and watched Gina and Catrin speak together off to one side, a discussion that ended up with

Gina blowing her nose a few times, followed by a prolonged hug.

Warlow threw Gil an appraising glance. 'That reminds me. I understand you bumped into Gina's brother.'

Gil, glasses perched on his forehead, answered without pausing, 'Dan? Yes, bumped into him on the street.'

'Do you know him of old?'

'Never met him before in my life. But he bore a remarkable resemblance.'

'To Gina?'

'No. To someone on the slippery slope to deep do do.'

Warlow glanced over at the younger officers, sharing a moment that underlined their closeness. 'Gina is very grateful to both of you.'

'I know how bloody awkward brothers can be.'

Warlow shot Gil a glance. 'You have brothers?'

'One. Did little with his life. Pathologically indifferent.'

'Oh?'

'Yeah.' Gil's nod was best described as sage. 'I found out later that it ran in the family. It would probably make him feel better if I told him that, but I can't be bothered.'

Warlow had just groaned an 'Oh, God,' when Catrin joined them.

'Why the long face?' Catrin asked.

'I'm sitting here with Gil,' Warlow said.

'Fair enough.'

Craig and Rhys were laughing at something.

'What's up with them?'

'Probably discussing the joke that Rhys texted Craig last night after he'd had a call from you.' She turned an accusatory expression towards Gil.

'I wanted to cheer him up after the PAVA spray,' Gil explained.

'It's not even a funny joke,' Catrin said.

Warlow saw that both Rhys and Craig disproved that theory, neither of them quite able to speak as they doubled up. 'Is it the one about the blacksmith dog who always makes a bolt for the door?' Warlow asked.

'No.' She turned to Gil, her lips pressing together in a thin line. 'Go on. It sounds better coming from you.'

'I can't see why.' Gil's eyebrows arched.

Catrin tilted her head and dropped her chin.

Gil sighed. 'Alright. My testicle used to be in the Guinness Book of Records until the librarian asked me to leave.'

Warlow wheezed out a laugh, his eyes crinkling at the corners.

Catrin remained stony-faced, her expression unchanging.

'Fourteen-year-olds find it hysterical,' Gil said.

Catrin gestured towards Craig and Rhys with both hands as if to say, and there they are. But then she recomposed her features and smiled brightly. 'I hear that things have taken a turn towards some kind of gang killing in your case.'

'You hear correctly,' Gil said.

Warlow grunted, shifting in his seat.

'You're not convinced, sir?' Catrin asked.

'It's looking more and more likely.' Warlow's voice was low, but his gaze distant.

She pouted slightly. 'Not exactly sending a message, though. I mean, if it's meant as a warning from a rival gang or as retribution, drive-by shootings have a lot more impact.'

Warlow imagined a drive-by shooting in Solva and promptly buried the scenario.

'Did someone want to make him suffer?' Catrin persisted with her train of thought.

'There's a long list in that column,' Warlow said.

'But they all have alibis,' Gil added.

'Then it sounds more like someone wanting to sell the suicide angle to muddy the waters.'

Warlow stared at Catrin.

Damn if she wasn't right. If it had not been for those remnants of zip ties around the leg, the water would have remained very un-muddied with suicide very much on top of the list.

Warlow ran the idea around his head, hearing it pinball against the objections and obstacles.

'Well, by the time you're back, it'll be sorted,' Gil said. 'You still keen on part-time?'

'For the first twelve months if they let me.'

'Good idea,' Warlow said.

'Is it, sir?' She shot him an anxious smile. 'I mean, will it jeopardise my work here? Or the team's?' She picked up a pen from the desk and rotated it between her fingers.

Warlow shook his head. 'I've spoken to Sion Buchannan. If Gina is happy to come on board as and when, all well and good. And we'll try to get Rhys through his exams as soon as possible to make him into a proper sergeant.'

'What about you?' Catrin looked at Gil. 'Are you back fighting fit?'

'Another month's physio should do it.' He worked his arm in a shoulder roll with an expression of wary trepidation. 'Now, any chance of me having another cuddle with this baby, or am I going to be yet another victim of the privileged matriarchy?'

'Good point.' Warlow glanced at his watch. 'However, I have a Zoom meeting with a superintendent in Cardiff in fifteen minutes, so I am first in the cuddle queue.'

He got up and crossed the room, speaking with a playful authority. 'DI Allanby, hand over that baby.'

Jess complied, albeit reluctantly.

The meeting dragged on until well after six. By the time Warlow got back to Nevern, he was dog tired. The good news, though, was that his dog was not.

'Fancy a quick walk down the estuary?' he asked Jess as he walked through the door. 'Unless it spoils supper.'

'It's a salad.' Jess smiled back. 'Besides, it's been too hot to take her out.'

'Just as I thought.' Warlow bent to the dog. '*Ewn ni am wac, fach?*'

The dog, fluent in two languages and even more fluent in vocal tones, responded with all four legs off the floor in the affirmative at this suggestion of a walk.

Warlow took the Jeep and drove for five minutes to the south side of the river and walked in towards Parrog on this balmy evening. One to relish being alive with his two favourite females. He said as much.

'And which one is *the* favourite?' Jess asked.

'Oh, is that a fence I see? I'll just take a seat if I may.'

'Smart answer.' She laughed softly.

They spoke little. They didn't need to. The pleasure came from being in each other's quiet company, watching a dog living its best life, chasing balls, greeting other dogs and walkers. But on the way back to the car, Jess asked the inevitable question.

'Are you happy with the way the Gittings's case is going?'

'You've been talking to Catrin?'

'She comes at it with a fresh pair of eyes.'

'Happy, no. Suddenly, it's messy and now we're fishing in a much bigger pond. We'll be lucky if we get some forensics back on the package dropped in the airfield. But even then, it's likely to be a foot soldier, not a gang leader. I mean, the head of the snake probably doesn't even know where St David's airfield is.'

Cadi, tongue lolling, walked ahead of them, carrying a blue and orange soft frisbee that she'd caught out of the air a dozen times on a stretch of estuary sand.

'I've seen what gangs can do to one another in Manchester,' Jess said.

'But it's the MO that gets me.' Warlow had an edge of residual disbelief in his voice. 'Someone orchestrated this as a suicide and went to a lot of trouble. Do you think organised crime gangs are capable, or even as fussy?'

'Not usually,' Jess agreed. 'But what's the alternative?'

'At the moment, I can't think of one.' His words petered out as he contemplated them.

They walked on, arm in arm. 'Nice to see Catrin and Craig and the little one today, though.' Jess smiled at the recollection.

'She's coming back part-time, you knew that?'

Jess nodded. 'She reminded me. I had forgotten.'

'Forgetting stuff is getting to be a hab—' Warlow stopped and stood stock still.

'What have you forgotten?' Jess recognised the expression.

'Talbot.' Warlow uttered the name in despair. 'The poor chap was having his surgery this morning. It slipped clean out of my mind. I'm going to ring the hospital.' His hands reached for his phone.

Warlow got through to the ward and spoke to the same nurse he'd spoken to the night before.

'You were with him last night, right?' Her tone was brisk.

'Yes, why do you ask?'

'There is no next of kin. But you are Evan Warlow? The police officer?'

A cold something slithered in Warlow's innards. 'What's happened?'

'Surgery went well. He came back to the ward this morning. But at around three, he developed pain in his leg. Looks like he's got a DVT.' She said all this with a serious calmness.

Deep vein thrombosis.

Warlow'd heard that term before. And it never earned a cheer.

'We're monitoring him now. He's comfortable. I suggest you ring in the morning.'

When the call ended, Jess read something in his face. 'Not good?'

'Complications. Remind me to ring in the morning, will you? Poor chap.'

'Yet another one of Gittings's unwitting sodding victims,' Jess said.

Warlow didn't answer, but took solace when Jess looped her arm through his, and they headed back to the Jeep.

CHAPTER THIRTY-EIGHT

WARLOW WOKE UP VERY EARLY. His sleep had been fitful, not helped by a muggy night with no breeze to temper the heat. He'd thrown off his half of the bedclothes soon after midnight. But thoughts of what had happened in the airfield kept intruding, jostling for position in a harrowing top ten that included Gittings's torched corpse, slithering snakes, Talbot's thin frame lying in the hospital bed, and cyclists in masks and goggles.

The cyclists kept coming out on top. Wriggling their way in and out of his thoughts like parasitic worms.

He got up and simply stood there.

The room was dark and, for the briefest of moments, he felt he might he might have to lie back down again. Not the first time he'd felt a bit yippy on getting up fast this last couple of weeks. But then he wasn't exactly sleeping like normal people. The swimming sensation only lasted a few moments and then passed.

He took Cadi out into the dawn light, much to her delight. But even that did not clear his mind completely.

Jess had not surfaced by six forty-five. He left her a note and drove to Carmarthen and the hospital as he wanted to see Barry Talbot. Wanting to reassure himself that the surgery had gone well. Partly to dispel his guilt at having encouraged the man to undergo the procedure in the first instance, and partly to ask him a couple of questions if he'd be up to it.

Questions only he could answer.

Sheer luck saw the orthopaedic registrar, Bo, walking out of the ward as Warlow walked on.

'Are you ever off duty?' Warlow asked.

'We're short staffed,' Bo replied. But the expected accompanying smile did not appear. 'You're here to see Barry?'

'I know it's early, but—'

'He's in ICU.'

'What?' Surprise made the word sound loud and angry in Warlow's own ears. 'But I spoke to someone last night.'

'Complications can spiral quickly, unfortunately. He had a DVT. That became a PE … a pulmonary embolus. They took him to ICU in the early hours. I was up there an hour ago. He's being ventilated, and they suspect he's developing DIC.'

Warlow's forward jerk and his narrowed eyes stopped Bo there.

The registrar let out the thinnest of sighs. 'Disseminated intravascular coagulopathy. Thrombin from the clot in the pulmonary artery triggers a cascade of clotting factors. Blood clots abnormally inside the blood vessels, blocking blood flow to vital organs. This paradoxically uses up the blood clotting factors, causing severe bleeding in other parts of the body. Unfortunately, the prognosis is … not good.' He paused before adding, 'Not good at all.'

'Oh, God,' Warlow whispered.

'We're keeping him comfortable. He's unaware of what's going on, and …'

Bo didn't need to explain that Talbot's future had not been bright. However devastating this DIC thing might be, it could be looked upon as something of a release.

Bo did not shy away from telling Warlow all of this. Not his first slide down the helter skelter, for sure. For that, Warlow felt a pang of gratitude.

'I was going to ring you,' the doctor continued. 'Barry left a letter with the ward sister addressed to you.'

'Me?' A vague and unsettling feeling crept over Warlow, like a half-forgotten nightmare calling its way back into consciousness. 'A letter?'

The news stirred something in him – a fleeting suspicion he'd entertained and quickly dismissed days ago. But as the reality of Talbot's condition sank in, that discarded notion began to take shape again. The detective in him bristled.

'Hang on.' Bo retraced his steps and came back with a manila envelope. 'He told me, and Sister Hargreaves, to give it to you if he didn't make it. It sounded a bit dramatic, and I said so … But he insisted. Now … Well, he's having the last laugh. Though no one is exactly laughing. Anyway, clearly a very organised bloke, Barry. I wondered if it had something to do with him being ex-army?'

'Might be,' Warlow said. But the worm wiggled some more inside him. 'Can I see him?'

'He's not conscious.'

'I'd still like to see him.'

Warlow followed Bo along the corridor and some stairs to ICU. A big room with large bays packed with equipment. One bay had pale-grey drapes drawn across. Bo pulled them back.

Talbot lay motionless in the bed, his face swollen, unrecognisable from the gaunt but cheerful figure Warlow had spoken to just a few days ago, now surrounded by the paraphernalia of modern medicine. An endotracheal tube secured with tape protruded from his mouth, connected to a ventilator that rhythmically hissed and sighed. Multiple IV lines snaked into his arms, delivering vital medications and fluids, while a continuous beeping from the heart monitor underscored the fragility of his condition.

A nurse in blue scrubs and a white plastic apron fiddled with the drip's fluid regulator.

Warlow saw instantly there was little point in staying.

Bo, recognising this, led the way back out.

Warlow thanked him and made him promise to keep him informed.

He opened the letter in the car and, as he read it, the

wriggling worm turned into something cold that wrapped itself around his pulsing heart.

Then he rang Jess and asked her to meet him at Barry Talbot's house in Solva.

———

TALBOT HAD INCLUDED a front door key with the letter. An hour and a half after seeing the man in an ICU bed, Warlow and Jess sat in front of a laptop in a room in the house.

Unlike the living room he'd sat in previously, this room looked well-used. A study— more accurately, a den. Shelves stuffed with books, several by Chris Ryan and Andy McNab, stood next to an old CD player with a floor-stacked library of music from the 70s and 80s. On the shelves, too, next to the man in uniform at his wedding with his wife, were photographs of Talbot as a strapping youngster in uniform and wearing a maroon beret. Other photos, with groups of other men, some bearded, with watch-caps and rifles, but no insignias or badges or names written beneath. Groups with eyes squinting against the sun, against desert-bleached walls, or up in mountainous regions with scattered snow.

Warlow handed over Talbot's letter, and Jess had it open on her knees as she read it.

'In the event of my death, my laptop password is Marlene54. Open folder MG and then the video file Quarry. Life is too short. Barry Talbot.'

Her eyes shot up.

'He knows what's happened?' she asked as Warlow fired up the computer.

'I don't think it's just knowing.'

Puzzled, Jess waited while the computer folder opened and Warlow clicked on the file named Quarry. An MP4 player appeared, and he made the screen full size.

Talbot came into shot, taking a seat in front of the laptop camera. The computer screen bathed his already gaunt face in blue light. But the backdrop he recognised as this very room. And Talbot's appearance looked recent. Hollow cheeks and wispy facial hair. Just as Warlow remembered him from days ago.

'If you're seeing this, then it's likely I'm not around. I am not usually a dramatic sort of bloke, but I thought best to make this video now while I still can. Matthew Gittings was a monster. Let's get that straight.

'There are other files here relating to when he moved in. At first, with his wife and kids around, things were good. But when his career took a dive and he moved in full-time, left his family in the Midlands, things were not so good. He didn't like my security lights. He didn't like the fact that he thought my fence intruded on his property line. He'd stand, scream, shout, throw things over the fence. I didn't want to fight him, I've done enough of that, but quickly I realised that what he enjoyed was exerting control. He was a control freak. Literally. He enjoyed making people feel small and inferior. If I'd have been younger, I wouldn't have put up with it. But I was pretty down after losing Marlene, and then the bloody cancer and the chemo … Still, I can't turn the clock back.'

Talbot coughed. He took a sip of what might have been lager from a glass before continuing.

'These last twelve months, things changed. He had visitors. Young men, sometimes an older woman. They never stayed long and often they'd be carrying small bags. The woman stayed longer, sometimes half an hour or more. I have all this on video in the files. I suspect this is all drug related.

'But that's not the worst side of him, not by a long way. In the pub, he'd sit with me because he thought we were friends. We weren't friends. I listened, that's all. And he needed an audience. Never showed any interest in anything I said. Initially, all I wanted was a quiet life and a bit of company. The chemo … it ended up being brutal. But Gittings would come in to the pub every other Friday evening after being away, clearly high on something. He'd want to chat. Or rant. He'd have a drink and get worse. More belligerent, more argumentative. These were the nights he'd talk about the girls. The local skirt, that's what he called them. He fantasised about finding somewhere he could take them. I didn't realise he meant it until he mentioned names. I remember one night he talked about people and films he liked. Silence of the Lambs, Kiss the Girls. Of how Fritzle could have got away with it if he'd been smarter. The idea fascinated him. These monsters fascinated him. He caught me looking horrified and shrugged it off with an "I'm only kidding".

'But he wasn't. I could tell. And then he started mentioning a waitress. I knew her vaguely from when she was a kid because her mother had been in a choir with Marlene. Two weeks ago, he came into the Anchor and started talking. Telling me he'd found a place; an old munitions block on unused farmland on the coast not too far away. He'd been there. He'd hacked a way in through the brambles. A hidden spot where no one would think of looking. His eyes lit up when he told me and it made me sick.

'Shortly after that, the girl turned up at his house. Iona. A pretty girl. Really upset, too. She came to the house to beg him to stop pestering her. Lucky for her, he wasn't there. I mentioned I knew her mum and so she spoke to me. Poured her heart out to me. Just a kid. That's when I knew Gittings was truly dangerous. He pretended to be a fantasist but seeing that young girl made it all real for me. That's why I decided I had to do something.'

Jess and Warlow exchanged a quick and horrified glance. But Talbot kept speaking to the camera.

'Marlene was on medication before she passed. She took sleeping tablets, Zolpinam. We had loads of it in the bathroom cupboard, all out of date. I should have got rid of it, but I didn't. I took it to the pub and put it in his drink on that Friday night. I hoped it might make him sleepy. Shut him up, so that I didn't have to listen. It worked, and he left early. I hoped he might have an accident in the car. Smash himself up. Get him off the road and give me time to think.

'An hour later, I got home and saw his car in the driveway with the lights on and the engine running. He'd fallen asleep alright, just as he got home. I couldn't wake him. I couldn't shift him.

'That's when I had the idea.

'We'd done the same sort of thing in Afghanistan a couple of times. When we needed to get rid of some bad actors and make it look like an accident. I'm not proud of it. But it was what we were there for. What we were trained to do.

'It's much more difficult if the car is not automatic, but his was. That was the game changer for me. If you want to drive a vehicle with the driver in the seat and incapacitated, tie their feet together and strap them away from the pedals with a bungee cord. You sit in the passenger seat and use a walking stick to compress the accelerator and brake. I put my electric bike in the boot and used another bungee to secure it with it not completely shut. Useful things, bungees. All the taxis in Hong Kong do luggage that way, too. Doesn't matter how big your case is.'

A brief smile flickered over Talbot's face. Some half-forgotten memory of a time gone by. Then he began to speak again.

'I recorded as I did it. It's called Quarry 2, and it's all there, but I'll tell you now what I did.

'The road to Whitchurch was empty that time of night, so I took my time. I drove up to the field behind the quarry with bolt cutters for the gate. I had petrol I used for my mower and poured that into the car and left the plastic can in the car to burn. It was on fire before it went over the edge. I set it up to get seventy-five yards of acceleration, with a block of wood wedged under the accelerator. The car was in gear when I got out. I had a nylon rope tied to the block of wood under the accelerator that went through the window on the driver's side. I threw in a match, slipped the column shift into drive and pulled the block of wood under the accelerator free. Gittings's foot zip-tied to the accelerator and the weight of his leg did the rest.

'I waited for the fireworks and then rode home on the bike with no lights. I met no one. Everything is on video. No one else was involved. Please keep the girl, Iona, out of it if you can. She deserves none of Gittings's stink upon her.'

All the while, Talbot kept his face expressionless.

'I am a killer,' he said. 'That's what my country paid me

to do. Getting him off the face of this earth is me using up the last of my foreign currency. I was too ill on chemo to do it before. What little strength I have left is for now. That's my excuse. As if I needed one.'

The screen went blank.

Neither Jess nor Warlow spoke for several seconds, then Jess turned to Warlow.

'What were you going to ask him at the hospital?'

'If he'd ever been to Middle Hill quarry.'

'You knew?'

Warlow's expression remained grim. 'I thought he'd be the one with the expertise.'

'He could be covering for someone?'

Warlow turned back to the computer. 'One way to find out.'

The pointer clicked on another video.

It took thirty seconds for them both to see that Talbot had been telling the truth. The video of the car, flames already licking at the interior, rolling towards the edge of the quarry shook and wavered. But there was no doubting the truth of it.

They were still in the study there an hour later when Warlow's phone rang. He didn't recognise the caller's number, but the voice, when it came through, was sombre and familiar.

It was Bo—calling to tell that Talbot had died half an hour earlier, without ever regaining consciousness.

CHAPTER THIRTY-NINE

WARLOW CALLED the team together that Saturday afternoon. Jess had stayed in Solva at Talbot's property, *Am-Nawr*, to liaise with the CSI team and Povey, but the DCI wanted to tell the others himself. They deserved to know firsthand.

A background check on Talbot revealed that he was actually seventy-five, born in 1949, and joined the parachute regiment in 1970 after earning a degree in history. By doing so, he followed an uncle who had fought and died with the Paras in the Second World War.

The two thin blue stripes on the military plaque Warlow had noticed on that first visit should have signalled that. But it had been of no significance then. Talbot had said he'd worked in logistics. What he'd meant was private security. Bodyguards for high-profile diplomats and media personalities at home and abroad.

In a drawer, they found an SAS cap badge, but it provided no details, or dates. However, what it did explain was how, and why, a thirty-seven-year-old Talbot had been to Afghanistan in 1987.

Officially, there had been no military UK presence there then. The preferred term was covert operations.

Gina, Rhys, and a snazzily dressed Superintendent Sion Buchannan, straight off a golf course, listened in complete silence as Warlow detailed the findings and the events leading up to their meeting that afternoon.

'A full confession,' Buchannan said, echoing the others' wonderment.

'Of course there's no trace of the plastic fuel container. That would have burned up. But, there will be a lot of other evidence. He's given us motive, his MO, the works,' Warlow added.

Buchannan could only shake his head. Not so much in disgust, more in disbelief and driven shock.

'It's a bit *Minority Report*, this,' Rhys said.

The team, well used to Rhys's lateral thinking manifesting as non-sequiturs, waited.

'You know, the Tom Cruise Spielberg film from Philip Dick's novel. Where they arrest murderers before it happens because they can predict who's going to do it? Since Talbot got rid of Gittings before he could do anything awful.'

For once, Gil's response was less than scathing. 'Some people might want to give the bloke a medal instead of calling him a murderer.'

Rhys's hand rose to pat down a stray strand of hair. 'Hard to believe, though. It's such a cliché. Why are all politicians self-serving narcissists or ideological headbangers?'

'They're not,' Warlow said. 'Like any group, they possess diverse personalities. What they need to have is ambition, good communication skills, and networking abilities. Most of them probably want to do some good, too. At least to begin with.'

'So, why is there something in the press every week about someone taking a bribe or cheating the system?' A flush appeared in Rhys's cheeks.

'Power and access to privileges does funny things to people.' Buchannan was the one who spoke. The senior view, and one Warlow suspected would be worth hearing. 'They are human, and so most of them want to be liked. As a result, you will get some who have latched on to a very shouty group and hear nothing but the clamour of an echo chamber in their own heads. They tend to gravitate to the Twitter side of the universe. Some are indeed narcissists who simply cannot shut up and send signals into the ether only to be surprised to find out that not everyone agrees with them. Others see it as a natural career progression from the right school to the right university and a job in the Cabinet. Mix that in with intense media focus and human fallibility and it can be an irresistible urge.' Not the most complete of answers, but there was no mystery here. Just a simmering melting pot under public scrutiny.

'Who would want to do that job?' Rhys asked.

He got a stony silence by way of answer.

'This changes things, of course,' Buchannan said after a while. 'We hand off the drug running to Vetch and his team. But I think we can scale down the murder hunt, can we not?'

'Do we stop looking, then, sir?' Gina asked.

Warlow smiled. Again, another good question cutting straight to the chase. Gina was coming along nicely in the team.

'We cannot prosecute a dead man.' Buchannan sighed. 'There will be an inquest where we can present evidence. The press will, no doubt, make a meal of it all. But the official line from today will be that we are no longer looking for anyone else in connection with the Gittings case.'

Warlow's nod of agreement was tempered with a caveat. 'But, now we have Talbot. If the pathologist says he died as a *result* of his injuries, then the driver of that black BMW is culpable. Let's talk to the drug squad and CID again for links. But my guess is that driver and that car are probably in London, or Liverpool, or Ireland by now and with a different set of number plates.'

'Is there a chance we can keep Iona's name out of all this?' Gina asked.

'The coroner can impose reporting restrictions. I'm sure that could be arranged.'

'But do we think Talbot was of sound mind?' Gil looked from Buchannan to Warlow. 'If you say he had brain secondaries, could they have affected him? Made him imagine all that stuff?'

The DCI's mind drifted to an OS map they'd found at Gittings's house. A map of the local area with crosses marked on it. No one had looked too closely at what they might mean yet. Now he thought it might be a good idea if he got a copy and he, Cadi, and Jess checked them all out.

'Perhaps,' Warlow said. 'That isn't for us to say. But it means that we can definitely stop chasing up all these threads.' He stared at the scattered pieces of information pinned to the boards.

Each photo, each scrap of paper, told a part of Gittings's story—and those whose lives he'd corrupted. His gaze drifted over to a photo of a man in uniform. A dead man trained in some very dark arts.

A conflicting mix of emotions swirled around in Warlow's head: relief at closing the case, relief for the victims, a pang of guilt over what had happened to Talbot.

Perhaps Rhys was on to something when he'd mentioned *Minority Report*. They'd never know if Gittings's fantasies would ever spill over into true depravity. But Warlow found himself unexpectedly empathetic towards Talbot himself.

'Sir?' Gina's voice broke through his reverie. 'Are you alright?'

Warlow flicked his eyes over to acknowledge the young DC, offering a wan smile. 'Just thinking, Gina. About what drives a man to take justice into his own hands.'

He picked up the photograph. Talbot resplendent in his Para uniform.

'Gil's right, in another life, this man would have been celebrated as a hero. He wasn't—because black ops seldom are. Instead, he'll be remembered as a killer. It's complicated, isn't it?' Warlow said.

Gina nodded, understanding dawning in her eyes. 'You see it as a brave act, don't you, sir? A dying man's last stand against the injustices he couldn't bear to leave unchallenged.'

Warlow set the photo down. 'It's not our place to judge. But I can't help thinking … how many lives might have been tainted, even ruined, if Talbot hadn't acted? How many more victims might there have been? And I'm not only talking about the young women he'd targeted, was still to target. I'm talking about a marijuana farm under an Engine House in Mwnt. I'm talking about some poor kid overdosing in a squat thanks to him facilitating the drug trade. Gittings had blood on his hands alright.' He shook his head. 'It's a grey area, this job of ours. Sometimes, the line between right and wrong isn't as clear as we'd like it to be.'

'One less snake,' muttered Rhys.

'What?' Gil asked.

'Oh, nothing, sarge.'

As they stood there, Warlow couldn't shake the feeling that Talbot's actions, however misguided they were, had stemmed from a deep-seated desire to protect the vulnerable. In his own way, perhaps Talbot had been fighting the same fight as they were –just from a different angle.

'At least it's over,' Gil said. 'And Catrin told me the other day that more files have come across from Napier's estate. I am going to go digging next week.'

'Like a Detectorist?' Rhys asked.

'In a way. But I'm interested in the dirt more than the treasure.'

———

SUNDAY

Jess did not want to make a fuss. That's why she'd been up since 7am preparing slow-roasted garlic and lemon chicken for lunch. Fresh flowers appeared on the dining table, and the noise of vacuuming came from Molly's room.

Warlow did not object. But when, at eleven, Jess appeared in a summer dress with full makeup to join him for coffee, he felt obliged to compliment her. After a fashion.

'If this is not making a fuss, I'd love to see it when you push the boat out.'

'I prefer making an effort, not fuss.'

'Well, you've certainly done that.' Warlow grinned his appreciation and watched as Jess touched both earrings and the necklace she was wearing with the middle finger of her left hand while holding her coffee cup in the right.

She smelled wonderful.

'Nervous?' He grinned.

Jess's shoulders dipped. 'I know it's silly. She's only my niece.'

Warlow nodded. 'But that's not true, is it? She's not just your niece.—she's your link to the darker chapters of the Cardinale family. You have every right to be nervous. I think it's misplaced, but …'

'What if she doesn't like me? What if I don't like her?'

'Now you're just being daft.' Warlow downed his coffee and got up.

'Where are you going?'

'To change. Make an effort.' He deliberately echoed Jess's words. 'I'm in Sunday dog-walking fatigues. I'll put on some chinos and see if there's any of that bottle of Springfield aftershave left.'

'Springfield? Is that a new one?'

'No, it's old. Just means if I put it on, I'll be able to say I've been Spruced Springfield.'

Jess smiled, but it took some effort, partly due to nerves and partly because it had been a bloody awful joke. She suspected Gil had a hand in that.

Molly and Nina arrived at 11:45. Warlow watched the car through the bedroom window. By the time he got into the living room, Molly was walking in, and as soon as she took one step inside, she was immediately love-bombed by the dog, leaving Nina hesitating on the threshold.

The image he'd seen of the girl, sent by Molly, did not do her any justice.

'Oh, and did I mention a dog?' Molly said with a laugh, which implied that she had not forgotten at all as Cadi attempted to get as much contact with her as possible while still gyrating like a spinning top.

Nina stood awkwardly, a half-smile on her lips.

Molly realised her gaffe and said, 'OMG, Nina, Jess. Jess, Nina.'

It was a frozen moment as the girl remained where she was and Jess remained rooted where she stood five yards away, her eyes wide, one hand covering her mouth. Fleetingly, Nina's smile faded in doubt.

'Auntie Jessica?' she said, her voice small.

Two words. But by far and away the nuclear option. With a strangled sob, Jess strode forward and grabbed the girl in an all-encompassing hug.

After several long seconds, Warlow heard the whispered, 'You look just like your mother.'

'You look just like Molly,' Nina replied.

The accent was strong, and the words heartfelt. But as usual, it was left to Molly to break the tension.

'Oh, and the bloke who has sidled in at the back of the room watching it all and wishing he was a million miles away is Evan. Cadi's daddy.'

Nina looked up, breaking Jess's embrace. She walked over confidently and embraced him, too. 'I know everything about you. Molly says you speak Italian.'

Warlow threw Molly a piercing glance. She grinned in reply. 'You said you did.'

'I do. Primitivo, Chianti, Amaretto.'

Nina laughed. Full throated and husky. An Italian laugh if ever Warlow had heard one.

'No, don't do that,' Molly objected. 'You'll only encourage him.'

'I love your house,' Nina said. She turned to Molly. 'Can I have a tour?'

'Won't be a long one,' Molly said, still with one hand on the dog.

With the girls out of the room, Warlow turned to Jess. 'You okay?'

She smiled, relief etched on her face, her eyes moist. 'She's so beautiful.'

'I've got news for you,' Warlow said. 'It's in the genes.'

Jess broke into a wide smile.

'Thank you.' She kissed him on the cheek.

'Shall I open a bottle of red, then?'

'You had me at open a bottle,' Jess said.

'Tell you what, I'm thirsty. How about a G and T?'

'I won't say no.'

'Good. Because I have a bottle of *Jin Talog* – Welsh for Gin Talog – Talog being where it is made. Gil's Lady Anwen is partial, especially now that they've stopped making it. Has rarity value. I called in to the butcher's in Whitland and there it was.'

'In a butcher's?'

'Exclusive stuff. Not available everywhere. It was locally made. A classic London Dry gin.'

Jess laughed. 'You sound like an expert.'

'I am not, but I know a man who is.'

'Now I am excited.'

'Of course you are. You're from Manchester.'

'Oy.' Jess flashed him a warning, albeit a very tame one. She took his hand, squeezing it gently. 'Thanks for this. For making me and Molly feel safe.'

'This is a new chapter for you two. Try to enjoy it,' he said, his eyes softening.

'You're right. I think I'm ready to see where it leads,' Jess agreed.

They stood in comfortable silence for a moment, one that, followed by the sounds of giggling drifting in from the next room, finally made the tension of the morning melt away.

Warlow studied Jess as she looked around the room, a newfound sense of belonging evident in her eyes.

'To new beginnings,' she said, raising an imaginary toast.

'To new beginnings,' Warlow echoed. 'And keep that pose while I find you a proper glass and fill it.'

ACKNOWLEDGEMENTS

As with all writing endeavours, the existence of this novel depends upon me, the author, and a small army of 'others' who turn an idea into a reality. My wife, Eleri, who gives me the space to indulge my imagination and picks out my stupid mistakes. Tim Barber designs the covers, Sian Phillips edits, and other proofers and ARC readers sort out the gaffes. Thank you all for your help. Special mention goes to Ela the dog who drags me away from the writing cave and the computer for walks, rain or shine. Actually, she's a bit of a princess so the rain is a no-no. Good dog!

But my biggest thanks goes to you, lovely reader, for being there and actually reading this. It's great to have you along and I do appreciate you spending your time in joining me on this roller-coster ride with Evan and the rest of the team.

CAN YOU HELP?

With that in mind, and if you enjoyed it, I do have a favour to ask. Could you spare a moment to **leave a review or a rating**? A few words will do, but it's really the only way to help others like you discover the books. Probably the best way to help authors you like. Just visit my page on Amazon and leave a few words.

A FREE BOOK FOR YOU

Visit my website and join up to the Rhys Dylan VIP Reader's Club and get a FREE novella, *The Wolf Hunts Alone*, by visiting the website at: **rhysdylan.com**

The Wolf Hunts Alone.

One man and his dog... will track you down.

DCI Evan Warlow is at a crossroads in his life. Living alone, contending with the bad hand fate has dealt him, he finds solace in simple things like walking his neighbour's dog.

But even that is not as safe as it was. Dogs are going missing from a country park. And not only one, now three have disappeared. When he takes it upon himself to root out the cause of the lost animals, Warlow faces ridicule and a thuggish enemy.

But are these simply dog thefts? Or is there a more sinister malevolence at work? One with its sights on bigger, two legged prey.

A FREE eBOOK FOR YOU (Available in digital format)

Only one thing is for certain; Warlow will not rest until he finds out.

———

By joining the club, you will also be the first to hear about new releases via the few but fun emails I'll send you. This includes a no spam promise from me, and you can unsubscribe at any time.

AUTHOR'S NOTE

So, a story about a dodgy politician—what a cliché, right? And yet, before you know it, every uncomfortable suspicion you've ever had about the little tinkers unfolds vividly before your eyes. If you catch my drift.

My story may take place on a local stage, but it confronts the bigger question: how do lying, irresponsible, self-serving narcissists manage to convince others of their sincerity and rise to power? I genuinely hope you never cross paths with someone like Gittings—though unfortunately, we encounter versions of him daily on television screens and in newspaper headlines.

What truly sets these thick-skinned individuals apart is their profound lack of remorse and empathy. Thankfully, there remain some who still embody altruism and genuine public duty—though, regrettably, their numbers seem to dwindle by the day. Still, as the bard Bonnie Tyler famously said, we're all *Holding Out for a Hero*. And never mind being fast or strong—he or she better hurry the heck up, is all I can say.

All the best,

Rhys

P.S. For those interested, there is a glossary on the website to help with any tricky pronunciations.

READY FOR MORE?

DCI Evan Warlow and the team are back in…

A Word With The Dead

What happens when healthcare reform meets murder? In the shadow of Welsh mountains, DCI Evan Warlow investigates a death that will expose the darkest corners of a community fighting for survival. With acid attacks, arson, and more bodies piling up, the race is on to catch a killer before they strike again.

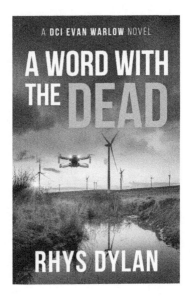

Made in the USA
Coppell, TX
29 April 2025